ALPHA
DIVIDED

AILEEN ERIN

First Published by Ink Monster, LLC in 2014
Ink Monster, LLC
34 Chandler Place
Newton, MA 02464
www.inkmonster.net

ISBN 9780996086424

For my husband,
Thank you for being patient and endlessly supportive
as I wrote two books at once.
I can't do it without you.
I love you tons.

Chapter One

The sun burned bright against my face. I sat on the teak table, reclining on my elbows in my parents' backyard. The scent of sizzling beef made my mouth water. My stomach growled, and I knew I'd eat at least a dozen burgers before all was said and done. For the first time since I'd been turned into a werewolf, that didn't feel totally weird.

My birthday barbecue was off to a solid start. Everyone had been goofing off since we got here. I let their voices wash over me as I grinned. Axel—my brother—and Adrian were talking witchy stuff as they tossed a football back and forth. The rhythmic slapping of their hands against the ball was unexpectedly soothing. Mom was inside, making side dishes to go with the burgers. Dad was at his usual post, tending the meat.

Chris and Meredith were asking Donovan about strategies he'd used against vampires. Donovan showed them a move that sent Chris flying into a nearby tree and I snickered.

"Way to show him," I yelled.

Dastien sat on the bench beside my feet, running his fingertips up and down my leg and sparking waves of goose bumps. His ever-present calmness seeped into me, and I was content to close my eyes and sit in the quiet, soaking up some rays while we waited for food.

"Tessa. You know you can't get tan anymore?" Meredith broke me out of my Zen state.

I cracked one eye open. She was nearly recovered from her run-in with the curse gone bad. It'd only been two days, but she'd managed to gain back some of the weight she'd lost during the ordeal. She'd changed her dyed hair from pink back to blue, and I liked it better. The color made her bright blue eyes pop. But then I was a little biased. I'd kill for blue eyes. Mine were dark brown.

Meredith munched on chips as she hopped onto the table next to me.

"What are you talking about? Of course I can get tan." I bumped her shoulder with mine. "This is me sitting under the sun, getting a healthy dose of rays. I'm half Mexican. My skin browns."

"Not anymore." This from my mate, Dastien.

I sat up. I liked having a little color. I'd been a pasty shade of white, but I wanted to rectify that before the weather turned cold. "What? Why not?"

"The sun has to damage your skin before it can tan. You're healing your skin cells too fast to tan," Meredith said.

I groaned as I stared down at my pasty legs. I'd worn shorts specifically so I could get some color. "I'm seriously never going to tan again?"

"Nope."

Oh, man. Just when I thought I had the whole being-a-werewolf thing figured out, something else popped up. "Dastien?"

"Yes, *cherie*."

"You bit me and now I'll be pasty-pale for the rest of my life. I officially hate you. The ceremony's off. Call Mr. Dawson. Tell him it's done-zo mugun-zo." I tried to pull my foot away from him, but he gripped my ankle. I gave him my best I'm-pissed-at-you face, but the jerk grinned back at me, showing off his dimples.

Those two dents in his cheeks got to me every damned time I saw them. It was a little pathetic how easily he could win me over.

Dastien's gaze roved over my bare legs, taking in my shorts and tank top, before meeting my eyes. Heat burned me from head to toe. He stood and leaned over me, running his nose up the side of my neck. "You love me," he whispered against my ear.

"Not anymore," I lied.

He placed a kiss on my neck. "I can hear your heart racing." His voice was gravelly and I shivered. He moved to kiss my lips but hovered a centimeter away and then pulled back.

I grabbed his T-shirt, tugging him back to me.

"Kisses are for people who actually love me," he said, but he let me pull him down anyway.

"Fine. Ceremony's back on. Against my better judgment, I love you. Even if I'm going to be pale for the rest of my life." I stopped him right before his lips touched mine. "And I better be the only one who gets kisses."

He chuckled. "From me? Of course." He pressed his mouth to mine, and my stomach did a nice flip-flop.

3

A chorus of gagging noises sounded around us, but I didn't care if we were grossing out our friends. I deepened the kiss for a second. His tongue barely touched mine before he moved back.

"Your dad's over there," he whispered.

Whoops. "Right. Well, maybe you could stop trying to make out with me."

"And maybe you could stop pretending you don't love me anymore."

"Touché, Mr. Laurent."

A throat cleared next to us. I pulled back to find Dad giving us the stare down. "Sorry, Dad." I gave him a sheepish smile. "But hey, it's my birthday. I'm eighteen. I can do what I want, right?"

Dad raised an eyebrow. His hip was cocked to the side, and he held out a grill spatula, ready to smack Dastien if he got too handsy.

"Within reason, of course," I added.

"Mmm." He sounded skeptical, but the apron he was wearing, which read 'Why you all up in my Grill?' killed some of his intimidation factor.

Time to change the subject. "How're the burgers?" My stomach rumbled again, and Meredith put a giant bowl of Doritos in my face. I grabbed a handful and shoved them in my mouth.

"Nearly done, kiddo. We're five away on this batch."

That meant that thirty burgers were almost ready. Dad had upgraded to a giant custom-made grill after the whole going wolfy thing. Even though I lived at St. Ailbe's—everyone's favorite boarding school for werewolves—my parents liked me to come home for Sunday lunches now that I was considered stable and

4

allowed off campus. I was welcome to bring friends, but werewolves ate way more than humans did. Thus, the super-sized grill.

"I'll get the buns ready." Meredith helped me line up plates and we dropped two buns on each one.

"Who wants cheese?" Dad called out.

Everyone yelled out some form of 'yes' or 'me'.

Dad chuckled. "How about this, then? Anyone not want cheese?"

Silence. As it should be.

I handed Dad the stack of cheese slices and he got to work.

Once everyone had burgers and Dad had reloaded the grill, we settled down around the table. Meredith sat next to Donovan. His chin-length wavy brown hair was tucked behind his ears, and he couldn't keep his eyes off his new mate.

"You guys are so cute," I said.

Meredith tossed a chip at me, and I successfully caught it in my mouth. I raised my hands in the air. "That is how it's done, ladies and gentleman." I couldn't believe how much my coordination had improved over the last few weeks. Before, I'd have been extremely lucky not to get an eye full of salt and vinegar.

Adrian kept chatting about magic stuff with my brother. Axel looked a lot like me. We had the same dark brown hair that tended to curl more than either of us liked. Adrian had darker skin, and his black hair was a little spiky. I liked that they got along so well. For the longest time, Axel had been my best friend— my only friend. I didn't want him feeling excluded now that I was a Were.

Mom scanned the table, making sure that everyone's plates were full. She smiled and turned to Chris. "How is your latest piece coming? The sculpture of the tree?"

Chris waved his hands as he described the way he was constructing the limbs.

I sat between Dad and Dastien. It was a good spot. Two of the most important guys in my life.

Looking around the table made me feel full, not because of the mountain of food, but because of the changes that'd happened in the past few months. This was the first birthday I'd ever had friends over to celebrate with me. It meant a lot.

So much had changed, and even if it had been hard, it felt like all of that was for a purpose. Now that I got to have moments like these, I really truly appreciated them for what they were.

Mom once told me that the bad days were there so you could really enjoy the good ones. It'd been at a time in my life when I was having nothing but bad days, and it hadn't gotten any better. For years.

I could see her point now. She was right. If I had to go through years of bullying to get here, then that was okay by me. This was amazing.

Maybe it wasn't much. A handful of friends and some burgers. But to me, it was everything.

Dastien kissed the top of my head. "You okay?" He could feel my emotions through our bond, and when I wanted to, I could speak to him through it.

I looked up into his amber-colored eyes. "Yeah. Really okay."

"You sure?"

"Absolutely." I took a big bite of my burger.

Then dad dropped the bomb. "So, I want to talk to you two about the ceremony tonight."

I started to choke. Yup. Today had been going just a little too well. A little too perfectly. This was probably the last thing I wanted to talk about with my father. Especially in front of everyone.

The blissful moment was officially over.

Dastien patted my back as I coughed and gulped down Mom's homemade lemonade. "Sure," I said when I could talk again. "What about it?"

"From what Michael's told me, this is like getting married. You turned eighteen today, which means you're still way too young to be so serious—especially about someone you barely know."

Oh jeez. The problem was that I used to agree with him, so I didn't really have a leg to stand on. Even a week ago, the thought of going through the whole bonding ceremony had given me severe heart palpitations, but somewhere in the last forty-eight hours, my perspective had changed. When I finally shifted forms, I'd let go of what I thought my life was going to be like and accepted what it was now. Being wolfy no longer scared me, and I was more than ready for the ceremony. It would cement my bond to Dastien, and that was something I wanted more than anything.

Dad was right about one thing, though. It was like getting married, except for werewolves, there was no such thing as divorce.

Do you want to wait? Dastien asked through our bond.

You bit me. I think it's a little too late for you to back out.

7

I'm not backing out. I'm just trying to consider your father's position.

"If I might say something." Chris smiled, but I was all too aware of the apology in his eyes. He was going to say something I might not like.

"Sure," Dad said.

My heart sped. I had no idea what might come out of Chris' mouth—he could be a little unpredictable at times—and if Dad was already worried…

"They can talk to each other without speaking and read each other's emotions," Chris said. "So they're pretty much as together as they can be already."

Why the hell was he bringing this up? It only made us sound like freaks. And honestly, it was something that I was still adjusting to.

Dad twisted to stare at me more fully. "You can?"

I shoved my burger in my mouth, not sure what to say. "Mmm."

"John. Leave them alone. She's going to be fine," Mom said.

"She will be," Donovan agreed. "I know it seems rushed and odd, but this is totally normal. Especially for True Mates. You couldn't find a better match for your daughter. He's financially sound, responsible, and would do anything to make sure Tessa's happy."

Great. Now they were talking about me like I wasn't there. This was too awkward. I jammed another bite into my already full mouth so that I couldn't be expected to say anything.

"Am I the only one who thinks this is completely insane? She's—"

"John." Mom's voice was a warning to drop it.

"No. She's *my* daughter. She's still practically—"

"She's eighteen—"

"Exactly. Still a child. People change so much between eighteen and twenty-five. She doesn't know who she is yet or who she even wants to be. She—"

"Stop it. Like it or not, Teresa's legally an adult. If she hadn't been bitten, she would've been starting her transition as leader of the coven." Mom blew out a breath.

God. This was mortifying. Did they have to do this now? On my birthday? In front of everyone?

"I know you're worried, but I'm not," Mom said. At least that was something. "This is her life now, and we need to at least try to be understanding and supportive."

I swallowed the last bite as I looked between them.

"She's only eighteen." Dad muttered as he got up to flip the burgers.

I caught Mom's attention as I swallowed. "Thank you," I mouthed.

"Give him time," she said softly. "He didn't think his baby girl would be moving on so fast."

"Me neither," I said under my breath.

Dastien poked me in just the right ticklish spot, and I barely suppressed a squeal.

"What? It's true," I whispered to him.

Dad cleared his throat. "Who wants more burgers?" His voice was a little gruff, but he at least he didn't try to argue anymore. Thank God.

All the werewolves held their plates up.

Dad shook his head. "I gotta say, it's impressive how much you kids eat."

Donovan chuckled softly. He looked like he was in his mid-twenties, but I was pretty sure he was older than a few of us put together. As one of the Seven—the council governing all the packs—he was extremely powerful. From what I understood, he had to have been around for a long time to gain the power for that position. It felt rude to ask his actual age, but I was curious.

Once we were done with the burger portion of the meal, we cleaned up and moved inside. Mom went into her room with Axel and came back with two giant sheet cakes.

"Whoa. That's a lot of cake," I said.

Mom laughed. "Well, I wasn't sure how much to get." She looked at Donovan. "Too much? Not enough?"

"I'm sure it'll be just grand, Gabriela."

Mom blushed at Donovan's accent. I had to admit, it was pretty hot. I lived for the times he said 'ehm'—the Irish version of 'uh.'

The doorbell rang. I paused what I was doing. Pretty much everyone who knew where I lived was already here. "I'll get it." I cut through the house to find my cousins Claudia and Raphael on the porch.

I never saw them unless something was wrong. "Hi. What's going on?"

"We just wanted to stop by and wish you a happy birthday." Raphael wore his usual khaki shorts and flip-flops. His black hair was cut short, and he rubbed his hand back and forth over the top of it as he spoke.

That was a surprise. I didn't think they knew when my birthday was. "Thanks." I swung the door wide and waved them in. "You got here just in time for cake."

Claudia gave me a hug. Her hair was pulled back

in two braids, like always. She wore a flower-print sundress. "*Felicidades.*"

"Is that Claudia?" Mom asked from the kitchen.

"Yes. And Raphael."

Mom appeared and gave them both hugs. "Come on in. We're lighting candles."

I cringed. "Oh, we're not doing the whole singing thing, right? Because that's really not necessary. We can skip straight to the cake part." I hated getting sung to. It was embarrassing.

"We absolutely are singing." Mom pushed me into the kitchen. "Get in there," she said as she slapped my butt.

I jumped. "All right. All right," I said as I rubbed my stinging tush.

As soon as I got back in the kitchen, everyone started singing. I wanted to shrink into the ground. I'd never had so many people be around for this, so I avoided their gazes and stared at the cake. When the song was done, I leaned down, made a wish, and blew out the candles.

Dastien pulled me into his side while Mom cut the cake. "What'd you wish for?"

I glanced up at him. "I can't tell you. That'd nullify my wish."

"Does it have anything to do with tonight?" He squeezed me, and all I could see was him.

"Maybe." I gave him what I hoped was my best flirty look.

"What's happening tonight?" Raphael asked, dragging me back to reality.

I wasn't sure how I should answer the question. *La Alquelarre*—the coven—had been pretty pissed about Dastien biting me. My cousins had been cool though, no matter what the rest of the other *brujos* thought. They'd even helped me out a few times.

Dastien gave a small nod and I took that as the okay to tell. "The full moon is tonight, so we're formalizing our bond."

The twins shared a long look, before Claudia turned to me. "I thought you were waiting until after the Tribunal." She said the words carefully.

I knew that the relationship between the pack and *la Aquelarre* was strained, but the way her hands fisted at her sides made me realize she was a little more upset by this than I'd thought.

I should've kept my mouth shut. This was totally going to come back to bite me in the ass. We were rushing things because Dastien and I wanted a stronger case when we defended ourselves at the Tribunal for the whole biting thing and all the drama that had happened afterward. If the *brujos* started interfering... "No. We're doing it tonight," I said as casually as possible.

"Are you sure about joining into this kind of a bond? Once done, it can't be easily undone. Not even by us," Raphael said.

I didn't like the threat of them breaking our bond, let alone the fact that that was even possible. *Should I lie?* I asked Dastien through our bond.

He shrugged.

Way to be helpful. I'd grown up being told honesty was the best policy. Guess that applied here. "Yeah. I'm sure."

The twins gave each other another long look.

A horrible sinking feeling crept over me. It was

like someone had just walked over my grave, and all the hairs on the back of my neck stood on end.

I'd come to know that feeling well. It usually meant bad things were coming. It wasn't exactly a premonition—I didn't have those. My visions were only of the past and present, but every once in a while I got really good gut feelings about what was going to happen.

As soon as I answered, I knew in my soul that I should've lied. "Everything okay?"

"Yeah, but we should go. Let you celebrate with your friends." Raphael smiled, but the expression wasn't real. "*Felicidades, prima.*" The way he said it, all soft, made it sound like an apology.

They left without another word.

The room was quiet. Frozen. We all knew how the rest of the coven felt about Dastien and me, but I hadn't realized that extended to my cousins. It had to be a recent development—as in the last couple of days.

Had I majorly screwed up? And if so, when? I'd borrowed their books to help Meredith, but I'd give everything back if that would fix whatever was wrong.

Or maybe I was being too sensitive? Dad's reaction already had my defenses up.

I swallowed. "Anyone else think that visit was off?"

Donovan nodded. "Aye. I think we'll be hearing from them again soon."

"They couldn't stop the ceremony, could they?" I asked.

"I don't think so?" Dastien said.

"You don't *think* so? Was that a question?" The

13

wolf in me rose to the surface and I buried my face in Dastien's chest before I started sprouting claws. I couldn't let my wolf free in the middle of my parents' kitchen. I inhaled deeply, letting the scent of him calm me.

He wrapped his arms around me and squeezed me tight. "It's going to be fine," he murmured in my ear. "Dono, should we call in some reinforcements?"

"We'll have plenty on campus, but I'll let word out that we might have trouble headed our way. We'll get you through this, Tessa, even if your coven shows up."

I pulled away from Dastien and scanned my friends' faces. No one would meet my gaze except for Donovan. His arms were crossed as he frowned. Not exactly encouraging.

"Shit. My birthday just got sucky, huh?"

"Who wants cake?" Mom said in a false cheery voice.

"Me," I said. Might as well head off this bad feeling with a massive sugar high. "I'll just take all of one sheet and maybe half of the other."

"Eating your bodyweight in cake isn't going to fix this," Axel said.

"I disagree. Cake will totally help," Meredith said. "Ice cream, too."

I laughed, but it was forced.

I'd spent weeks dreading the full moon, but now that I'd finally shifted for the first time, I was pretty damned excited about the ceremony. I wanted it so badly that the thought of it not happening made me feel stabby. There'd be another chance next month, but I didn't want to wait. We needed it now so we could get through the Tribunal.

Hopefully Dastien was right and we were overreacting, but I had a feeling we were exactly right. With just a few words, I'd screwed over both my birthday and my first full moon ceremony.

I'd bet my life that we'd be seeing more of the coven before the moon rose.

Chapter Two

Everyone took off back to campus after the cake, leaving only my family and Dastien. My parents wanted a little alone time before I went back to the dorm. Even though they knew what was going to happen tonight in a vague sort of way, they couldn't be there. It was a Were-only thing.

The tension in the house was only getting worse thanks to the cousins' visit. As I did the dishes, Dad started whispering to Mom about how they should stop the ceremony. Suddenly, the kitchen seemed too small.

I moved to the wraparound porch and sat on the swing to soak in a little bit of quiet. The screen door screeched. My eyes were closed, but I didn't need to open them to recognize Dastien sitting down beside me. I could sense it through our bond and the scent in the air—that lovely mix of forest and dirt and him. I rested my head on his shoulder and he nuzzled against me.

"Nervous?" he asked after a moment.

"A little." Straddling the lines between human, wolf, and witch was hard. Each part pulled me in a different direction. Being with Dastien was easy.

Natural. I wasn't worried about that, but the ceremony symbolized taking the final plunge into my life as a Were, letting it take precedence over everything else.

I knew why Dad was having so much trouble with it. Everything was changing for me. Fast. "I still feel like a kid, you know? And we're basically getting married tonight. When I think about it, it's kind of crazy."

He lifted his arm so I could scoot closer. I pressed my head to his chest, and listened to his steady heartbeat as he ran his fingers through my hair.

"What's making you nervous exactly?"

I blew out a breath. "Honestly?"

"I only ever want the truth from you." His chest vibrated under my ear as he spoke, his voice low and rumbly.

"Just don't laugh."

"*Cherie.* I would never laugh."

That wasn't true at all and we both knew it. He laughed at me all the time. It was a good thing I didn't take it personally. I poked his side.

"I laugh *with* you," he said as he chuckled, and batted my finger away.

"Everything's changed so quickly. I feel like I'm always racing to catch up." My nerves wound tighter as I talked, which was why I'd been avoiding this discussion. "I want to hit pause for a bit. Enjoy this moment. Have some time to grow up."

His fingers continued to run through my hair, soothing me. I swung my legs over his to get a little closer. I felt his smile through the bond—a jolt of pleasure because I wanted to be closer to him. It made

Dastien happy, which settled my nerves a little more.

"No one said you have to have everything sorted tonight. We still have time to grow up, but we'll grow up together. As a team." He pressed a soft kiss to my forehead. "Don't forget, I'm only two years older than you."

"I know, but you feel a lot older."

He laughed again. "Thanks?"

I slapped his stomach. "That's not what I meant. It's just that you always seem to have it all figured out."

"I don't have it all figured out, but I'm not a worrier. Don't put so much pressure on yourself to know how everything's going to work out. It's impossible." He tugged on my hair a little, and I swatted his hand away.

The guy had a point, but that didn't mean I'd stop worrying anytime soon.

I smelled the jasmine in Mom's perfume a moment before she stepped onto the porch. She sat on the swing on my other side, careful not to touch me. It was still ingrained. Growing up, any brush of skin was enough to bombard me with flashes of thoughts and memories. Of everyone in the family, Mom had always been the best at controlling herself around me, mostly because she grew up with my grandmother—the source of my talent.

"So, what's the ceremony like?"

Dastien's hand found mine, and he squeezed, sending me his support.

"Well, there's one every month. Apparently, everyone gets together and shifts and runs, but some pack business gets taken care of, too. Anything that changes the pack structure." I hadn't been sure I was going to go through with the ceremony until after I shifted. Since then, I'd finally had time to ask questions about the process. Dastien and Meredith had been pretty great about filling me in over the past couple of days.

The only part that I wasn't too into was biting Dastien. Apparently, I had to eat a little bit of the flesh and blood of my mate—completely barbaric and disgusting. Dastien had done his part when he bit me, but I still had to return the favor.

Yuck.

I figured vague was best for the icky part. "We recite some words—kind of like marriage vows—and then it's done. We shift and take an evening run." I sat up, moving my legs from Dastien's lap. "I know it's a lot to accept, but Dad seems pretty not okay with the whole thing."

She shrugged. "You're still his baby. We figured we'd have years before we had anything like this come up, and that was if you could ever let someone get close to you."

Yeah. I hadn't been too sure about the whole being-able-to-have-a-boyfriend thing either. Before, it'd seemed like a long shot at best. "I don't want to upset him."

"He's not upset."

I sat up enough to look at her. "We both know he is."

"One of the hardest things about being a parent is letting go," Mom said. "We lost your brother to college this year, and that was hard, but very expected. We didn't expect to lose you, too. Not like this."

God. She made it sound like I was dying. "You're not losing me."

She brushed her hand across my forehead, sweeping a piece of hair behind my ear.

I was suddenly in my parents' bedroom as a vision took hold.

"She's my little girl. I don't want her to grow up so fast," Dad said. He wore the same clothes he was wearing today. Tears glistened in his eyes. "Can't she wait?"

I jerked away from Mom's touch. She was the only one with enough control to show me exactly what she wanted me to see and no more, but that I didn't mean I wanted to see anything. It felt too intrusive.

"Is this where the party is?" Axel came out to the porch and handed me an ice-cold Diet Coke, breaking the tension. He was my savior when he wasn't being a pain in my ass.

I popped the tab on the Coke, and took a long drink. I needed to consume more calories as a wolf, but I still liked diet sodas. I'd gotten used to the taste and regular Coke tasted wrong now.

He handed Dastien and Mom root beers and leaned against the railing on the porch. "So, what's the drama now?"

I rolled my eyes. "No drama."

"You guys look pretty serious for a drama-free zone."

I plucked the tab off my can and threw it at him. "Jerk."

"Nerd," he countered. "So, what's up?"

"Nothing. We're just talking about growing up."

Axel made a face. "Yeah. That's a mood-killer for

21

sure."

"Look. I know you're worried, but nothing much is changing tonight," Dastien said.

I scoffed. It seemed like a lot was changing tonight.

"We're formalizing what's already happened, so it's like getting upset over the past. Not worth it. She doesn't even have to move in with me."

Uh, I was kind of looking forward to that, I said through our bond. *And I wasn't really going to tell them that part.*

We have to be honest with them. You're lucky to have two great parents who care about you, and they're freaking out right now, so we have to be considerate.

What they don't know won't hurt them...

No. We're not going to lie to them. I just think—

"They're talking to each other in their heads." Axel scrunched his nose. "They're making all the faces they would if they were talking aloud, except without the words. It's so fucking creepy."

"Axel! Language!" Mom swatted his leg.

My cheeks burned. It felt like being caught doing something really intimate.

"Sorry. That was rude." Dastien took the blame, but I was the one who'd started the conversation.

"My bad." I took a long sip from my drink.

"Just don't knock up my sister."

I nearly spewed Diet Coke all over him.

Dastien patted my back as I nearly choked again. I was on a roll today. "Jesus, Axel. Shut up."

"Who's talking about knocking my daughter up?" Dad said as he stepped outside.

I groaned. If he owned a shotgun, I was pretty

22

sure he'd be cocking it right about now. "No one is getting knocked up." I'd need to have a sex life to get preggo and we hadn't gone there yet.

And God. Could this be more embarrassing?

"Just be *safe*," Mom said as she patted my hand.

I was wrong. It could totally get more embarrassing. "Please. For the love of all that's holy, everyone just ixnay on the exsay alktay."

"If you can't say it, honey, you shouldn't be having it."

Jesus Christ almighty.

I set my drink on the ground and covered my face with my hands. "Did no one hear what I just said? Shit. And it's my *birthday*…"

I heard Dastien's laugh through the bond. I peeked at him and his face was a perfect mask of serious.

This isn't funny.

It's extremely funny.

"No. It's humiliating."

Just think, this time next week, we'll be getting ready for some Paul van Dyk.

I grinned. *Can't wait.* "Hey." I kicked Axel's foot. "We're going to PvD next Saturday. If you wanna go, you're gonna need tickets."

"Dastien warned me a while back. I guess I'm going to suffer through yet another night of Nintendo music for you."

Axel had always been my dancing partner, even if he didn't like the music. Hitting the clubs had been my one release when we lived in LA. "Awesome. Thanks." The tickets were Dastien's birthday present to me and I couldn't wait. We had the same taste in music—a heavy rotation of trance and house with some breaks and ambient mixed in. I never thought I'd meet someone who shared my passions, but Dastien did. He got me.

"Can we have a moment with our daughter before you go?" Dad asked.

I started to protest—whatever Dad said to me he could say to Dastien—but Dastien stood before I could say anything. "Of course. I'll wait by the car?"

We were quiet as Dastien stepped off the porch. I knew he could probably hear whatever we said—werewolves had fantastic hearing—but he gave my family the illusion of privacy as he leaned against his black Porsche Cayenne at the end of the driveway.

"Are you sure you want to go through with this?" Dad asked. "If you want to wait, I'm sure we can talk to Michael."

Mr. Dawson, a.k.a. Michael, was Dad's boss, the head of St. Ailbe's and the local pack. Even if I wanted Dad to step in—which I didn't—it wouldn't do any good. It wasn't Mr. Dawson's decision.

I cracked my knuckles as I stared across the driveway at Dastien. The way he leaned against the car made my heart race.

He wasn't even doing anything and my whole body flushed. How could that get me so riled?

"I'm not nervous about it. Dastien…" God. My face burned because I knew he'd be listening to this. "Dastien is kind of perfect for me. I'm a worrier and he's mega calm. We have the same interests in music and dancing and whatnot. I'm not good at the fighting stuff and he's not good at the magic stuff. It's like we balance each other. We fit."

I couldn't even explain what I'd felt when I first saw him. From that moment, it was like I already knew him. I'd never felt something so strongly. And when I left him at the mall, the longing that drew me to him… I couldn't help but hope he felt the same.

"I know it's fast and we're all still adjusting to everything that's happened, but I need to do this. I think once I do, I'll feel more settled. But right now, it's like something could happen and I dunno. I'm nervous. I'm on edge." The more I tried to pinpoint my feelings the more illusive they became. It wasn't just growing up that was bothering me.

I blew out a breath. "I don't know what to say, but I want you to trust me. It's going to be okay."

Dad pulled me in for a hug, and I wrapped my arms around him. Dad was always free with his hugs. He didn't understand my visions the way Mom did, so he didn't keep his distance. But I didn't care anymore. Now that I finally had more control, I could relax into his embrace. "You want away from the pack, then we'll find a way," Dad said.

I kissed his scruffy cheek. "Thanks, Dad. But seriously, I'm going to be okay."

He blinked, not letting tears fall. "Okay, big girl."

Mom pulled me in for a hug next. "*Te quiero mucho.*"

"I love you, too."

I turned to Axel.

"God. It's like it's a fucking funeral."

"Axel!" Mom said.

"What? It's true." He pulled me in for a hug, too. "I love you, kiddo. Good luck tonight. And happy birthday. You finally have friends, you awkward dork."

"I love you, too." I shoved him away as I laughed. "I'm gonna go. Gotta get ready."

"Don't miss dinner next Sunday. Even if you're tired from dancing," Mom said.

"Will do."

I walked to Dastien's car, and he opened the door for me.

"Hey, Dastien," Axel shouted.

"What?"

"Take care of my sister or I'll be forced to kick your ass."

I laughed. We all knew that the only way Axel was kicking Dastien's ass was if Dastien let him.

When I looked back at Dastien, he wasn't laughing this time. "I'll protect her with my life." I heard the resolve in his tone and felt it through the bond—he was making a serious promise.

"Good," Axel said.

Were they for real having a macho handing off the little lady convo? Because that was just so…fifty years ago.

Dastien closed my door and walked around to the driver's side.

"You ready?" he said before starting the car.

I took one last look at the house—my family standing on the porch. Dad had his arm around Mom. Axel leaned forward over the railing, resting on his forearms. It was weird. I was leaving one family for another, yet I was still part of both. It felt like I was being pulled in so many directions lately.

But I was being overly dramatic. I shook myself free of my thoughts and placed my hand on the window. "Yeah. I'm ready." Mom lifted her hand in an answering wave.

"Nothing's changing tonight."

"That's not true," I said as I stared into Dastien's amber eyes. "I really feel like I shouldn't have told my cousins the truth. As soon as they left, I got this overwhelming feeling of dread. I don't like it."

He raised a brow. "Is it a vision? Is that what I'm feeling from you?"

That was impossible. "I don't have visions of the future. Only past and present."

"You could, though. Your powers are still growing. Don't limit your perceptions."

I rubbed my sweating palms on my shorts. "It can't be. I just get the feeling like something's about to change, and that it won't be good. But that has nothing to do with how I feel about the Full Moon Ceremony. I want to be with you. I'm already in your head. It's not like it'd change anything except the way the pack sees us."

"Then it's not the bonding you're worried about?"

"No. I actually can't wait for that part, but there's this feeling. The only other time I felt like this was right before I met you." I paused. "Do you think we should be worried about the Tribunal?" I asked for maybe the millionth time. There was a lot riding on it. Our punishments could even be death, although everyone kept saying that wouldn't happen to us.

"No," he said patiently. "People will make their statements. Then there will be a question and answer session—that's going to be the hardest part. Then, we'll get to say what we want. Biting you was a serious offense, but we've already passed the Seven's test, and

Sebastian and Donovan themselves pardoned us. This is just a formality. It'd be different if that hadn't happened yet. We'd need to prepare defenses and arguments, but I can't think of a reason why it wouldn't go our way now. Just tell everyone what happened, and they'll get it. It's going to be fine. Trust me."

"Okay." I'd been working on my speech for the past couple of days, but it wasn't going very well. The Tribunal wasn't until Monday night, so I still had some time to get it done. But if Dastien wasn't too worried, then I shouldn't be either.

He started down the dirt road. "It's going to be okay. Whatever happens, we'll deal with it together."

"Right." I squeezed his hand, but I wasn't sure I believed that. I'd never been lucky enough to have things go smoothly. Something told me this wasn't going to be as easy as Dastien thought.

Chapter Three

The drive from my parents' house didn't take long. The baseline of Andrew Bayer's "Bullet Catch" rattled the speakers, and I grinned. I freaking loved this track. The dirty beats made my heart race every time. When the breakdown hit, Dastien squeezed my leg.

He was smiling. I love this one, too.

It's kind of perfect, right?

He cranked the volume as he hit the gas, and we wound through the curves of a back road, pushing his fancy-ass car to its limits.

This. This was why I was with him. He'd totally played this track for me—for us—because he knew it'd make me happy.

The greens and browns of the forest blurred past. As we neared campus, a brick fence loomed. The gates to St. Ailbe's were just ahead. I held my breath, waiting for Dastien to slow down, but he blew straight past.

I gripped the door handle. *You missed it.*

Did I?

He sounded a little more than mischievous. The guy was definitely up to something. *Where are we going?*

I want a little time with you before tonight. Is that okay?

Alone time with Dastien? *You read my mind.*

He laughed, because that wasn't far from the truth. Ever since I'd gone furry for the first time, we'd been using this form of communication more and more. It was easier than talking aloud. Or maybe I just liked it better. It felt special.

Dastien finally slowed as he turned the car onto a dirt road.

Huh. I'd never been down here, and for good reason. The "road" was practically a deer path.

A loud thunk rattled the car as it bottomed out. The scratching noise pained me. "Holy crapola! That sounded like it hurt."

"Eh. I'm sure it's fine."

The guy had lost his mind. After ten minutes of holding onto the "oh shit" bar, he finally stopped the car in the middle of the forest.

I unbuckled and got out. "Where are we?"

He gave me a small smile, and a wave of his nerves hit me. "This way."

Why was he nervous?

I sighed. Sometimes Dastien wasn't the most forthcoming person. I could've dug into his mind and figured out what we were doing. At least, I was pretty sure I could do that now that our bond had strengthened, but being patient was the better route. Snooping of any kind was rude, especially the mental kind.

I followed behind him as he wove through trees. After a little bit we hit a clearing.

The grass, brush, and flowers were wild and overgrown. I could hear and smell the wildlife that lived there. The view even had a small lake—okay maybe a pond, but whatever—it was amazing. "Wow. This is awesome. How did you find this?"

"You like it?" He was still nervous.

Not going to pry. Not even going to think about it. The temptation was too strong.

I was quiet for a second as I walked closer to the pond. The clearing was massive. Acres. *It's beautiful.*

Dastien's cheeks reddened.

Holy shit. He was blushing. My mate was actually blushing.

Something was up. Something was special about this land, and I wasn't getting it. I looked around again, trying to figure out what this was about, but nothing sprang to mind.

He closed the distance between us and pulled me into a hug. "I know I said we didn't have to move in together, but I thought one day, this could be a good place to live."

I laughed. "Here?" There wasn't anything around except for a forest and a pond.

"Here." The nerves were back.

What was he talking about?

"It's kind of like a dual birthday and bonding present."

"My brain isn't functioning." I blinked a few times, trying to process his words. "This—all of this land—is a present? For me?"

"For us. The spread is about fifty acres. We could build a house near the lake. There are fish and it's quiet. Plenty of room to go for runs. Not too far from your parents or brother—if they stay in Texas. Obviously, it's a long-term thing. But my cabin won't work forever, and when we start to think about a family and—"

Wow. My mind was blown.

He'd bought me acreage. For a house. So we could raise a family here. The guy was light-years ahead of me, but that wasn't anything new. Still, I was worried about growing up and taking the next step, and he was onto building a house and raising a whole pack of kids.

It was a little absurd. I stepped away from him as I took in everything.

"You don't like it?" His tone was more than a little pouty.

"That's not..." I didn't know what to say. "I mean, I love it. I just wasn't prepared. I didn't expect anything like this." I was totally messing this up. "Am I supposed to get you something? Because I definitely didn't buy you a farm or two goats or whatever."

He grinned, and the dimples deepened in his cheeks. "No. You're giving me you. That's what I want. It's tradition that the guy gifts his mate the home they'll share. This isn't exactly a place to live yet, but I think it could be perfect."

I tucked myself to his side and scanned out at the land again. A house. A lake. I could handle that. "It's perfect."

Dastien put his arm around my shoulder and I reached up to link my fingers with his.

One thing that he'd said stuck out though. "Kids, huh?"

"In a few years?"

"A few years?" Now *that* was something I wasn't ready for. "You realize *we're* kids."

"We're also werewolves. We can wait twenty years, but I see you and I see the future. I want to be prepared. I want to give you everything."

That was sweet, but I really didn't need all of it. "I only need you." I stood on my tiptoes and pressed my lips to his. "But umm...I won't have puppies will I?"

He pulled away, looking at me like I was nuts. "Puppies? We're not dogs."

"I know...but you know—" I waved my hands around, trying to ease the tension. "The babies...they won't come out furry, right?" Because I didn't know if I could handle that.

Dastien started laughing. Hard. Like he probably was busting a gut. He fell to the ground when I shoved him.

"It was a valid question!" My cheeks were burning. Okay, so it was a dumb question, but it was a fear of mine.

He pulled me down beside him. "No. They won't be furry." He chuckled again. "We don't change until puberty. Remember? That's why the school exists."

Oh. Right. "Well, I got carried away for a second. You buy me land and start talking about a family and my mind is still sort of in pieces. I mean...I can barely think about what's going to happen post-St. Ailbe's— or post-next week really—and you're talking family."

His rough hands ran up my arms and I shivered. "I thought the girl was the one who was supposed to be all into the family thing."

"That's a cliché. And if there is one thing I refuse to be, it's a cliché." His mouth was inches from mine, and I couldn't look away from his lips.

"No one would ever think that, my *bruja*, alpha werewolf, human. You are anything but normal."

Done waiting for him to close the distance, I brushed my lips against his quickly and my heart kicked into gear. "Isn't it grand?"

"It sure is, *cherie*," he said with his lips a breath away from mine. His hands on my cheeks, he deepened the kiss. I lost myself in it. The warmth of him. I ran my fingers under his shirt, and wrapped one leg around his hips.

It wasn't enough. I wanted more of him. It was like I was drowning and he was my air.

We rolled until I was under him. "I love you."

"*Je t'aime.*" He ran his nose along my neck and I moaned. Goose bumps spread out along my skin as he muttered something in French.

I loved it when he did that.

He nipped my earlobe, and I pulled him back to me. I needed his lips. Again.

My cell phone started ringing, playing a loop from Above and Beyond's new track.

Dastien pulled back from the kiss just long enough to say, "Ignore it."

I was with him. His hips ground into me and I moaned. My body was burning up.

My phone went off again. *Ignore.*

His hand ran under my shirt, and I swear I saw stars as he lightly teased my nipple.

When my cell rang a third time, I pulled back. "Damn it." I panted. Trying to catch my breath, I checked the screen. Meredith had called three times.

Oh shit. "We're so late!" I said as I plopped back

down on top of him.

"What time is it?" Dastien sat back enough to pull his phone from his pocket. "Oh. Wow. It's almost seven. We should head back."

"But I was having such a good time." These days, time alone with Dastien was mostly made of stolen moments here and there. It was frustrating. Or maybe I was just frustrated.

He brushed the hair from my face. "Me, too." He quickly pressed his lips to mine and stood. "Come on. If we don't go now, we'll stay forever."

I took his hand and he pulled me up. I scanned the clearing one last time before heading back to the car. "Thank you, Dastien."

He squeezed my hand. "Thank you. I'm excited about living here with you."

"Me, too."

His answering dimpled grin made my heart soar. I felt so full I could burst.

***

As soon I stepped onto my floor in the girls' dorms, Meredith's door swung open. "Where the hell have you been?" She stormed down the hall. "Is that a twig in your hair?" She tugged so hard she practically ripped out a piece of my scalp.

"Ouch. Watch it."

"It is…it's a twig." She studied it for a second. "What have you been up to?" This time the anger was gone, replaced with a heavy dose of curiosity.

"Nothing," I said, but I was sure my cheeks were a lovely shade of red, totally giving me away.

"Mmm-hmmm. Nothing my ass." She held out the twig and I snatched it from her.

I started down the hall to my room. The dorms were set up so everyone had their own room, but two rooms shared a bathroom. Meredith and I shared ours. I'd been nervous about it at first, but she'd ended up being the best part of the dorm. I'd never really had a girl friend before.

My room was still decked out in all white. Even though I could probably add stuff now that I didn't have to bleach the emotions and memories from everything, I was still a little paranoid.

I tossed the twig in the trash. "So, Dastien kind of bought me a bunch of land?"

"He bought you land?" She sounded excited.

I grabbed a brush from the bathroom and saw my reflection.

Yup. I was looking crazy. My hair was one giant rat's nest. I started attempting to fix the tangles. "Yeah. Fifty acres so we could build some sort of monstrous house and start a family."

"Nice!"

Picturing the pond and what could be there made me smile like a moron. "I know, right? But it's a little nuts." I pulled a leaf from the brush.

"And romantic. Most people who do the Full Moon Ceremony have estates to move into. Dastien's parents have a place somewhere in France. I don't think he's been in years, though. But if the mate doesn't come from a rich family, then the guy makes sure they have a place to share post-ceremony. I was expecting him to give you the keys to something, but land to build on is a nice touch."

"So, when you and Donovan do your ceremony, you'll move to his place? In Ireland?" I said, taking a wild guess. I had no idea where Donovan usually lived.

She shrugged. "I hadn't thought about it, actually. I guess I should've. I don't even know where Donovan lives."

I grinned. It was nice being on the same wavelength with her.

Meredith was quiet for a second, but then she laughed. She was totally asking him using their bond. "He just told me that I'm ruining surprises by asking him questions, but I have options. He says he has a place on every continent but Antarctica. Although he favors the one in Ireland in County Clare, I get my pick." She plopped down on my bed. "I like the sound of that."

I gave up on my hair. It wasn't going to be fixable without a shower. I tossed the brush on my bedside table. "When are you two gonna do the whole ceremony hoopla?"

She snorted. "Ceremony hoopla? We're going to do it at the Full Moon Ceremony next month."

"Why wait?"

"We could do two in one night, but usually it's one couple at a time. Plus, I wanted to give you and Dastien the chance to have your own special time. You've worked hard for this."

I sat next to her. That was nice, but made me feel a little guilty. "I don't want you to wait because of me. It's not like you've had an easy time either." That spell she'd been under was horrible, and not being able to shift for years…

"No, but Donovan and I have both been Weres our whole lives. We always knew what we were and the dangers around us. This life wasn't at all what you were expecting, and you've had to make huge adjustments."

No kidding. I hadn't imagined that werewolves existed in my wildest dreams, let alone that I'd *be* one.

"Plus, this is my first Full Moon Ceremony in years. I'll actually get to run with the pack now that the curse is gone. I'm happy enjoying just that for now." Meredith popped up from my bed. "Okay. So you need to shower, and then we'll get you ready. I got the robes from Mr. D in my room."

"Robes? Really?" I knew that there were some in the boxes of clothes stashed around campus, but it still seemed totally weird.

"Unless you want to shred what you're wearing or undress before you shift in front of everyone, the robe is the best way to go."

Shit. "I'll take the robe."

"Thought so."

Meredith headed into her room, and I closed the door behind her. I flipped the shower knobs, putting the water as hot as I could stand. Showering was one of my favorite things. I did some of my best thinking in there.

The past week had really been a blur. Between breaking the curse on Meredith and the birthday and everything else, I hadn't had time to catch my breath. The nerves that I'd felt since my cousins showed up at my parents' house finally started to settle down. No wonder I was feeling so anxious. It was natural to be worried when it came to them. But Donovan and

Dastien had it covered. Everything was going to be totally fine.

I was happy with the way my life was going. Had things been a little hectic? Yes. That only made life interesting. Soon, everything would settle down. It had to, right?

When I was done showering, I worked on detangling my hair. Maybe rolling around on the ground with Dastien hadn't been the smartest choice hair-wise, but it sure had been fun. I was pretty sure we'd move on to the next step in our relationship soon. And then I'd be spending more nights in his cabin. We'd just been sleeping so far, but waking up next to Dastien was kind of perfect on its own.

"All right, girly. Time's up."

I tightened the towel around myself as Meredith opened the bathroom door. She held a red robe. It was long, floor length, and hooded.

"I got this one altered for you."

I was at least half a foot shorter than the shortest werewolf. "Thanks. I wouldn't have thought of that."

"No worries. I got your back." She set the robe on the counter. "Let's fix your hair, put on a little makeup, and then head out."

I forced myself to take steady, even breaths. "Right." My voice was a little squeaky.

"It's going to be fine. This is no big deal. You're already bonded to the hotness."

"Right." Still squeaky.

"And you love him."

I let the breath go. "Right." Not even a little squeaky.

"I'm thinking we do some braids. That way you

can put on the hood and not mess it up too much."

I shrugged. My normal style was leaving the hair down and letting it air dry or tying it up in a totally sloppy knot. I wasn't one for fixing myself up, except for special occasions. But this totally counted as one.

"Whatever you think." Because I couldn't think about anything other than what would come next. My mind was already a million miles away, going over the steps of the ceremony.

Meredith clapped her hands. "Perfect. Go sit at my desk. I'll bring everything over."

I was fidgeting too much as she worked. "You've got to stop moving."

I chewed on my lip. "So, did you see the latest episode of *The Soup*?" It was a total non sequitur, but it kept me distracted when all I wanted was to be outside with Dastien, and fully bonded.

I borrowed Meredith's computer to show her the latest clip of *Finding Bigfoot*. We were laughing when I realized that maybe I was the dumb one. Could they really be onto something?

"Wait. Is there a bigfoot?"

Meredith snorted. "No. Not that I've ever heard of."

"Thank God. If those morons were right, I wasgoing to freak out."

"Even if they were real, I doubt leaving a half-eaten donut in the middle of the forest is going to attract one. And what is with that crazy screaming bigfoot noise that guy makes? Does he really think that it's going to attract a bigfoot? I mean, how does he know that's what a bigfoot even sounds like?"

I laughed. "I know! Right? Because they're not

real. It's horrible."

Meredith stepped away from me. "Okay. Done."

"Really?"

"Yup."

I got up to look in the mirror. My hair had gotten pretty long—the dark brown wavy-curls reached halfway down my back. Meredith had shaped the mess into lots of little braids that twisted together and formed a crown. "Wow. This is amazing."

"Thanks."

"How did you learn to do this?"

"The same way anyone learns anything these days—the Internet."

I picked up a compact mirror so I could see it from all angles. "Seriously. I'm impressed."

"Happy to be of service. So, makeup?"

I gave myself an honest once-over. Ever since I became a werewolf, I hadn't used much. My complexion was pretty perfect—which it had never been before. I put on a little shadow, some eyeliner, and mascara.

My hands were sweating as I slipped the robe on over my towel.

This was it. Today was the day that I was going to do this whole werewolf ceremony thingy.

You okay? Dastien's voice rumbled through the bond.

I tied the robe and ran a hand over my trembling stomach. *Fine.*

I'll see you soon, okay?

I closed my eyes as his love and support washed over me. *Okay.*

The nerves were still there, but lessened. I still had

41

the nagging feeling like something bad was going to happen, but I hoped that was just me being a pessimistic worrier. I was ignoring my gut and trusting my heart.

What could possibly go wrong?

Chapter Four

The pack was supposed to meet up in the quad. The whole area was grassy, and on nice days people lay out doing their homework. Besides the cafeteria, it was probably the biggest gathering spot on campus.

I wasn't sure how many people went to a typical ceremony. I assumed everyone in the school pack, but since we had so many visitors, I wasn't sure. Maybe everyone would come.

I'd avoided the ceremony during the last full moon. I was still a little weak from the vampire bite and not at all comfortable with the idea of shifting, so I'd let Dr. Gonzales at me with one of her needles. I'd slept through the whole thing. Meredith and Dastien had explained that everyone got together as a pack, shifted, and ran. I had an idea of what was going to happen, but knowing about it and actually doing it were two totally different things.

As soon as I stepped outside the dorm, I stopped walking. "Oh my God." In the hour or so I'd been inside, campus had become a zoo. People streamed into the quad from the path to the parking lot. Already, a crowd of at least a few hundred filled the square plot of grass.

How had everyone even found parking?

Meredith bumped her shoulder against mine. "Bonding ceremonies don't happen very often, and people really like to see them."

"I thought all the girls got paired up." Even if I thought it was odd that girls got matched before they turned eighteen, that was the norm among the Weres. That meant my ceremony was nothing special—or at least it definitely shouldn't have been such a big draw.

"Lots of people are mated, but only True Mates do this exact ceremony. It's been a long time since the last formal bonding. Plus, people are already in town for the Tribunal and you made a lot of people interested... So..."

"This blows. And I totally blame you." Only the students had really heard about me before Meredith's curse fiasco.

"Me? No. You should be blaming Dastien. Breaking the spell was one thing, but he bit you and that was a huge freaking deal. Word's gotten around about the True Mate thing."

True Mates were extremely rare, but that was what Dastien and I were. Nothing could've kept us apart. We were two halves. And apparently 'True Mate' was Were for 'freak show.' I wiped my sweaty palms down my robe. I wished I wasn't totally nakey under the damned thing. It must've been wishful thinking that the ceremony was only a big deal to Dastien and me. Crowds weren't my thing, but since I showed up at St. Ailbe's, I'd found myself in the center of a few of them. It never got any easier.

I made my way through the quad and past the stares. Each surrounding building was only a few stories tall. The dark brick was lit by lights hidden in the trees. People stood around, chatting as they waited for the ceremony to start. Everyone was dressed in robes, but theirs were plain black like the one Meredith was wearing.

"This looks really cultish."

Meredith laughed. "You'd rather see everyone in their birthday suits?"

"Well…I mean some of these guys—"

A growl rang through the crowd, and I rolled my eyes. I recognized that special timbre. "It was a joke. Jeez."

"*Cherie.*" Dastien's voice had more than a little wolf in it.

The crowd parted and I finally saw him. He wore a red robe, too. His dark curls were tucked back behind his ears. I met his golden gaze. There wasn't any turning back now, and crowd or not, I didn't care. I didn't want to turn back. "Let's do this."

We moved as a group to a clearing in the woods. The moon rose as we walked, and I could feel its energy burning through me. My skin itched as the wolf rose to the surface. Only Dastien's firm grip on my hand kept me from shifting.

Why do I feel like I can't hold this form?

It's hard during the full moon. That's why we have the ceremony. It's important to be together as a pack and get out in the wild. The newer or less dominant the wolf is, the harder it is to keep the human form. It gets worse as the moon rises.

Perfect. I scratched my arm, but it didn't help alleviate the itch at all.

When we got to the spot for the ceremony, I was

surprised that I recognized it. We'd held the meeting here when we discussed whether to kick Imogene out of the pack. The moon provided more than enough light to see by, illuminating the unlit bonfire area off to the side. Slightly deeper into the woods, piled rocks and boulders from the nearby creek formed a circle of seats, and a stone dais sat in the center of the ring. The platform part probably weighed a million pounds.

Mr. Dawson, Donovan, and Sebastian all stood on the oblong stone wearing black robes with the hoods down. Donovan and Sebastian were both members of the Seven—the council that ruled all werewolves—and Mr. Dawson ruled the local pack. All three were seriously strong alphas. I was sure some of the other alphas called in for the Tribunal were around, but I wouldn't know them if I saw them. Not unless they tried to push their power at me.

Dastien pulled me along until we were standing in front of the dais. Everyone else crowded around behind us, some taking seats on the stones, others just standing, waiting for the ceremony to be over so they could shift.

Mr. Dawson and Donovan stood in relaxed poses, while Sebastian stood a little off to the side. He was grinning, and his blue eyes glowed bright.

Donovan had been really easy to get along with. He was only intimidating when he needed to be, but Sebastian was a little more so. When I first got to St. Ailbe's, he'd pushed himself into my mind, which wasn't fun at all, but ever since that one unpleasant experience, he'd been really nice. Super smiley. It was kind of weird, but I'd take that over scary Sebastian any day. I'd never fully gotten over that first impression.

Donovan stepped forward and the few whispers of the gathered wolves immediately died. "The moon has risen, and the ceremony shall begin. Have you both approached clear of heart and mind?"

"Yes," Dastien said.

Donovan turned to me.

Right. I had to say something now. "Yeah." My voice cracked. "I mean, yes." God. I'd been over it in my mind a million times the past couple of days and I still managed to mess it up.

Donovan gave me a wink. "Good. Then let's get started."

Sebastian stepped to the edge of the rock. His white-blond hair looked even whiter against his stark black robe. "This is the joining of two wolves whose like I've not seen before. Both more alpha than Dono or I were in our youth. When I was called here to assess them and determine what had happened, I was not prepared for this one." He pointed to me. "Her strength and magic will do well for the pack."

I was really grateful that my hood blocked out my peripheral vision. Only the three on the stage could see my face and how red it was getting.

Donovan held up his hands, and the whispering crowd finally settled. He looked at me for a second and it felt like he was seeing into my soul. I struggled not to move under his inspection. "Before we proceed with the incantation, you must complete the exchange of flesh."

Dastien turned me so we were facing each other. He held out his arm.

Oh God. This was going to be a disaster. I suddenly felt cold. I wiped my sweaty palms on my robe. "I can't bite you." I'd known it was part of the ceremony, but hearing it and actually having to tear into Dastien's arm were totally different. "That's just...nope...not gonna happen."

His eyes flashed to bright yellow. "You don't want this?"

Was he messing with me? Of course I didn't want to bite him. That didn't mean I didn't want to be with him. "No. I mean. Yes. I mean." God. I was sounding like a real moron tonight and so many people were here listening. I let out a shaky breath. "I don't want to hurt you. Because it totally hurt when you bit me. More than a little bit. It was not cool. At all."

A few chuckles rang out through the crowd and I stared down at the ground.

"I thought we were different than vampires..." I muttered softly, but everyone heard me. Full on laughing came from the crowd.

Who knew I was such a freaking comedian?

Shit. I had to do it. And not make an idiot of myself in front of everyone. I wiped my hands on my robe again. "Fine. But don't get all pissy when it hurts. I don't want any whining."

Dastien gave me a small smile. "I'm not going to whine."

"Sure you won't."

He held out his arm for me again and I grasped it with both hands. I met his gaze and sucked in breath.

I so didn't want to do this. Not even a little bit. My stomach churned at the thought.

I started to bite down, and then stopped, whining

a little. I hopped from foot to foot. "This is so messed up."

"Just do it."

I started to put my mouth on him and then pulled back. "I can't. Shouldn't we just skip to the spell?"

You can do it. I'll be okay, he said through the bond. *One little bite and it's done.*

My stomach churned as I tried again. "Fine. Count to three. I'll go on three."

I rested my teeth gently against his skin.

"One."

I squeezed my eyes tight.

"Two."

Just do it, I told myself. *Don't be an idiot in front of all these people.*

"Thr—"

An explosion cut off Dastien's word.

Dastien jumped to action, shielding me as I covered my ears. My hands shook as I lowered them, looking to see what had happened.

"She's not yours to claim." A familiar voice called out.

Dastien growled. His spreading fur rippled under my hands. His anger was making my blood burn. I was angry, but he…he was pissed the fuck off. His emotions were so strong that the nearby Weres started wolfing out.

That couldn't happen. Whatever was going on, I needed him in human form so we could deal with it. "Dastien. You have to calm down. Please."

The crowd parted and suddenly our roles reversed. Dastien grabbed my arms as I lunged forward.

Luciana wore all white. A dress, flowing with many layers. The spell that lit her hands made her look like an avenging angel, but I knew she was the opposite of anything angelic. Behind her were at least ten other people dressed in white.

How in the hell had she managed to sneak up on all these wolves? Especially with the extra guards Dastien and Donovan had posted.

I felt it then. It wasn't just the moon that was making me itch. Magic hung thick in the air. "I don't know what you're doing here, but you weren't invited. Leave now." Wary of the *brujos*, the wolves who'd already shifted flattened their ears and a few still in human form slid away, leaving space between themselves and whatever magic Luciana was working.

"No." Luciana looked past me, dismissing me. "We had a deal, Michael."

"I'm not aware of any deal that would affect anything we're doing tonight."

"You gave your oath that the coven would be allowed to speak at the Tribunal. Now you're breaking your word?"

Mr. Dawson pressed his lips together in a firm line. "Both this ceremony and the Tribunal are Were-only events. Outsiders can't participate without a pack sponsor assigned on a case-by-case basis. You might have a sponsor for the Tribunal, but not for tonight. You don't have the right to be here."

I nearly gave a fist pump. Thank God for rules I was totally clueless about.

"I'll sponsor her." A voice rang out from the crowd.

The pack separated to show a woman in a black

robe. Her brown hair fell in waves around her face. "I'm her sponsor for the Tribunal. I'll sponsor her tonight as well."

What? No. This wasn't happening. *Who the hell is that?* I asked Dastien through our bond.

Sophia Hoel.

Related to Rupert?

His wife.

Perfect. Rupert Hoel was the asshole who'd tried to take over the pack and failed. He'd chained up Sebastian, Donovan, Mr. Dawson, and Dastien, and left them in a vampire cave. The douchebag was still on the run, but his family couldn't be punished for his actions. Now I kind of wished they could be. They had two daughters—Imogene and Nikki. I pretty much hated both of them. Big time.

Mr. Dawson crossed his arms. "This ceremony and the Tribunal are entirely separate matters, and sponsorship for tonight wasn't given proper notice."

Luciana waved her hands, and fire licked the ground. "You think I don't know what this means? The second she bites him, the second the words are said, she's yours for good. It makes the Tribunal worthless."

The Weres that had gone wolfy prowled around the members of *la Aquelarre*. The rest were watching. Motionless, but ready for action.

"Everyone knows mated wolves can't be separated," Luciana said.

She was right. That was why we were doing this. With the completed bond and Sebastian and Donovan's approval, we were golden for the Tribunal. It was just a technicality. But if we didn't cement the bond…

Mr. Dawson grinned, and I shuddered. There wasn't even a little bit of warmth in his expression. The man was scary when he was pissed. "If you think I will allow two of my *already mated* pack alphas to be separated, you're sorely mistaken."

No way. She wasn't getting between Dastien and me. I wouldn't let that happen.

"Teresa isn't just any pack member you can mate off. You stole her from our ranks—not only our leader, but our strongest coven member. The Tribunal was our chance to make our case using your methods, but by your actions, you'd obviously prefer we take her back using force."

I knew Luciana wanted me to join the coven. She'd even tried spelling me to get her way, but it hadn't worked. I stupidly thought she'd just wanted to speak at the Tribunal to make Dastien's life hell. Boy, was I wrong. *Did you know they wanted to talk at the Tribunal to get me back?* I asked Dastien.

No. I knew they wanted to talk, but I didn't know anything about this. I swear.

With the amount of panic and anger I was feeling through the bond, I believed him.

"But now…You've gone too far, Michael."

Lady had lost her damned mind. No way was I leaving Dastien or the pack. I was done listening. "We've been over this." I made sure to enunciate so there'd be no misunderstandings. "I'm not going back to the coven. Not when you were so quick to try manipulating me with magic. Not when you nearly killed my friend without a whisper of remorse. I don't want to be anywhere near you let alone join your coven."

"But you'll take our help when you need it."

That was low. Claudia and Raphael had helped me more than once, but they were family. And to be honest, the first two times I hadn't even asked for it. "If you're referring to my cousins, then yes. I'll take my family's help and I'll help my family. But you— you're not family. This—" I waved my arms toward the assembled Weres—"is my family."

Fire shot from Luciana's fingertips, and she wavered. A coven member—also dressed in white— came to help her stand. Whatever flashy spell was lighting her hands must've been costing her.

"Donovan. Sebastian. I know you remember the last time our people fought. Surely you don't wish to repeat that."

"Are you threatenin' us? With war?" Donovan jumped smoothly down from the dais, his Irish accent thickening with his anger.

I'd never seen Donovan so furious, but when his eyes flashed to blue, I knew he was not someone I ever wanted to piss off. I stepped back, giving him room.

"It's not a threat. It's a fact," Luciana said.

What the hell was going on? Why did she fucking care so much where I was? What was her endgame? It didn't make any sense. If she forced the pack to make me go with her, then I'd do everything in my power to tear her down. To get back here. I was nothing if not stubborn.

Could she be that dense?

No. Not being as high in the coven as she was. Which meant that she had to be up to something. The big question was what?

"Luciana," I said. My voice sounded much calmer than I felt. "I want nothing to do with you. Forcing me to go with you will not end up with me helping you in any way, shape, or form. I will never be like you." I paused to let my words sink in. "You need to leave. Now."

The spell on her hands strengthened, and I blinked my eyes from the sudden bright light surrounding her. "I think Donovan and Sebastian would disagree. Is it worth it to fight now? Why not complete your ritual at the next full moon? Give us the chance to make our case."

"Or else?" I asked.

She held up her hands. "I'll do what I must."

The circling wolves moved forward, but knocked into an invisible barrier that surrounded the *brujos*. They snarled and a few more Weres shifted as they ran at the barrier.

One of the coven members threw a bottle filled with red powder at the closest wolf, and it cut through the invisible wall. The wolf yelped as the glass smashed against his hindquarters and he went down in a whimpering heap as magic flashed.

They were going to fight. Over me. People—my pack—could get hurt. I had to stop this.

"Wait." I took a breath.

"*Non.* You can't—"

The fight started to grow around us. Wolves crashed into the invisible barrier, bones crunching as they hit. The witches threw potions into the pack. Some sparked in blazing fire. Others were more subtle, casting shadows or fog. But every vial sparked a chorus of whimpers. Pain rippled through the pack bonds and for the first time, I could feel each wolf—and every injury.

I had to stop this before it got out of control. I grabbed Dastien's hand. "We get through the Tribunal and in a month, we're right back here. Nothing will change, except this fight."

He pulled me close, running his nose along my cheek. "I don't trust them," he whispered in my ear. "If we don't press this now, I could lose you."

I pulled back. "Impossible. We'll get through this." I cleared my throat. "We'll wait," I said to Mr. Dawson.

Sebastian shook his head. "Let us handle this."

One of the coven members yelled an incantation in language I didn't know. The ground exploded off to my right and howls rent the night.

At once, Sebastian shifted. A spell flew his way and he dodged it, but a blast of light hit another wolf who collapsed to the ground.

Wolves were getting hurt. Arguing about this was a waste of time.

I spun to Mr. Dawson. "We have to stop this."

"I'm with Dastien. That's a huge mistake. You give in now, you'll be giving in to them forever."

Non. Please. We have to do this now. You can't let her affect our actions. Dastien protested through our bond, but I tuned him out.

It was too much. Spells flew, crisscrossing the night in streaks of jagged light. Wolves circled the coven, slamming their bodies into the barrier. It was chaos, and all because I couldn't wait one month?

"Stop." I yelled the word as loud as I could and backed it with alpha powers. Every wolf froze in place.

I held my breath, hoping that the *brujos* would stop, too. When no one moved, I said, "This isn't worth fighting over. I'll promise not to finish the bonding ceremony tonight if you'll leave now."

"Are you sure?" Mr. Dawson said softly to me, but every Were heard the question.

The night was quiet as everyone waited for my answer. I knew that what I was doing was right. I couldn't let any more wolves get injured because of me. But that didn't make this any easier. "Yes," I said finally.

Mr. Dawson gave me a solemn nod before turning to Luciana. "You're getting this much from us, but nothing else."

She raised her head in the air, like she thought she was the queen of the universe, and I wanted to strangle her. "I need your word. The spell please."

Spell?

Fur sprouted over Mr. Dawson's face. "We won't finish this bonding ceremony tonight. You have my word. I shall break it only on punishment of death by the gods above and below." His voice was growly with the wolf. "Leave now, Luciana. Or we will remove you from our land."

The fire went out of Luciana's hands. "That's all we ask." She grinned, and my stomach flip-flopped.

I knew that smile. The feeling of dread that it invoked in me. That was what my premonition had been about. This moment.

She and the rest of *la Aquelarre* walked away, but I knew whatever they were plotting was far from over.

"Oh God," I muttered. My heart was racing so fast that my hands shook. Dastien hugged me to his chest.

"Did I do the right thing?"

"I don't know," he said. "I don't think we had any good option, but I was ready to fight for you. For us."

"I know."

"You gave up." His sadness and disappointment flowed freely through the bond, and my eyes welled.

This wasn't what I wanted to happen. "Did you hear the wolves in pain? It wasn't about giving up. It was about not causing a huge blow up if it could be prevented."

It took a while for everyone to calm down. A few wolves shifted back and Dr. Gonzales led them as they took the injured to the infirmary. I hoped whatever spells had been cast could be easily removed.

"Lass," Donovan said beside me.

I pulled away from Dastien enough to see Donovan.

He looked shaken, with his skin a little paler than normal and his eyes glowing bright blue, signaling his wolf was ready to take over. "It was a hard choice, but I think it was the right one. Even I was ready to fight, and it wouldn't have been pretty. The last war with the witches...suffice it to say it took a few centuries before the world recovered. Thank you for keeping your head when no one else did. You'll be a good leader."

"Thanks." But I was still hung up on war. It was such a strong word. "Is that what's going to happen now? War?"

"You may have stayed it for a while, but it could be unavoidable if Luciana calls the other covens for aid." He clasped Dastien's shoulder. "Hang on, you two. If it's you they want, they'll have quite a battle in store for them."

I took a breath. "Thanks."

He nodded. "The moon is high in the night. Let us run together and renew the friendship and bond that takes us from lone wolf to pack." He raised his arms, and power flowed through the pack. It hit me, rushing along my skin. My inner wolf rose up and there wasn't anything I could do to stop it. I let go, and within a breath, I was on four feet.

Wolf-Dastien butted his head against mine and took off running.

The power of the full moon filled me with energy and I took off after him. The trees whipped past as I let the power of the pack take my worries away. It was almost like I had no problems as a wolf. Everything was simplified.

A wolf howled off to the left, and the group moved as one in that direction.

I caught the scent of the deer a second before I smelled its blood.

The wolf wanted to go after it, but I didn't.

I shouldered into Dastien, and he led us around the kill. He howled again, and the pack followed.

I caught the moonlight and the wolf took over. I lost myself in my senses, the feel of the run, and the pack around me.

Chapter Five

I woke up the next morning in Dastien's arms. His cabin was just one big room. The blackout curtains had parted a little bit, letting a sliver of light in. I tried to pull away, but he tightened his grip, and nuzzled his nose against the back of my neck.

"More sleep." His voice rumbled.

I sighed and closed my eyes. After the run, we'd come back here to eat. That'd always been our plan, except that we hadn't gone through with the ceremony. It was supposed to be romantic. We were supposed to take the next step, but Dastien didn't want to do that until after the ceremony. I'd been scared about it, but excited too. Now that was all shot to shit.

As I lay there, my nervous anticipation kicked into overdrive. Tomorrow was the Tribunal. I knew Dastien was worried about it, but I didn't think the worry I was feeling was his. A lot of it was mine. There was so much more on the line now that we hadn't cemented our bond.

"How much do you think we should worry about Luciana?"

Dastien growled. "*Merde*. She's a pain in the ass."

I rolled my eyes.

"I saw that."

"That's literally impossible. Your eyes are closed and you're spooning me. You can't see my face."

"Fine. I felt you do it."

"That's creepy."

"I'm not creepy. I'm your mate. Remember?"

I rolled my eyes again, and he squeezed me tighter.

"The thing is, Luciana isn't stupid. She's conniving. I felt like postponing the ceremony was my only choice, and it wasn't that big of a deal to—"

Dastien flipped me onto my back. He hovered over me, balanced on his forearms. His eyes were bright yellow. "Not that big of a deal?"

I reached up, cupping his face with my hand. "What are a few more weeks when we have a lifetime ahead of us?"

He sagged down beside me. "I didn't want to wait. And now we have to fight to be together during the Tribunal. If we'd gone through with it, we'd be together. End of story." His words were gravelly, thick with the wolf.

I winced. Okay. So it was a big deal. "I know. But she came to fight, and I didn't want to go there when waiting a few weeks will protect the pack. What could change?"

We were quiet for a second.

"That's the thing, though. What could change? What is she going to try to do?" I asked.

"She's going to the Tribunal to make a case stating that I took you from them."

"Which is kind of true."

Dastien huffed. "I know. Which is why I wanted to do the ceremony yesterday. You're pack now, so it's a bit of a moot point, but she wouldn't have wanted you to wait if she didn't have something up her sleeve. I wanted that extra protection."

I chewed my lip as I thought. "I want to know why she's doing this."

"We've been over that. She wants you back with the coven."

"I know. But why?" There had to be a bigger picture, but I wasn't seeing it. "So she gets me back over there. Then what? Is she really that delusional that she thinks she can convince me to take over? And if she hates wolves so much, why would she even want me? Hello. I go furry and I'd never let her curse me like she did Meredith."

"She wouldn't exactly need your permission to curse you." Dastien cut me off before I could protest. "Okay. If she doesn't want you to run the coven, then why's she doing this?"

I backhanded his stomach. "That's what I've been asking." Damn it. That hurt my hand more than it hurt him. Dastien rubbed his thumb along my skin, soothing the sting. "There's one more thing I don't like."

"Just one more?" He asked.

"When I begged her to save Meredith, she said she'd only help if I stayed at the compound. I didn't go for it. Even with Meredith's life on the line. So, what's she got that's worse than killing someone I love?"

"Killing lots of someones."

"War?"

61

"Yes. War."

A chill ran through my body, but the question remained the same. "Why, though? I'm not that important."

Dastien ran his fingers through my hair. He was quiet for a second. "She knows something about you that we don't. Or she wants to use you somehow."

He was on to something with that one. "Like what? What could she know? How could she use me?"

"I have no idea, but if she'd risk centuries of peace over this, it's got to be big."

I rolled over and pressed my face against his sternum, breathing in his scent. "I'm sorry."

"For?"

"For the way things went last night. For not fighting for us."

He ran his fingers through my hair. "It's never a good idea to fight when it can be avoided." He tugged on my hair a little until I looked at him. "But I wished we'd gotten to do the ceremony."

"Me, too." I pressed my lips gently to his. "Me, too."

***

Since I still hadn't fully moved over to Dastien's cabin, I made my way back to my room to shower and change. And call my parents. They'd want an update.

Mom was shocked about what'd happened. She didn't trust Luciana at all. It was the whole reason she'd kept me away from the coven growing up. She made me promise to keep her updated before hanging up.

I plopped down on my bed and stared at the ceiling.

This wasn't how my day was supposed to be going. It wasn't like we were going to get a honeymoon or anything. We had to stick around for the Tribunal, but I'd been looking forward to relaxing the day away with Dastien. Instead, he was revising his speech, which I should've been working on, too, but I couldn't. The words weren't there. How many ways could I say 'leave me and Dastien the fuck alone'?

I dug through my bedside table until I found my red and blue bouncy ball. I threw it against the wall by my tiny window as I thought.

There had to be something more that I could be doing. This was my fault…well, not exactly my fault, but still. I wanted to fix it. I wanted to make this whole situation with Luciana go away.

When I tried to talk to her rationally about the curse she'd put on Meredith, it'd been a disaster. A complete waste of time.

Damn it. Why had I told my cousins we were doing the ceremony? That was so dumb. They'd been so helpful before, I'd just thought they were my friends. They were my family.

A blur of movement caught my eye before the ball was snatched out of the air. "You're killing me with this." Meredith wore a pair of pink camo sleep shorts and a tank, and her hair stuck out all crazy.

"Sorry. I didn't mean to wake you up."

"Donovan already left, so I was up-ish. Just not physically up." She sat on my bed. "You're not doing so hot, huh?"

When I first got here, she'd walked right into my room and made me feel better about everything. It was pretty damned awesome of her to do that for a total stranger. But this time she had her work cut out for her. It felt like I couldn't catch a break. All I wanted was a little peace. I wanted to enjoy Dastien and my friends. It'd taken me so long to get to where I was—a really good, happy place—that I really resented what was happening.

Meredith nudged her shoulder against mine. "Brunch? I'm feeling like it's omelet time."

"I seriously don't think food is going to fix this."

She scoffed at me. "A good meal can fix just about anything."

Werewolves and their food addiction…

My stomach growled. The traitor.

"I'm going to throw on some clothes." She jumped up from my bed. "I won't even shower. Give me five."

"Cool." I reached my hand out. "Can I have my ball back?"

She narrowed her gaze at me. "Are you going to bounce it against the wall again?"

"No?"

"No. I don't trust you with it." She threw the ball in the air and then caught it. "Your bouncy ball privileges have been revoked."

I pouted. "But I had a really bad birthday."

She pointed a finger at me. "Don't give me that face. It's not going to work." She closed the bathroom door. "Read one of your steamy romance novels. I'll be ready in a sec."

By sec, Meredith definitely meant at least fifteen minutes. It'd been a while since I'd actually had time to sit down and read a book. I scanned my shelves, picked up a random one, and flipped through. The scent of forest and wolf filled my senses. I put my nose to the spine and inhaled.

The books still smelled like Dastien. When I'd first moved in, he'd brought all my stuff. He even made sure to put all my books in order alphabetically by author and separated by genre.

I grabbed a Christine Feehan book, one of her Sea Haven novels. That series was seriously awesome. I got swept away by the sisters that all had special powers. Kind of like the coven.

That got me thinking. If I'd met the coven first, would I have wanted to be part of it? Would I have drunk their Kool-Aid?

I hoped I would've been able to see through it, but it was possible that I could've been blinded by their powers.

It was dumb to sit around thinking about what-ifs. That hadn't happened. I was here with the pack, and I liked my life. I doubted the coven could've helped me gain control of my powers so fast. I would've been stuck on their land, living in their middle-of-nowhere compound—that sounded terrible.

I liked running with the pack. I liked being with Dastien.

No. I *loved* being with him.

I sighed and tried to focus on the words as I read the first chapter.

I was fully sucked into the story when Meredith popped back into my room. "Ready?"

"Yes. I'm starving, Miss I-said-I'd-be-a-sec-and-meant-half-an-hour."

"Shut it. Not everyone can be as naturally gorgeous as you." She laughed at her own joke.

Werewolves were all kinds of hot. Probably because they all were ripped and had naturally healthy skin and hair. They looked like the best versions of themselves at all times. When I first showed up, I'd thought I'd walked onto Mount Olympus. Each Were was a testament to perfection. It was sick. And I was from LA. I was used to people working hard at looking good. But the Weres made it effortless. Tall. Fit. Graceful. My five feet and change couldn't ever really compete with that, but I didn't care. I didn't mind being different. I was used to that.

We chatted about the ins and outs for the watching order of *Firefly* as we walked to the cafeteria, agreeing that the chronological order, not airing order, was best. The cafeteria was next door to the dorms. I smelled the food before I saw it. Cooks worked at different stations while workers on the line kept heaping more into the trays of prepared food. It was enough to drive my senses crazy. I ignored whoever was in the room and went straight for the buffet. Turned out, I was hungrier than I'd thought.

We made our way around the stations, loading up our trays until they were piled high. When I turned, I found a mostly full cafeteria.

That was weird. Sundays were usually the most laissez-faire time on campus. People slept in and came and went throughout the day. They were my favorite days for that reason. No packed cafeteria.

This Sunday wasn't my favorite. Not only were there a bunch of new people, but someone in particular caught my eye as I made my way between the large round tables.

Imogene Hoel.

She'd helped her father nearly tear the pack apart a month and a half ago, and she was the whole reason we were having the Tribunal. Sure, I'd attacked her, but she'd gotten in my face. And it wasn't like she hadn't tried to kill me in return. If Claudia and Raphael hadn't stepped in, she might've succeeded.

Her father, Rupert Hoel, was still on the run. No one had heard from him since his failed attempt to take over, but that didn't mean he was gone for good. His wife butted into the whole Luciana thing last night—sponsoring the coven for the Tribunal and at the ceremony—and now his daughter was back from her mandatory leave of absence. That whole family was trouble, and I had a feeling I'd be hearing from Rupert before long.

It was stupid to be blindsided by the sight of Imogene, but I'd totally forgotten that she would be here for the Tribunal. Or maybe I'd been hoping I wouldn't see her. We'd kind of made peace with each other before she left, but I still didn't trust her. It was one thing to forgive, but another to forget.

And now she was sitting with Dastien. *My* Dastien. Her hand was on his arm.

"Calm down," Meredith said. "No need to rip her throat out again. We all know Dastien's yours."

I took a breath. "Yeah, but does she know that?"

"She'd be dumb to not know that now."

Meredith was right. I'd forgiven her, so I needed to stick by that. The only reason she was bugging me was because I hadn't seen her since she left, and her parents were trying to make my life miserable. This was not the time to act like a jealous girlfriend. Even if I kind of was one.

Dastien looked up, and his glowing eyes met mine. He scooted away from Imogene. *I don't like what you're feeling right now.*

"Me neither," I muttered to myself. Jealousy sucked. It made me feel petty and weak and insecure. I didn't like it one bit.

There's nothing to be jealous of. You're my mate. It's not a secret.

Sorry. I started toward him. *I'm feeling a little unsettled after last night, and she's not bringing out the best in me.*

Dastien pushed out the chair next to him. As soon as I sat, he brushed his lips against mine. "I was going to come get you in a few if you didn't show up."

"Really?"

"Yeah." He held up his phone. "You barely made it." The countdown had less than a minute on it.

"Why the time limit?"

He sat back in his chair. "You wouldn't eat on our run again. You're still going too long between meals."

Ripping into a live, fur-covered Bambi wasn't something I wanted to do, no matter how natural everyone else thought it was.

I kissed his cheek. "Thanks."

Meredith plopped down next to me. "Hey, Imogene."

"Hey." She drew out the word a little too long for it to be mistaken as anything nice. "Well, I'm going to get going. Good to see you Dastien." She put her hand on his arm again and squeezed. I wanted to rip her hand off her body.

I shoved a giant bite of omelet in my mouth to keep from talking to her.

"See you, Tessa."

"Mmm-hmm," I said around my bite.

Dastien leaned back in his chair. "You're kind of adorable when you're jealous."

My cheeks heated. Shut up, I said through the bond. I glanced over to Meredith, who was nodding and staring off into space. "How's Donovan?" I said when I was done chewing.

She jumped a little in her seat. "Oh. He's fine. He's on his way. Sorry, was I doing it again?"

"Yeah, but I'm just as bad."

"He wants to talk to you two."

I dropped my fork. I didn't like the sound of that. "Anything bad?"

"He didn't say."

Perfect. The way the last twenty-four hours had been going, chances were on a scale from one to ten the news ranked somewhere around fifteen, a.k.a. mega-terrible. I just knew I wasn't going to like whatever he had to say.

Before I could worry too much, Donovan appeared at the table and settled into the chair next to Meredith. He didn't say hello. Instead, he put his arm around her, drawing her close. "How're you two doin' today? Feeling okay?"

Dastien stiffened beside me, and I put a hand on his leg. "We're going to be okay, provided that we don't have the same problem next month."

Donovan sighed. "I can't promise anything. What I can say is that Luciana's up to something."

I clasped a hand against my chest. "No! You don't say?"

The side of his mouth tilted up. "All right. I get it. But I want you to be prepared for what may come. Don't be afraid of fighting for what you want."

I met his gaze and couldn't look away. "Even if it puts other people in danger?"

"Yes."

I shook my head. No way. "That's too selfish. I don't know that I could do that."

The only sign that Donovan was pissed was the sudden glow in his blue eyes. "Fine. Don't completely ignore the good of others, but don't be a martyr either. I've seen that look in Luciana's eyes before. Seen it in others, too. I know this is going to come down to a fight. It's just a matter of how big."

I broke his gaze. Not because it was too intense, but because I was confused. How was I supposed to know what move to make when he was contradicting himself? What was right? "You really think it's going to be a fight no matter what?"

He settled back in his chair. "There's a delicate balance between us supernaturals. Any one gets too big for their britches and it's bad for the lot of us. Last time it was us who were in the wrong. We wanted too much control. Too much power. An evil wolf came to rule all the packs, and it went downhill from there."

"What about the Seven? Didn't they do anything about it?"

"That's exactly why the Seven were formed. One person can't know everything. One person shouldn't be able to make a choice for a whole. It's the individual that can be corrupted, but by conducting open discussions between equals, we can decide what's best for all packs." He blew out a breath. "It works better this way. Trust me."

That sparked something. "Mr. Hoel wanted to do away with the Seven."

"That's right. And I'll not be surprised if he's working with this local coven."

More fantastic news. "So worst case, we fight with my coven and whoever is still backing the Ass-Hoel. Some stand against us. Some don't. That's that."

"Not quite. You see, we did some bad things to the witches before. We attack one group, they'll all come calling. And they won't be thinking rationally. We're sending messages. Some will believe us. Some won't." He paused. "One fight, one little misstep, and the balance will be thrown off."

This sounded way more tenuous than I'd thought. "You say not to give up and be selfish, but how am I supposed to do that and keep it from being a fight?"

"I'm not sure there's a way."

Great. *Let me work up a miracle.* "I thought you were supposed to be in the all great and powerful Seven. Don't you have a plan? Shouldn't you…I don't know…figure something out?"

"Ehm. Well. We're trying, but a lot now rides on the results of the Tribunal. We're talking to our contacts and gathering some witches to our side to counter whatever Luciana has planned, so don't worry too much. More importantly, have you written your speech for the Tribunal? Thought about what you want to say?"

I wish I had it done, but that just wasn't the case. "I've got a few points, but I'm having writer's block."

Dastien squeezed my hand, and I appreciated the support, but I needed to stop procrastinating. Not doing it wasn't going to make the Tribunal go away. It was only going to make me unprepared. "You know, you supernaturals are really making it hard for a girl to enjoy her life. All these fights and battles and coups."

"It usually isn't like this," Meredith said.

"Yeah. That's why you have the Cazadores. Because everything is usually sunshine and rainbows." The 'hunters' took out all the bad supes that preyed on humans—they wouldn't exist if they weren't needed.

"Eat," Dastien said. "I can help you prep. We'll come up with something to make sure we're together."

I hoped so. Going back to the coven's compound was not something I ever wanted to do, but Donovan didn't have a clue how I was going to avoid that without a fight. And fighting wasn't an option. At least not yet, it wasn't.

I dug into my omelet, wishing that Meredith had it right and food could fix things.

If only it were that easy.

Chapter Six

The day of the Tribunal started like any other day. I went through the motions, but I felt like a zombie. Like it wasn't really happening to me. I wasn't sure how I expected to feel, but being resigned and numb wasn't exactly helping. I needed to be ready with my arguments. So, I did what any other nerd might do. I studied.

Research was going to help me figure out what I needed to say. I read that whole damned *Werewolf Bible* front to back. And then I read a couple other reference books that Mr. Dawson had given me. I took notes, and at the end of it, I wasn't numb anymore, but I was a little pissed.

I stomped my way from my room to the cabin. Dastien had said he'd be there prepping for the questions with Mr. Dawson. They believed that I wouldn't be held accountable for anything, but Dastien had known better than to bite me. And after I attacked Imogene, that was on his head, too. The whole thing was bullshit; Imogene's father had only registered his complaint to take the focus off his attempted coup. Which had failed.

As long as Dastien could be held accountable, so

could I. Dastien couldn't take the blame for me and my actions, like almost ripping out Imogene's throat, but I knew he'd try.

The truth was we were both in serious shit, and he'd known all along. Everyone had been patting me on the head saying it'd all be fine and not to worry.

Fur rippled and disappeared along my arms with every step I took. When I got to Dastien's cabin, I didn't knock. He sat at the table with Donovan, Sebastian, Mr. Dawson and an old man I didn't know. But I didn't care.

I threw the book at Dastien, but he caught it before it hit him in the face. "We're so fucking screwed. According to Chapter Seven, paragraph fourteen, what you did is inexcusable. IN. EXCUSE. ABLE. Not even a little bit okay. As in of course they have a case. I read about four other cases similar to ours—minus the whole True Mate thing—and they were killed. As in no longer breathing! And you've been telling me not to worry? Just write the speech, you said. They'll let us be together, you said." I paused to catch my breath. "Are you insane? High? What? Please tell me. Because from what I've been reading all morning, we're in a whole heap of shit."

"*Cherie*—"

"Don't you *cherie* me! I know what I read. How could you lie?" I spun to Mr. Dawson, pointing a finger at him. "And you. You said everything would be fine." I turned to Sebastian and Donovan. "And you two didn't say a damned thing either. I talked to you yesterday, Donovan. Told you I was worried. And you said to write from the heart and it'd all be grand. *Grand*," I said the last in my best Irish accent. I was coming off as a little crazed, so I took a moment to catch my breath. "Don't think I'm scared of you and won't say anything. Everyone treats me like a child. It'll be fine, they say. Don't worry, they say. Well fuck that."

My blood was on fire. Fear and anger and frustration had all melded together to form one giant ball of bad emotion. I was out of breath again, panting hard.

"You done?" Mr. Dawson said.

"I don't know." I couldn't think behind the mad.

Donovan started to laugh, and I shot him a look. "Stop laughing! It's not funny." I backed power with the command before I could stop myself.

Donovan's laugh instantly died. "Well, that's the first time someone's put me in my place in quite a while."

"Did the command get you, Dono?" the stranger asked.

"I'll be damned, but it did. Shite. It definitely did."

Maybe that wasn't the best thing to do, but I couldn't help myself. Now everyone was watching me like I was some fascinating creature. I didn't like it one bit. "What?"

"What, indeed."

"This is what I mean," Sebastian said. His thick German accent turned the 'w' to a 'v' sound.

The staring made me calm down a little. "Sorry." I paused. That was a lie. "I'm not really all that sorry." I crossed my arms, waiting for someone to address the real issue at hand.

"What he did was bad. Yes, inexcusable. But there are exceptions to every rule, and we agreed that you were the exception," Sebastian said. "That's why Donovan and I came to see you. If there had been a need for all of this, we would've said so then. We would've called the Tribunal and made an example of the two of you, but instead we found you. Your bond with him was weaker then, but even so, we suspected what would happen if it were to strengthen."

I swallowed. Sebastian's calm words got rid of most of my anger, but all I was left with was fear. "Do I need to be worried about this? Beyond whatever Luciana is going to say? Be honest."

"Maybe," Sebastian said. "If you'd gone through with the ceremony yesterday, then no. But now…"

It felt like someone had punched me in the stomach. The panic made it hard to breathe. My chest was so tight that it felt like an elephant was sitting on it. At least he was finally being upfront with me. "So, what's next?"

"We're all behind you, but I've a feelin' that the Hoels will be a problem. That the coven will be a bigger problem. But we're all behind you," Donovan said. "Except Ferdinand. He's been causing problems."

"Ferdinand?"

"One of the Seven."

I looked around the room. I'd made a really great first impression on the old man. His skin was so wrinkled that he looked a little like a Shar Pei. His eyes were bloodshot, giving him a sickened look. Whoever this guy was, he wasn't doing well. Something was wrong with him.

"This is Muraco, another member of the council of Seven," Mr. Dawson said with a small smile.

Oh, that was just fantastic. I'd flipped out in front of one of the guys who would be deciding my fate. I stared at him for a moment before looking back at Mr. Dawson. "What can I do?"

"What do you want?"

"To stay here. To be with Dastien. For everyone to leave me alone."

I suddenly realized why Muraco being so visibly old was so shocking. I'd never seen an old-looking Were. They always seemed young despite whatever their ages were. But Muraco looked ancient, and his skin reeked of leather and tobacco.

He leaned forward over the table and it was like everyone paused as we waited to hear what he would say.

"No one with any amount of power will ever be left alone. You might've seen it before you moved this way. Humans were drawn to you. Maybe not in the way you would've hoped, but they didn't leave you alone, did they? And the second Dastien saw you, he couldn't leave you alone. You can't walk into a room without everyone looking at you. It will always be that way. More so now that you're both alpha and witch. You will be a magnet for all things. The sooner you accept that, the happier you'll be." Muraco coughed, hacking loudly. I found myself holding my breath, waiting for the noise to stop.

Sebastian handed him a glass of water. "Here you go, old friend."

Muraco downed the water, and then cleared his throat. "But keeping you with your mate, that is something that we should be able to achieve."

I let out the breath I'd been holding. "Okay." For

whatever reason, I trusted him—maybe it was the age or the aura of wisdom around him. "Okay," I said again, as I let his words sink in.

The book had been pretty clear about the rules. No exceptions. It contradicted what everyone else had said, but three of the Seven were saying that I was the exception to the inexcusable act: turning an innocent who hadn't been approved by the pack. The abomination was punishable by death in all cases. Sometimes both people involved were killed, but the biter was always executed.

There was nothing worse than ignorance. I swore I'd read every book I could about the coven and the pack. I couldn't be left in the dark anymore. Sure, for a while my ignorance had been pardonable. It'd been more than I could do to adjust to this new life. But that time had passed.

Dastien stood from the table, still holding the book I'd thrown at him.

I'm sorry, I said through our bond as he crossed the room to me.

No. I'm the one who's sorry. I haven't forgotten that this is all happening because of me.

"Is it really, though? Is it really all happening because of you? Or is it because of me?"

Muraco waved his hand through the air. "People do what they do. We're all responsible for our own actions. Now, we should go over what you're going to say tonight."

"Okay." I sat on the arm of the couch. "I was going to talk about what it was like to transition. The change and overwhelming emotions of the wolf. And about Dastien and our bond." Dastien stood next to me, his hand in mine.

"You also might want to think up some counterarguments for anything Luciana could come up with," Mr. Dawson said.

That seemed like a good idea. And I knew who I should call. I couldn't believe I hadn't thought of it sooner. I blamed my procrastination. "I'm going to head out. Sorry for interrupting." I headed out the door before anyone could stop me, but as soon as I stepped on the front stoop, Dastien had his hand on my arm.

"Where're you going?"

If I was going to gain the confidence I needed to get this speech done, it wasn't going to be in a room full of alphas. I needed to be somewhere that I felt safe. "I'm going to go talk to my dad."

He nodded. "Want me to go with you?"

I always wanted him around, but for this, I just wanted to be home with my family. "Seems like you're busy."

"Are you okay?"

No. "Yes."

He stepped closer to me. "You're lying."

"I don't think I'll be okay until all of this is over." That was the truth. I wanted to get back to my life and not have to worry about defending it. "Don't keep things from me, okay?"

"I didn't—"

"You sort of did." I waved off his protest. "It's fine, but I need to know what I'm dealing with. I feel like I'm in the dark all the time and you're only giving me half the story." If I'd known all this last night, I might've made a different call. Whatever the consequences, I doubted I could've stopped the bonding ceremony if I'd known Dastien's life was at risk.

"I'm not keeping anything from you. Every time I brought it up, you changed the subject."

He had a point. In his defense, he'd brought it up almost daily. "Well, I'm ready now. So no holding back. Even if I don't want to hear it. Promise?"

"I promise." He pressed his lips to mine. "Come back here when you're done."

Where else would I go? "Okay."

"Call me if you need me."

"Sure." He was looking at me so intently, I knew something was up. "Are *you* okay?"

He stared up at the sky. "I don't want you to go."

I laughed. "I can tell." I yanked him down for a kiss that he quickly deepened, but I pulled away before I got too breathless. "I'll see you in a couple hours. Meet me for lunch?"

"*D'accord.*"

When I looked back at him, he was watching me walk away. The expression on his face was one of love, but also longing. I knew exactly how he was feeling. I'd been planning on spending the day snuggling with him, and now I needed to prepare a defense. Definitely not as fun.

Soon, he said.

Can't wait.

***

It was still hot outside, but I drove with the AC off and the windows down. My hair was tied back in a messy bun, but a few loose pieces of hair whipped against my face. There was no more time for quiet reflection. Even in the odd spare moments I'd had alone in the dorms, I could hear the conversations in the rooms around me.

The overwhelming lack of privacy had only gotten worse. And now, if I concentrated, I could feel the pack. It was faint, but I'd borrowed energy from the wolves to help break Meredith's curse, and my awareness of the pack bonds had never fully disappeared since then. With the mate bond getting stronger every day, I felt like there was no room in my head for my own thoughts. After a lifetime of visions, I should've been used to it, but those few heavenly weeks of peace—before I realized what being in the pack and mated really meant—had spoiled me.

A few months ago—hell, a few days ago—I couldn't figure out why Dastien was with me. He had the pick of any girl. But now I knew. Being an alpha weighed on him more than anything else. Having me around kept him grounded. Helped him keep control.

The more I found out about him, the more I realized that the two of us were a good match. Luck wasn't my thing, but I was starting to think that fate was.

I saw the turn off for my parents' house and kept on going. I wasn't ready to end the drive yet.

When I pulled up to the yellow house, I couldn't believe it'd been nearly an hour. My dad stepped onto the porch as I pulled up, and I turned down the music. My ears were ringing, but it was worth it. I felt a million times better. Music really did soothe my soul.

"You trying to kill your eardrums? I could hear you about a mile out."

"Eh. They'll heal."

"How about sparing the rest of us, then?"

Funny, Dad. "I'm sure from a mile away, you're safe."

"That's what you'd think, but with your music…" He hugged me, and I smelled his aftershave. He'd used the same one since I was a little girl. It was one of my favorite smells. "How're you doing?"

"I've been better." I pulled away from him. "I wanted your legal advice. Plus, I figure your PR spin could help, too."

He nodded. "I heard there was a little trouble last night. This Tribunal thing sounds not good." He put his arm around my shoulders. "Let's go in the kitchen and we can talk about it."

Four Diet Cokes, three bags of Cheetos, seven grilled cheeses, and one and a half packages of Oreos later, I had a solid plan. Dad had even given me notecards. We'd gone through them three times, and he'd drilled me on questions—even the hard stuff. I'd been uncomfortable with the role-playing at first. It'd been hard for me to answer his questions, but by the last time, I had my answers down. I was ready. The Tribunal seemed slightly less scary.

I sat on the kitchen island, kicking my feet. The cool marble felt good against my warm Were skin. I still wasn't used to being so hot all the time. It was something I wasn't sure I'd ever adjust to.

"You're pretty good at this stuff."

Dad laughed. "It's my job, kiddo."

I stared at my feet. "What if none of this works?"

"Do your best." He leaned against the kitchen counter across from me. "But don't forget that no one can force you to do something you don't want to do."

I ate another Oreo. "That's not true."

"Maybe before it wasn't true, but you're stronger than everyone else now. That's why they're making such a fuss over this. Don't be afraid to use that to your advantage if it comes to it."

I didn't feel that strong. Sure, I was more in control than I used to be, but I didn't really know anything about my *bruja* side. And I was just starting to understand the Were part of me. I'd only shifted for the first time a few days ago. It wasn't like this was a home run.

I was new. I felt new. I felt the opposite of empowered, but I needed to get there if I was going to win. So, how was I supposed to do that before tonight?

I wasn't sure at all. It seemed like every time I took a step forward, I took five back. Eventually, maybe I'd get somewhere, but it was a trudge. I didn't want it to be a trudge. I wanted to own it.

"You're a smart girl, Teresa. You can do anything you put your mind to."

I was fully committed to both staying alive and being with Dastien, but the rest…

It was going to take more than visualization to come out of the Tribunal unscathed.

Chapter Seven

Ever since the second I'd stepped into my new town, Marion, Texas, I'd been in danger of some sort or another. Bitten. Vampires. A coup. A curse gone wrong. Coven politics. Basically everything that had led to the Tribunal had been an overwhelming clusterfuck of bad. And yet, even as scared as I was, I didn't regret moving here. When it came down to it, I was dealing with bullies. I had plenty of experience with that. Only these bullies had claws and fangs.

And spells. *Mustn't forget the spells.*

Dastien and I stood on the same dais used in the Full Moon Ceremony, but it had been pushed to the side of a massive bonfire. Weres crowded the stone benches, sitting or standing all around, filling the air with nervous energy. As big and overwhelming as the gathering had been last night, this one was bigger.

So, if they decide they want us dead, then what? They throw us in this massive fire?

Dastien looked at me like I was crazy.

What? It's a valid question.

No. The fire's for light.

Yeah, but we have crazy good eyesight. Do we really need it?

He shrugged. *It looks more official with the fire.*

Official. Sure. Because what this whole mess needed was to be more official.

Mr. Dawson stood on the other side of the fire. "A charge has been raised against two of our pack. One against Dastien Laurent, for turning a girl without pack permission and without providing her with the proper warning and education. One against Teresa McCaide, for losing control of her wolf and attacking a fellow member of the pack."

I expected some whispering or murmuring among the Weres, but no one said a thing. The only sounds were from the woods and the crackling fire.

"Tonight, we'll hear testimonies from a handful of people. This includes Luciana Alverez from the local coven. Letting a witch speak here is highly unusual, and Luciana will only be allowed to say her piece before she's escorted off pack lands. Once everyone involved tonight has spoken, we'll break to debate our course of action, and then Muraco and Ferdinand of the Seven, along with five randomly selected pack alphas who've traveled here, will decide what's to be done."

Why weren't Sebastian and Donovan voting? That made me way more nervous. I thought I had at least a few votes in the bag.

Donovan continued like he'd been reading my thoughts. "A point has been raised that myself and two of the Seven are biased toward the couple in question."

Bastards.

"In fairness, we've decided not to vote, but we will speak on their behalf. After all parties have spoken, questions can be addressed to Dastien and Teresa. Then, they will each have a chance to say their final words."

I swallowed. *Final words?* This was going to be a long night.

"Once a decision is reached, the matter will be closed. Anyone seeking retribution will answer to me." Mr. Dawson's threat rang out in the still of the night. No one dared to say anything against him.

I wasn't sure who reached for who, but the second Dastien's skin touched mine, I felt calmer. A drop of sweat rolled down my face. I itched to wipe it away, but didn't want to show even the littlest bit of weakness. Besides the handholding.

The first part of the Tribunal was fine. Mr. Dawson talked about when Dastien and I first saw each other. I'd never forget seeing Dastien through the screen door. I'd been so afraid of him—of what he might mean—that I didn't want him to see me. But he had.

"I don't think even the most in control Were could've resisted the call of his mate. The way Dastien went about this was not in order with our laws, but an exception was made once we found that he and Teresa were True Mates."

I swallowed. Hopefully everyone here would agree with the exception.

Sebastian stepped forward next. His voice was smooth and clear as he spoke. "As most here know, I am descended from a line of sorcerers, which is why I was specifically called to Texas to assess Teresa. What I have to tell you about her might shock you, but I believe that letting someone with her particular ability leave the pack would be a detriment to us all."

I was surprised my eyes didn't pop out of my head. *A detriment to us all?* He really was laying it on thick. I tried not to laugh as he continued. He made me sound like the second coming. Totally ludicrous.

A man I didn't know stepped forward from the front row. His hair was buzzed close to his head, but his blond beard was long and thick. "It seems to me that we've forgotten a big part of what this Tribunal is about. One of ours broke the rules. If we don't stand by those rules, then all our laws will become optional. Am I the only one who sees the error in this way of thinking?" He paused and a few people clapped in support. "Dastien bit a human. We can discuss whether or not to keep her, but him—that's another story. He should be punished. I understand that he's dominant, but that doesn't mean the laws don't apply to him. If anything, his power should be subject to added responsibility and repercussions. What's to say he won't bite again if let free?"

I gasped and Dastien squeezed my hand. *Don't react,* he said.

They're talking about punishing you. I can't help it. Who is that guy?

Ferdinand.

Great. The member of the Seven who wasn't so hot about us. His status meant that he had some sway over the rest of the pack. I just hoped it wasn't enough to discount Mr. Dawson, Sebastian, and Donovan's opinions.

Donovan stepped forward next. "I'm not votin' tonight against my better judgment. I hope that after I talk, you'll all have realized what a waste of time this is. And afterward, I'm lookin' to change the Tribunal system; the rule to stop Tribunals from being canceled was only put in place to stop corrupt alphas from sweeping charges under the rug, so to speak. This here is a gross misuse of the clause." His harsh voice rang out in the night. A ripple of his anger and frustration ran through the pack bonds, and I knew he'd meant for everyone to feel it. He wanted everyone to know exactly how mad he was. "The fact that a wolf who tried to overthrow the Seven, who drugged us and threw us into a cave of vampires, who associated with vampires, called this Tribunal shows what a sham it is. The coward isn't even here, and yet we still are."

I found Meredith in the crowd. She wasn't smiling exactly, but her head was held high. She was proud of Donovan, with good reason. I wasn't sure if the speech was her doing or all Donovan's, but regardless, they both deserved a huge thank you.

"Not a few days ago, Meredith was nearly killed by a spell placed upon her by the local coven. That they would strike out against my True Mate is…I'm still deciding what steps to take, but I wouldn't be here today—and neither would my mate—if Teresa wasn't in our pack as both wolf and witch." He paused. "As for what Ferdinand said, I don't agree. Dastien is in control, and his biting was reviewed and pardoned by both myself and Sebastian. In my opinion, it shouldn't be an issue tonight. For that matter, nothing would've stopped me from biting Meredith had she been human. Dastien is more dominant than any of us. Has he ever lost control? Have you ever even seen him lose his temper?"

Silence.

Clearly they didn't know how much I could rile Dastien.

"That's what I thought. Before you decide willy-nilly to kill off what could be a couple of our greatest leaders, think about who is manipulating you into this. About why we're here. Don't be a bunch of fuckin' morons."

I wanted to high-five Dono, but that wouldn't make our case look any better. I didn't dare blink. My heart was beating so fast that I couldn't feel my limbs. I was on the verge of passing out, but I stayed on my feet.

As Donovan continued to speak, I thought for a second that everything would be fine. We'd get through it after all.

Then Imogene stepped in front of the dais to speak, her back to us. I glanced at Dastien.

Did you know she'd be speaking?

I wasn't sure. Since she's part of the reason we're here, I knew there was a good chance.

Thanks for sharing the info.

As usual, Imogene looked like she'd stepped out of the pages of a magazine. Her hair flowed down her back in perfectly curled waves. Her white silk blouse didn't have a hint of a wrinkle on it. I always wished I looked as nice as that, but never managed to drum up the effort to make it happen.

"I always thought I'd end up with Dastien," Imogene said, and I gritted my teeth. It was going to take some major self-control not to attack her. "We'd talked about it for years, so I was surprised when I found out that he'd bitten Tessa. I mean, why her?

Why choose her instead of me, when we'd been so close for so long?"

She actually had a tear rolling down her cheek. I glanced around and saw that some of the alphas were nodding. Everyone had assumed that her and Dastien would be mated by now.

They were eating out of the palm of her conniving little hand. This so wasn't good.

"And then it hit me." Imogene spun to face me. "She's part witch. She had to have done something to enspell Dastien. I mean, right? It was the only answer. So, I went digging in her locker."

I couldn't believe I'd been so stupid. I'd defended her. I'd accepted her apology. I'd even told the pack we shouldn't kick her out, and all along she'd been gearing up for this?

Anger swelled inside me and until my skin felt too tight and itchy.

Dastien's hand squeezed mine. *Don't. You can't lose your cool now. We still have to get through Luciana's speech.*

Okay. Okay. I'm trying. But shit. Did you know about this?

No. The word rang in my head was more growl than voice.

"When she caught me and I asked about the spell, well, she tried to rip my throat out. Needless to say, I almost didn't survive. Keep that in mind. She's powerful. Really powerful. And that's dangerous."

I swallowed down the anger. That bitch was going down.

"I propose that she be separated from the pack for a period of time while we find out why one of our greatest alphas bit her. He risked his life by breaking the rules. No Were would ever do that unless they weren't in their right mind. Only time apart can help us assess the state of Dastien, our next true leader." No one cheered or clapped, but Imogene went back to her place and sat down with her head held high, like she'd won the day.

It was official. I fucking hated that bitch.

Mr. Dawson stood back up. "At this point, we're going to pause for a moment while the Coven is escorted to the Tribunal grounds. They've been allowed three minutes to speak and have agreed to leave us as soon as they're done. I'd like to remind all the alphas deciding today and the pack members watching to take what they say with a grain of salt. This is the coven that nearly killed Donovan's Meredith."

I cracked my knuckles as we waited for Luciana to make her appearance. I had some things to say about Imogene. Maybe I should even draw charges up on her. She'd tried to kill me, too. Or was everyone just going to forget about that part?

The crowd cleared a path and three guys dressed all in black led the coven's representatives toward the firepit. Luciana walked at the front of a group of five, and all of them were dressed in white. Her hands weren't glowing today, but the way she carried herself—head high, shoulders back—told me that she felt confident. That arrogance of hers always rubbed me the wrong way.

Who was I kidding? Everything about her rubbed me the wrong way.

"Luciana. As stated, you've got your time. Sophia

Hoel is responsible for your behavior. Anything goes wrong and it's on your head." He said the last to Sophia, who stepped down to stand beside Luciana.

Sophia nodded. "I chose to sponsor Luciana because I feel she has some valid complaints. Teresa's transition was poorly managed. I understand and accept responsibility for the coven's actions here tonight."

Luciana's gaze met mine through the fire. She grinned and I shuddered. There wasn't an once of good in that lady. And I was pretty sure she was insane.

"That one," she pointed to Dastien, without any lead into the speech at all—"took our next leader. You see, Teresa is unbelievably strong. Maybe some of you have noticed how strong?"

She paused, and I wondered if she and Imogene had coordinated their speeches.

"Her powers are only going to grow. As I understand it, Weres develop their powers over decades, but this is not the case with *brujas*. We don't have such long lives, so we gain a little power at birth, and then that power blossoms as we reach adulthood." Luciana spoke and the Weres gathered all hung on the edges of their seats. Even if the witches and Weres had a big history together, it seemed like both sides kept to themselves without sharing information. Getting to understand more about the witches was gold for the pack.

"Teresa was strong at birth," Luciana continued as she raised her had toward me. "Stronger than any we have ever known. She could see things that no one else could. Her powers have grown ever since, and will continue growing for the next few years. If you think she's dangerous now, just wait. If you can't control her now, what do you think will happen then?"

Control me? No one was going to control me. Not ever. No one was going to take away my free will. And I was a goddamned American. I didn't take too kindly to someone talking about taking away my freedom.

She started around the circle again. "That's not the worst of it. How would you feel if we took one of your Seven? That's what he's done." She paused to stab her finger at Dastien. "One of our great leaders, gone. And it's *his fault*." She finished another loop around. "Do what you will with him. It matters not to us. But her, she's ours. You will return her or face war with our kind."

Luciana paused before turning to Mr. Dawson. "I want you to think about that. About what's to come should you decide to keep—"

"Your three minutes are up. Yeats, please escort them off our land."

"I don't need an escort. We don't want to stay here a second longer than we have to." She stormed off, but the Cazadores followed her anyway.

That wasn't so bad, Dastien said.

Not so bad? She basically said I was too dangerous to be a wolf, and that if the pack doesn't hand me over, then she—and the rest of the witches of the world—are going to go to war with the packs.

Exactly.

So how is that not so bad?

Because all we have to do is say 'no' and she'll go away.

Was he being dense? *How does 'war' translate into 'go away' in your brain?*

She can't go to war with us. There's no way she has that much backing. It's a bluff. It has to be.

It really didn't sound like a bluff to me. Even if she was using me as an excuse to start a war, I don't think there was a bluff in what she said. *Are you sure?*

Pretty sure.

That would change everything. *How sure is pretty sure?*

I don't know.

Exactly. Because she wasn't bluffing. *If you think you're right, then give me a percentage. How likely is this to start a war?*

He didn't shrug but I could feel it. Like a mental shrug. *Sixty-two percent? Maybe sixty-eight percent.*

That wasn't very certain. *So you're thirty-eight to thirty-two percent not sure. That's a whole lot of not sure. Especially when we're talking war. War, Dastien. War.*

I understand—

A cry went up in the surrounding crowd and I knew I'd missed something. Everyone had been so quiet, that it was shocking to hear.

"—not go to war over something this petty. Let them have her."

Everyone started talking at once and Mr. Dawson growled. His power rolled through the woods, and it was suddenly silent again. "This isn't how things are run. You're breaking protocol by—"

"War with the witches isn't an option. Some of us here are old enough to remember what that means," Ferdinand shouted.

"Don't you forget, so am I." The ice in Donovan's voice made me shiver. "I might not be votin' tonight, but I'll not have this Tribunal interfered with—"

"Then you shouldn't have let the witches in," someone shouted. "Even with the sponsor."

"—more than it already has been," Donovan continued like nothing had been said. "Unless it's your turn to speak, you will be silent." The last word was so loud, so sharp, that I flinched. His power that backed the command was meant for all the Weres. He turned to me, and his face softened. "Sorry about that." His t's had become harder, which meant even if his face was kind, he wasn't over his anger. "We'll have the questions now. A warnin' to all of you, best to stay on topic. Any judgments in your questions and you'll be cut off. Identify yourself before asking, too. The lass is new and won't know your names."

It was quiet for a long time, and then the old man from the cabin stood up.

"I'm Muraco, alpha of the Andes clan, with a question for Teresa. We've heard a lot of people talking about you. What I'd like to know is how you felt about becoming the wolf?"

I hadn't been expecting that kind of question. I'd thought this was going to be more of an interrogation.

I couldn't lie—they'd smell it—so I had to be honest, but I wasn't going to sway anyone to my side with the truth. I cleared my throat. "I didn't want to be a wolf and I didn't like that I'd been bitten." I paused, waiting for something, but it was so quiet, all I could hear was the crackling of the fire. "I didn't know that werewolves existed before I moved here. I didn't even know that I was a *bruja* and that was why

I could see what I see. So, it was shocking when I woke up at St. Ailbe's." I went into the whole running away thing, and why I'd done that. It had been an adjustment, and I hoped that they'd understand or at least sympathize with the drastic changes I'd gone through. "So, it took me a while not to be afraid of my wolf. Now, asking me how I currently feel about becoming a wolf—I love it. I love shifting. I love it here. I love my mate, my friends, and my pack. I don't want to leave."

Dastien got the next question—about his level of control. I got one about what my powers were exactly, and then one about my interactions with *la Aquelarre*.

Then, someone asked me what I thought about Luciana and my relationship with her. "If being cursed by Luciana is a sign of a good relationship, then I'd say we were on the best of terms. I don't trust her and I certainly don't like her. You heard what she said. She wants to control me. She made it perfectly clear that she'll do whatever it takes to achieve that when she cursed me." There were some murmurs, and I was sure I'd get some questions about that before I was done, but for now, most were quiet. "As much as I would like to learn about being a *bruja*, I can't. Not from her."

I hadn't really realized that I wanted to learn until I said the words. After helping Meredith, I knew that I couldn't avoid that part of me anymore. I had to be able to use the gifts that I'd been given. I had to do better. Be better.

A bunch of people shouted questions all at once and I blinked through the heat of the fire. It seemed like with every question I answered, there were twenty more. I wasn't sure how I was supposed to handle this.

I think Donovan's about to call this to an end, Dastien said.

You think?

Yeah. Look at his hands.

They were fisted by his sides. His knuckles were white, and a fine sheen of fur covered over their tops.

He's itching to. He wanted to cancel the Tribunal from the start.

I'd known that, but it didn't change where we were today. It might be too late for us.

Yes.

"—your turn to say something," Donovan said.

Everyone was staring at me. Shit. I had to stop tuning out when I talked to Dastien through our bond.

That's your cue.

Right. I got out my notecards. My hands shook as I flipped through them. The words seemed to blend together, and I couldn't make sense of them. The paper crinkled as I flipped through them again, and I realized this was dumb. I didn't need the cards. I just had to speak from the heart.

I tossed them in the fire and watched as the cards curled, the flames licking along the edges until they were totally consumed.

This was it. Time for me to defend myself.

I cleared my throat, wishing I had a glass of water before I started. "I know that I've caused quite a stir since I showed up here. Believe me, no one expected me to be here less than me." I blew out a breath. "But now that I'm here, I don't want to leave. I know rules were broken, and that I lost my temper a bit with Imogene. It was wrong, and I was fighting the change. I'm not anymore. I've accepted my wolf, the pack, and my mate. I'd love it if I was accepted in return." I paused, trying to think of what I should say next. "Even if I wanted to feel bad about not joining the coven, I don't. Maybe it was a disservice to them that I was bitten, but I don't know how my life could be other than the way it is." I couldn't apologize for something I didn't feel. "I would apologize to Imogene for attacking her, but I was told that fights among students was a thing of the norm around here. She was digging through my things making insane accusations, and I lost my temper. I was new to being a wolf, and it was an adjustment. However, when she attacked me, after participating in a coup to take down this very pack, I didn't call a Tribunal on her. I forgave her and asked that the pack give her a second chance. I hope that some of you will remember that. Will put yourselves in my shoes. And when you're thinking about what to do with me and Dastien, it'd be great if you could remember that we can't go back in time. This—me being bitten—can't be undone. We can only move forward. And for me, that means I'm both wolf and witch. Luciana is hanging on to the fact that she can separate me from the wolf, but each of you should know how impossible that is." I glanced around the pack, hoping to see some kind of agreement, but got nothing. A sea of faces stared back at me. "I—" I cleared my throat. "I wanted to also make it known that I'm not completely unreasonable. I don't want anyone else hurt because of the choices that Dastien and I have made. Just know that any type of permanent separation will not be entertained by either of us." That was backed with just a little taste of power. I didn't want to push them, but if I gave them a little bit of weakness, they'd exploit it for sure.

"Are you done?" Mr. Dawson asked.

Was I done? I hadn't a clue if what I'd said had gotten through to anyone, but anything else I could say would be a rehash. "I think so. Yes."

"Dastien," Mr. Dawson said.

"Teresa Elizabeth McCaide is my mate." His voice was strong and clear. Not hint of fear tinted it. "I'd love to hear from one of you who could deny their mate. Who could refuse them anything?" He paused. "And she's not just my mate. She's my True Mate. My other half. I don't think any of you could understand what that means, except Donovan and Meredith. To get between mates is one of the biggest crimes in our world. No one would ever dare. Yet, here I am," he yelled the last. "Forced to stand here and beg for the chance to keep my other half. Our bonding ceremony was already interrupted. I'll not stand for one more thing to come between us. Know that before you decide anything." He sounded cold. Even I was a little scared of him in that moment.

He always said he struggled with control, but I'd only seen him lose it a couple of times, and never like this. Seeing him now... I wasn't scared for myself, but I was worried for him and the rest of the pack. What would happen to him if we were separated?

You're kind of intense.

Don't make me smile. It'll ruin the effect.

I started to grin, and he narrowed his gaze at me. *And don't you smile either. United front, Tess. It's all about being together on this.*

Dastien hopped down from the rock and reached a hand out to steady me as I followed. "When you have a verdict, send for us at the cabin."

We made our way through the woods in silence. I was too afraid to talk. I'd already overshared enough for the night and Were hearing was a little too good. They wouldn't get any more of me. Not if I could help it.

I didn't open up until we were well out of earshot. "So, what do you think?"

"About?"

I rolled my eyes. "About what just happened."

Dastien's eyes glowed amber. "It's all going to come down to how big of a stink they think the coven will make and how much the pack is willing risk for us."

I chewed on my lip as I thought. "And? What do you think?"

"I don't know. I really don't. But one thing's for certain, I don't want to be apart from you. That's not an option. So, we'll do what we have to."

A chill ran up my spine. I knew that Dastien was mega-alpha. Seriously strong. There was no way anyone but me could stop him from getting what he wanted. And there was our dilemma.

What if the pack decided to send me to the coven? What would Dastien do?

Could I stand against my mate for the sake of the pack?

I wasn't sure, but I had a feeling I was going to have to answer that question soon.

Chapter Eight

We snuggled together on Dastien's couch to wait for the news. I started working on a tub of Häagen-Dazs pralines and cream and tried to focus on the TV—currently a mom was yelling at her toddler as she teased the shit out of the little girl's hair. Poor kid. Dastien cuddled me to his side and absently rubbed my shoulder. I'd been pacing his cabin for the first hour, but it started driving him batty; thus, the ice cream and reality TV therapy.

Then the knock came, and all other thoughts vanished from my head.

"Come in," Dastien said.

I sat up and put the nearly empty container on the coffee table.

Mr. Dawson stepped through the door. "A decision has been reached. It's time for you to come back outside."

I reached for Dastien's hand and he squeezed it. *It's going to be fine*, he said through the bond. *You'll see.*

The walk back to the bonfire felt like a funeral march. No one said a word. Forest sounds that were usually so peaceful and relaxing suddenly felt suffocating. My breathing was heavy, and it wasn't because I was walking fast.

A thick silence greeted us as Dastien and I stepped into the circle. Everyone sat completely motionless.

Maybe it was because I was so used to my visions and being flooded with too much information, but all that silence and quiet made me antsy. The calm before a storm.

I hated it.

Dastien jumped back onto the stone and then reached to pull me up. Last thing I needed to do was look like a klutz in front of everyone. They were already here to judge me.

Mr. Dawson stepped forward. "I want to start off by saying that the original calls for the Tribunal—Tessa's loss of control when confronted by Imogene and Dastien's breaking of our laws—have been totally dismissed."

Thank God the pack wasn't made of total morons. If I got in trouble for that after everything Imogene had done, I really would've lost it.

"We've had a heated debate and are almost evenly divided on what we should do regarding Luciana's claim," Mr. Dawson continued. "The complication that the witches brought forth—their wanting you back and willing to go to war over it—has been divisive among pack members."

I nodded. How could it not be? I didn't like the idea of the pack having to fight for me either.

"However, most agreed that you two should be together. We understand that Dastien lost control only because he met his mate. No one is faulting him for that, but we can't let a war start because of it."

That wasn't something I wanted either. But what did that mean? I clenched Dastien's hand tighter.

Sebastian stepped up. "We've come to a decision to appease the witches. For a period of one lunar cycle, you, Teresa Elizabeth McCaide, will live on coven lands. You will have no contact with Dastien—"

"No." Dastien's voice was so harsh I jumped. "I reject this. I will leave this pack. Go lone wolf—"

Gasps rang out. I wasn't sure what being a "lone wolf" meant, but from the reactions, it was obviously a terrible idea.

"Dastien. You will wait to speak until I've finished."

"No."

I squeezed Dastien's hand. *Calm down. We have to know what we're up against.*

Dastien stared down at me, his eyes two glowing orbs of yellow. It wasn't him talking anymore. It was the wolf.

"No one takes my mate from me."

I don't know how I knew, but right then—it was like my life flashed before my eyes. If I didn't get Dastien to calm down and agree to this, he'd destroy this pack. They were nearly evenly divided. Among the ones that had mates, the desire to keep us together had to overshadow the desire to keep the witches satisfied.

The pack would fight. Fear leading some. Love, honor, and tradition leading the rest.

The witches would come. It would be war, and the pack would be too weak to defend itself.

Visions of blood and death flickered behind my

eyelids, but they moved too fast for me to pick out the specifics. All I knew was that we were about to head down a terrible path. Really, really bad.

I let out the breath I'd been holding.

While I'd been out of it, Dastien had started yelling. Others were shouting back.

"We're asking for a bit of leeway with you." Donovan's clear blue gaze met mine. "I know it's a lot to ask—"

"No! Would you ever let someone separate you from Meredith? Let them take her away?" Dastien stood up and leaned over Donovan. "She won't be going anywhere." His face contorted as he slowly began to shift. His jaw popped and expanded. Fingers lengthened into claws. It was a grotesque sight, and it hurt to look at him.

The bond revealed the full spectrum of Dastien's emotions. His gut-shaking terror. Anger enough to boil the waters of Antarctica. And a healthy dose of I-don't-give-a-fuck. He wanted what he wanted, and he wasn't going to let anyone tell him different.

He'd always told me he was more dominant than any other wolf. None of those gathered here could really make him do anything. And that was the problem. If someone didn't convince him that this was the right thing to do, no one could make Dastien follow along. He couldn't be ordered. He only obeyed orders out of respect for his elders.

But threatening me had taken away all that respect.

I was the only one who could fix this.

"You will obey us." Donovan shouted, power backed words, his eyes glowing bright blue.

106

As soon as Donovan said it, I felt Dastien's anger swell. He was never going to obey that order.

Dastien leaped off the rock, hitting Donovan with the full force of his alpha energy. The power rolled into the gathered crowed. Donovan hit the ground, and Dastien pinned him. But only for a second. Donovan rolled and sprang up, throwing Dastien into a tree. Branches crashed down.

I had to do something. I had to stop this before he tried to rip out Donovan's throat.

"Stop! Dastien!" He wasn't listening to me. I tried to get to him through the bond, but he was too much wolf, and not enough of his human mind was left to see reason.

My gaze slipped to Mr. Dawson. He was the only one not watching the fight. Instead, he stared steadily at me. Waiting for me to say something. To do something.

A sudden chill came over me and I hugged myself. "I'll do it. I agree to the terms."

"No!" The roar startled me.

Dastien had paused long enough for Donovan to get the upper hand. He pinned Dastien to the ground on his stomach, but Dastien's gaze was on me. "Why?"

The pain in his voice made my heart ache. "There isn't another choice. Fighting Donovan won't change that."

He was too distracted to notice Dr. Gonzales moving behind them. She darted in, using her Were reflexes to stab the needle into Dastien's arm and depress the stopper.

Dastien tried to thrash, but Donovan held him

firm.

My heart pounded as I stood there and let them sedate my mate. I felt like the worst person ever. Not worthy of Dastien and his trust and love. Not when I'd just quit so easily. I watched as Dastien's eyes slid closed within seconds and my knees weakened so much that I couldn't stand anymore.

Oh God. What have I done?

"Everyone. Leave. Now," Mr. Dawson said.

It didn't take long for the pack to file out, but Mr. Dawson, Donovan, Meredith, Sebastian, Muraco, and Dr. Gonzales stayed behind. I sat frozen, watching Dastien breathe from across the fire.

"Way to freak out, Dastien. What am I going to do now?" I muttered as I settled on the ground next to him, putting his head in my lap. His features slowly sank back to human as I held him.

"After our talk with him this afternoon, we thought he might react this way." Mr. Dawson squatted next to me. "It was always your decision to make, not his."

I rolled my eyes. "You're not dumb or naive enough to believe that, right? He's my mate. We're a team," I said, echoing all the times Dastien had said as much to me.

I knew what I wanted and I knew what I should do, but those two things were totally divergent. Like everything else in life, I knew it was going to end in a compromise, so I had to figure out what I was willing to give up and what I wasn't.

"Did Luciana agree with the decision? Did it satisfy her?"

"We haven't asked yet, but if she wants more than

one lunar cycle, the pack won't stand for it. I can't imagine her not agreeing."

But there was still a chance. Hope for me to cling to. "I'm going to leave it up to you to negotiate, Donovan." I'd helped him out with *la Aquelarre*, and I was calling in that debt.

"I'll do whatever it is you ask. I owe you more than I could ever repay."

I nodded. I'd usually deny that, but not now. I needed his help too badly. "I want to be back before the next full moon. I'll give the witches until then, max. No extensions for any reason. I'll burn the witches' compound to the ground before I miss the next ceremony."

"Are you sure that's what you want?"

I scoffed and bit my lip, trying to stop the tremble. "No." My voice was thick. "What I want is to be left the hell alone, but apparently I don't always get what I want." I ran my fingers through Dastien's hair. "He's going to be so pissed at me when he wakes up."

"Indeed."

Mr. Dawson put his hand on my shoulder. "I've taken care of him since his parents died. Don't worry. I won't let him lose control while you're gone."

"It's not for forever. Just a few weeks." I brushed away a tear that slipped free.

"Let's get Dastien back to his cabin." Mr. Dawson hauled Dastien over his shoulder and started back through the woods. The rest of us followed behind him in silence.

When we got to Dastien's, Mr. Dawson laid him carefully on the bed.

"I'm trusting you, Dono," I said as I sat on the bed

next to Dastien.

"Aye. And you'll not have misplaced that trust. I'll see what I can do." Donovan moved toward the door. "Let's go."

"Wait, Dr. Gonzales," I said.

"Yes, Tessa?"

"Can I have one of those shots? Just in case he's...you know."

She gave me a tight smile and reached back into her bag. "Here. Just do it quickly. If the needle breaks off in him, give me a call."

I nodded and stared at the syringe in my hand like it was a poisonous snake. "Sure thing." I placed it carefully on the bedside table.

"I'll be back as soon as we come to an agreement with the coven," Donovan said.

"Am I doing the right thing?" I asked without taking my eyes from Dastien.

Muraco nodded. "Yes, child. I think you're being very reasonable and responsible. Very adult."

Great. Because that was what I'd always wanted. To be more adult-like.

I hoped Dastien could forgive me for this.

***

I wasn't sure how much time passed, but Dastien was still asleep when Donovan returned.

The verdict was that I had to be on the coven's land by nine tomorrow morning, and had to stay until the day before the next full moon. While I was there, I had to fully suppress my wolf. The witches wanted me to live as a coven member, not as a Were. It was the stupidest thing I'd ever heard. Like it or not, I was a Were. Nothing was going to change that.

I'd been warned that the Internet was nearly nonexistent at the compound. Apparently, the witches thought technology was a crutch. An unnecessary distraction. I hadn't been without my cell in years. *Years.*

So, probably no FaceTime. No Skype. No video chatting. I wouldn't even get email.

Donovan had left me to break the news to Dastien. Smart guy. I'd seen Dastien pissed before—he'd nearly decimated a tree once when he punched it—but this was different. I knew he'd be angry, but he'd lost his shit. One hundred percent blown lid.

It was hours before Dastien's eyes blinked open.

"Hey," I said. "How're you feeling?"

He closed his eyes, and I wondered if he'd fallen asleep again, but he finally spoke. "Terrible." When his eyes opened again, they were golden. "What happened?"

"Dr. Gonzales knocked you out."

He laughed softly, and I wondered if the drugs were still making him a little loopy. "I got that much."

I swallowed. He wasn't going to like this. Better to rip off the Band-Aid than to drag it out. "I have to stay with the coven." He sat up and started to speak, but I put my finger over his lips. "I'm back the day before the next full moon. We're not missing the next ceremony. I told Donovan I'd burn the coven compound to the ground before I missed it, and I wasn't joking at all."

Dastien pressed his lips together, and his emotions swelled. But it wasn't anger that dominated him anymore. It was fear, which worried me. What was he so afraid of?

"It's only a few weeks, and then we'll get to be together. And—"

"I won't be able to feel you through the bond. It'll be like you died. I won't know if you're hurt or in danger or lonely. I won't know when you wake up or if you're eating enough." He traded our positions, lifting me into his lap, and nuzzled his nose against my neck. "I'll go crazy without you."

I rested my head against his chest so that I could hear his steady heartbeat. "Don't go crazy. We can do this." I sat up straighter so I could look into his eyes. "Humans do long distance all the time. It might seem like the end of the world, but it isn't. We have a stronger bond than humans do, and they manage." I cupped his face in my hands. "So, we can do it, too. It's not going to be super fun and awesome, but we'll be okay."

He closed his eyes and his shoulders hunched. "I don't know that I'll be okay." The words were little more than a whisper, like he was confessing something that weighed heavily on his heart. It was so sweet and so sad that it made my heart ache.

I rubbed my thumb along his bottom lip. "I love you so much."

"I love you, too."

I gave him a soft smile. "Say it in French, please."

That made him actually smile. No dimples yet, but it was better than the pout. "*Je t'aime, cherie.*"

I pressed my lips to his and stood up. "Help me pack?"

"I don't want you to go."

"I don't want to go, but I have to. We both know that *la Aquelarre* was never going to stop until they got at least a piece of me. So we give them this little bit. Plus, Luciana is up to something. What better way to find out than by being there? And if I learn some more stuff about my powers and being a *bruja*, well then, all the better."

"I wish you didn't have to go do all that." He huffed. He actually huffed, and it made me want to squeeze him tight and never let go.

"Me, too. But I do need to pack. It's getting late and I have to be there by nine." I got up and started back toward campus, knowing Dastien wouldn't be far behind me.

It took him a minute, but then he got up. His long stride caught up to me in a few steps. "I'll take you there in the morning."

"I want to have my car with me." If shit hit the fan, I wanted to be able to get away from the coven, and fast.

"Fine. I'll go with you and then I'll shift and run back."

That was over an hour drive. "It's kind of far."

He put his arm over my shoulder and pulled me into his side. His need to be close to me beat along the bond. "I've done it before."

That was true. "Okay."

"Did you tell your mom what happened?"

Maybe I should've called her, but I was too busy watching Dastien sleep off Dr. Gonzales' cocktail. "I haven't really had time."

"Wasn't I out for hours?"

My cheeks heated. He wasn't going to let me get

away with this one. "Yeah, but I was brooding and watching you sleep."

He squeezed me tighter. "Now who's creepy?"

"It's not creepy." I elbowed him. "I'm your mate."

He was quiet for a long moment. Almost so long that I thought he was done talking, but then he said, "That's definitely true. I'm your mate. And you're mine."

It didn't take us long to pack what I needed. I wasn't taking everything, only the essentials. It was like a long, mandatory vacation. Only it was definitely not my idea of a good time.

Meredith stopped by as we were about to get into bed. She fidgeted with the bottom of her T-shirt. Meredith wasn't one to fidget. "Are you guys okay?"

"Of course."

Meredith relaxed a little. "Good. I was worried after his reaction and it's kind of my fault—"

"None of this is your fault. At all."

"But you went to the coven to help me and—"

"No. They were always going to be upset about this. I'm surprised they didn't show up before now. So just push that guilt away because it shouldn't exist."

She hugged me. "You'll be back before you know it."

I gave her a small smile. That was something people said when they didn't know what to say. This plain sucked, no matter how I cut it.

"I'll see you soon. Okay?" I didn't meant to be short with her, but if this was the last night I was going to sleep in the same bed with my mate, then I wanted to enjoy it.

She gave me a tight nod. "Sure. Goodnight."

"Night," Dastien said. He was already under the covers, but he lifted them up for me as I walked to the bed. The bed was all nice and warm thanks to his body heat. I rested my head on his shoulder and wrapped an arm around his stomach.

"You still want to wait until after the ceremony to…you know?"

That got me the first laugh of the evening. "Your mom's right about one thing. If you can't say it, you shouldn't be doing it."

"Have sex." My cheeks burned.

"Make love."

"Same thing."

"No. It's not."

We'd talked before about his 'active' life before me, although I'd made him shut up halfway through the conversation. I didn't want to hear about him with other girls. It made me feel inexperienced and childish.

It also made me jealous. Extremely jealous. Just remembering a bit of the conversation had me grinding my teeth.

He kissed my forehead. "No reason to feel jealous. No one could ever compare to you."

"You don't know that," I said. Because it was true. He didn't know that.

"You're my mate. That makes all the difference." He opened the bond and all his emotions for me flooded my senses. It was like being wrapped in a blanket of love.

I put my leg over his, and scooted as close to him as I could. "I'm going to miss this."

"You better."

I bit his chest softly. "I'm sorry I have to go."

"It's my fault. If I'd done something differently, well...maybe we could've avoided this."

I thought about it for a minute, but all roads led to Luciana being a total asshole. It didn't matter how I became a Were. "I wonder if she ever would've let me go without a fight. I mean, I didn't even know anything about the coven when I moved here. When I met you, I didn't know that I was supposed to be leading them. So, how would I know to ask permission? Or even know that I needed permission? And even if I did know about the coven and my place in it and asked permission, she never would've said yes. Not in a million years." The more I thought about it, the more inevitable it seemed. "It is what it is, but I know we can really get through it. It's not forever, and we are."

He ran his fingers lazily up and down my arm. "I don't know that I can be okay with you gone."

I kissed him. "You have to be."

He was quiet for a second, and I felt a little strand of hope along our bond.

"What?"

"I was thinking about our land."

Our land. "What about it?"

"Just that. The future. I hope that we get to have it."

My bottom lip trembled, and I bit it. No use getting upset now. "Me, too."

"Sleep."

I sighed. I didn't want to go to bed. I didn't want tomorrow to happen. And yet, despite how much I didn't want to sleep, as Dastien trailed his fingertips lightly over my skin, my eyelids grew heavy.

I hoped I wasn't wrong. That we'd get through it. And that I wasn't putting my mate through hell for no reason.

If I didn't come back from my stint with some answers, heads were going to roll.

Chapter Nine

The morning came way too soon, and I wanted to spend every possible second with Dastien. Rather than going down to the cafeteria, we ate the contents of my mini-fridge for breakfast. Sure, not all of it was exactly breakfast food, but it did the job.

By seven we were both dressed and all my bags waited by the door. "I guess we should go."

"Wouldn't want you to be late."

His sarcasm annoyed me. "No. I don't want to be late. We made a deal, and we need to follow through. I'm not going to give them any reason to point fingers at us. I'll follow the rules, so that when I come back, they'll have no complaints."

"Do you really think that's going to happen?"

Honestly, no. "I have to hope that I'm doing this for a reason. That I'm not putting you—*us* through this for nothing. I'm trying to stop a war and keep people from getting hurt. I don't want to see anyone spelled like Meredith was." I pictured her seizure on the roof of the dorms. "That was a nightmare." I grabbed one of the duffels and started for the door, but Dastien grabbed my arm and tugged me to him.

"I'm sorry. I'm trying not to be a spoiled brat. I

just…You don't know how awful I felt when you snuck onto their land with Chris. It was the worst thing I'd ever experienced. Worse than my parents' deaths."

I dropped the bag. "I won't be dying. You have to remember that the bond is blocked, not broken. Every time you reach for me and I'm not there, remember that I'm okay and that I love you. All right?" Dastien was kind of adorable when he was being pouty.

"I'll try." He picked up the bag I'd dropped along with my other bag. "Let's go, before I lock you up in the feral cages and swallow the key."

I threw my messenger bag over my shoulder and took one last look around my room before I closed the door. *Be back soon*, I thought to myself.

If I'd been wondering where my friends were hiding, I shouldn't have. They were all sitting around my car. I handed Dastien the keys as I walked to them.

"Hey," Adrian said. "You need me to come down to the coven, you let me know. I think they might let me visit." Adrian was the only Were I knew who had *brujo* blood. If he hadn't been born a Were, he would've ended up with *la Aquelarre*.

Chris pulled me in for a hug. "If the coven gets to you, try drawing mean pictures of them. Always helps me."

"I can't draw." My 'art' made stick figures look like masterpieces.

"Even better."

I laughed.

Meredith hugged me hard, nearly suffocating me. "I'm going to miss you, roomie."

"Me, too. Keep an eye on my stuff for me." Both of us were choking back tears, but I wouldn't let mine fall.

"Will do."

Dastien closed the trunk. "Time to go."

I wouldn't cry. I couldn't let myself. I was doing the right thing and being an adult. That meant no crying. "See you guys later." I hopped in the passenger side. As much as I liked driving, I was sure that when we left the gates, the waterworks were going to start whether or not I was trying to be brave.

I wasn't wrong. The first sob slipped through as soon as we were turned on the main road.

"Please don't." Dastien gripped the steering wheel hard. "I'm barely holding it together. I can't take you there if you're going to cry like this."

I wiped my tears on my shirt. "I know. It's dumb. I just don't like goodbyes."

He squeezed my leg. "This isn't goodbye. Everyone will be there when you get back."

"I know. I'm being dumb."

"Not dumb at all." He handed me his phone. "Plug her in and hit play. The first song on Matt Lange's guest mix from ABGT eighty-five is amazing. You're going to love it."

My grin was a little watery, but I did what he said, and let Matt Lange's 'We Transcend' take me away.

"Is that Einaudi that he's mixing in?"

"Yup."

I turned it up. *Amazing*, I said through the bond.

I thought you'd like that.

Thanks. For distracting me. For driving me.

Anything. For you, I'd do anything.

I let that soak in as I leaned over the console to rest my head on his shoulder. No, it wasn't the safest way to drive, but I trusted him and I was a Were. Being near him, with the soft piano and deep rolling bass, took away a measure of nerves and sadness and frustration that burned through my veins.

Luciana was getting a fuckload more than she'd bargained for. If she thought I'd decide to stay forever and suppress my wolf, she was going to be disappointed. I'd only be biding my time, waiting until I could go home to St. Ailbe's, where I really belonged. With people who actually cared about me.

Things had a funny way of working out, and I was going to make sure they worked out the way I wanted them to this time.

***

As we pulled up to the compound, I felt only one thing. Dread. I'd been here twice in the past week. Neither time had gone well. I thought about having Dastien drop me outside the gate, but no one had told me he wasn't allowed to walk me to the door, and I wasn't about to tell Dastien he couldn't do this last little thing.

We went through the gate and that same icky barrier spell passed over me like a slimy curtain. I was prepared for it, and as long as Dastien was on the same side as me, our bond still held.

Beyond the gate was a long, straight dirt road. A line of two-story houses lined the road, with cars parked in front. *La Aquelarre's* land felt more rustic than St. Ailbe's, mostly because the dirt road was so bumpy and they'd barely managed to cut back enough forest to fit the houses. St. Ailbe's had nice landscaping around it. Even the forest immediately surrounding the campus was a little tame. But the forest here felt like it was about to swallow up the houses any minute.

The last two times I'd been here, the road was empty of people. This time I had a full-on welcoming party.

We got out of the car, and Dastien quickly moved to my side. He was tense, but not totally losing it yet. I just hoped he could keep his cool. A confrontation with Luciana on my first day wouldn't be the best way to start off.

Luciana stood front and center of the gathered crowd, with her son, Daniel, slightly behind her. I scanned the faces and found my cousins. They stood on their porch, away from the crowd. I wasn't sure if I was glad to see them or pissed.

Right then I was leaning toward pissed. I had trusted them when I told them what was going on in my life, and they ran home to tell on me?

I knew I needed allies if I was going to make it at the compound, but I wasn't sure that I could count on them anymore. It was more than a little disappointing.

Luciana stepped forward and Dastien's anger at her rippled through the bond. I gripped his hand to keep him from doing anything stupid. He'd been doing so well this morning, which was exactly what I'd needed, but he couldn't backslide now.

Luciana wore one of the long, flowing skirts she favored that I found impractical. Especially here with the dirt road. How did she manage to keep the hems clean?

"I'm so glad you've decided to join us," she said.

"You didn't give me much choice. I'm not here of my own volition." I fought to keep my voice calm and even.

"I'm sure once you get settled in, you'll forget all about the pack."

Dastien growled and I squeezed his hand harder. *Please, don't freak out. I have to stay here and I need you to be calm.*

I'm trying.

"You really have no concept of reality, do you?" I said to Luciana. "I'll be going home for the next full moon, and if I ever set foot on this land again, it'll be to raze it."

A few shocked gasps escaped the crowd and I wondered who here knew what Luciana was up to. The whole coven couldn't be bad, and by the reactions, not everyone agreed with her methods.

"Starting off with a threat isn't a good way to win over the coven."

Good thing I wasn't trying to win anyone over. "Threatening me and the pack with war unless I show up here isn't a good way to win *me* over."

More murmurs went through the crowd.

Daniel stepped forward. "Mother, I think it's best if she gets settled. It's been a trying few days for her."

"Good idea." Luciana didn't spare him a glance. "I was hoping you could stay with me and Daniel."

Yeah. There was no way in hell that was going to happen.

I looked toward my cousins. "I think I'll stay with

my family. I'm sure you understand." When I moved to the back of the car, Dastien followed.

First impression? I asked. As long as our bond was in place, I'd use it as much as I could until Dastien had to leave.

Not everyone is backing her, but there are a lot who are. Even through the bond, his voice had a hint of wolf. He was under control, but just barely. *You're going to have to watch your back at all times, and I'm not going to be here to do it.*

I never had any intention of letting my guard down. I grabbed my backpack and let Dastien handle the rest. *Do you think it's a mistake to stay with Claudia and Raphael?*

Anything is better than sleeping in the same house as her. But keep one eye open.

Always.

By the time we rounded the other side of the car, the crowd had dissipated. I made my way toward my cousins' place. Their door hung open. "Hello," I called as we stepped inside.

"Come on in," Raphael said. "Claudia is changing the sheets in the guest room. They were clean, but she wants them fresh, too." He shrugged.

"Thanks. Where to?"

"Up the stairs. First door on the right."

The stairs creaked with age as I walked up, Dastien close on my heels. The steps were covered with a patterned carpet that was a little threadbare in places. Claudia was in what I took to be the guest bedroom, rushing around the tiny twin bed. It had a white-painted iron frame.

"Can I help you do anything?" I asked.

"No. I've got it. Just one second and I'll have this all ready."

"You didn't have to—"

"Yes, I did," she said without pausing her quick movements. "You have every right to hate me right now, but we need you more than your pack needs you. The least I can do is make a clean bed for you to sleep in."

I dropped my messenger bag with a thud. "You need me?"

She kept busy as she moved around the room. A huge lace doily sat on top of the dark wooden bedside table, which was cluttered with an ornate lamp, some colorful dishes, a bowl of potpourri, and a lit candle. The potpourri and candle were going to have to go. The concentrated floral scent was already giving me a headache and I was barely in the door.

I stepped to the candle, blew it out and handed it to Dastien. He grabbed the potpourri and went back downstairs. Knowing him, he'd grab all the rest of the little smelly things around the house and chuck them out the window. *I hope they didn't leave any important potion stuff hanging around.*

Sure enough, I heard something crash. Hopefully, whatever it was wasn't irreplaceable. Raphael started talking downstairs, but he didn't sound angry, so I ignored it and focused on Claudia.

I felt awkward not helping as she rushed to make the bed, but if bustling around made her feel better, then I might as well let her have at it.

When she was done, she smoothed a hand over the white and yellow quilt. She was a couple years older than me, but she acted much older than that. It made me wonder how much responsibility she'd had to take over when her parents left the compound. "There. The closet is small, but empty. There are hangers, too. I don't have a desk for you, but I could—"

"This is fine. I didn't bring much. I'm not staying longer than the full moon."

Claudia finally stopped moving. "That's fine. If we can't do what needs to be done by then, it'll be too late."

I shot a look over my shoulder as Dastien came back into the room. He gave a barely there shake of his head. *I haven't figured out what Claudia's planning, either,* he said through the bond.

"What's going on?"

"That'll take a bit to explain. I'm sorry for what I did, but we're desperate." She pushed past me to exit the room. "Get settled, and then come downstairs." She checked her watch. "Luciana will be here soon to make Dastien leave. We can talk more once he's gone."

Dastien moved into the room and set my duffles by the foot of the bed. "What do you want to do? We can turn around now. I can take you home."

I shrugged. "It's too late to back out."

"It's never too late. I don't like you being used as some sort of pawn in whatever game the coven is playing." I could feel his desperation through the bond, even if he looked cool as a cucumber on the outside.

I can't, I told him through the bond. *Leaving would mean a fight.*

Dastien wasn't scared of fighting, but that was

exactly what I'd been trying to avoid. "At least we sort of know why they told Luciana." I bit my lip as I considered the situation. "They've helped us twice. I have a feeling these weeks are about repaying the favor."

"I have a feeling you're right."

The doorbell rang. "Time for the dog to leave." Luciana's voice filled the house.

Dastien growled and I stepped into him, wrapping my arms around his waist. *Calm down.*

I hate her.

I'm pretty sure the feeling is mutual.

Luciana was waiting in the living room, but neither of us said a word to her as we walked out the front door.

When we got to the front gate, Dastien took off his shoes, shirt, and pants, but left on his boxer briefs. He handed it all to me, but I wasn't paying attention. The sight of him took my breath away.

"*Cherie?*" He reached to cup my chin.

"Right. Sorry." I took his clothes and held them to my chest.

He pulled me close, and ran his hands through my hair. His lips came to mine, and I lost myself in the feel of them. His tongue ran along the seam of my lips, and I opened. Somewhere along the way I must've dropped the clothes because I wrapped my arms around his neck. My heart thumped in my ears, and I couldn't get close enough. I slid my hands down his abs and around his back.

This was what I was missing. We'd been too sad last night to really do anything, but I ached for him. My wolf craved him, and so did I.

Dastien bit my lip and rested his forehead against mine. "Call me if you need me."

I wished I could say the same, but I doubted I'd be free to leave the compound for anything related to the Weres. I kissed him lightly. "I'm going to miss you."

Since I'd stopped running from him and trying to escape St. Ailbe's, we hadn't really been apart. I saw him everyday.

As soon as he stepped beyond the gates, it was like he'd been ripped away from me. If I couldn't see him with my own eyes, I would've thought he was dead. The sudden break in the bond left both of us gasping.

"Holy shit. This is worse than it was last time."

"That's because you were distracted last time. Now you know what that feeling is like."

I ignored the icky sensation and reached over the gate to feel him. As soon as my hand touched his skin, the bond snapped back into place and I instantly felt better. "This is really going to blow."

He gave me a sad smile. It wasn't very reassuring. "I know." He stepped back and shifted. It took less than a second, and then I was staring at my mate in wolf form. His boxer briefs were under his feet. He nipped them up with his teeth and passed them to me through the gate.

I stood there and watched him run until he disappeared around the bend in the road. I tried to reach him along our bond, but it was gone. Not just muted, but gone. A side effect of being on separate sides of the barrier. It was meant to warn other supernaturals away, and it would've worked if I weren't being forced to stay here.

I closed my eyes for a second. My head knew that

Dastien was fine. He was running home, back to his cabin, back to the pack. And he was safe. But my heart, my gut, my bond, told me that everything was completely and totally fucked.

It was time I dealt with the coven for good. Maybe if I did whatever Claudia and Raphael needed, I could go back sooner than planned.

I let myself back into my cousins' house, and walked into the tchotchke-loaded living room. Claudia and Raphael were sitting on the floral-printed couch talking softly, but Luciana was gone.

Thank God for small favors.

First things first. "I can't deal with all the smells. Did Dastien get rid of everything?"

"Yes," Raphael said.

I could still smell the roses, orange, vanilla, cinnamon, cloves and a million other things from all the potpourri and candles that had been everywhere in the house. "Can we open some windows? Air it out?"

Claudia started into motion. "Yes. Of course."

We went through the house, opening all the windows. She had a fan in her room, and I snagged it for the living room. Texas didn't have a ton of wind this time of year, and the downstairs was the most offensive room in the house. I aimed the fan to blow out the window.

"Better?" Claudia said when it was all done.

"Much. I couldn't think with all that." I sat on the couch. "Let's talk. What's going on?"

"There's something wrong with Luciana—" Claudia started.

I snorted. No shit. "Sorry. Go on."

"Some of us think she needs to be replaced, but with you gone, it's a little hard. We're hoping that you can help us with a change of power," Claudia said.

"I would've done that regardless of my relationship with the pack. You didn't have to stop the ceremony."

"But we couldn't have accepted your help if you were fully bound to the pack," Raphael said. His voice was very matter of fact. I could've chosen to take offense at that. They wouldn't accept my help but they needed it. It made me want to thumb my nose at them and take off.

But for now, I was committed to being here, so I listened as Raphael continued. "The coven's divided, and the anti-Luciana group isn't the majority. Our side doesn't want war, but I think she does no matter what. Over the years, she's developed a thirst for power. It started out as restrictions on us, but now it's grown. She wants more territory. She wants to move off the compound and practice out in the open. She wants the wolves gone."

That wasn't going to happen. "I don't care how much land she has or where y'all live, but practicing in the open and taking out the pack? That's too far."

"We agree," Raphael said. "Things are like this for a reason. Humans...they wouldn't understand. We already had one season of witch burnings, and none of us want to go through that again."

I could definitely understand that.

"But she's our leader, and with you gone, it's like she has no end in sight for her rule," Claudia said. She leaned forward in her chair. "I'm not sure how she's done it, but every year she's gotten stronger. Other than you, she might be the most powerful living witch. I understand that you can't take your old place now, but could you help us find someone who could? Or at least help us find a way to take Luciana down?"

"I'd be happy to help. I'm just not sure how." Neither statement was a lie. I didn't want some crazy person with power going around doing God knew what, but short of taking over the coven like I was supposed to, I had no idea what to do to stop her.

"You know how we find our new leaders?"

I wasn't totally sure where she was going with this. "Yes. The previous leader goes to find someone, but it always skips a generation. So when Luciana took charge, my grandmother announced the following leader."

"Exactly. It's something that only you or Luciana could do for us. She's not going to find anyone. She never wants to step down. And your grandmother passed away...You're our only hope."

She wanted me to find them a new leader? "Don't you think someone from another coven would be better suited?"

"No," Claudia said. If she thought I was the best person to find a new leader, then she must really be desperate. I didn't have the first clue about anything that went on in *la Aquelarre*.

"We have a little bit of a rivalry between covens," she said. "It's not like a pack, where you're like separate states in the same country. We're separate countries. And not a lot of us are allies."

This seemed like great news for the pack. Donovan had made it sound like the witches were way more united. But I'd never known Donovan to be wrong. "So, if war starts with the wolves?"

"Then, we join together," Raphael said. "But that's it. Only when we have a common enemy."

So, not only would Luciana get rid of the wolves if she started the war, but she'd unify the covens and immediately take charge of all that power.

It was all starting to make sense.

I only had to stop a war, find a replacement coven leader, and then take down one of the most powerful, evil witches on the earth. And I had all of twenty-six days to work with.

Chapter Ten

With all the unpleasantness done, I went in search of food. It hadn't been that long since I'd eaten, but I wasn't giving the wolf any chances to take the upper hand. Claudia and I went to the kitchen, and Raphael left to go do something. I didn't ask what.

The kitchen hadn't been redone in forever. It wasn't eighties old, it was like thirties old. White tile lined the countertops and thick iron handles were mounted on the white cabinets. None of the doors closed properly, all of them hung a little open and drooped just a smidge. A round table with four chairs took up one corner and a backdoor led outside. Even though it was small, the space was efficiently used, and it had a ton of cabinets. The pale yellow paint was trimmed around the top with flowered wallpaper. It was peeling back along the edges, but it still had some vibrant colors. I could almost picture Mom growing up here, but that didn't mean it felt like home.

I opened the fridge and sighed.

"What's wrong?"

"We're going to need more food."

"What?" Claudia peeked around my shoulder. "I got twice as much stuff as I usually get just in case you stayed with us."

"I could eat all of this in a day." I closed it. "So, am I allowed to leave the compound? Because we're going to need to hit a Sam's as soon as possible."

"Really? You eat that much food? But you're so little."

I pulled up my shirt to show her my abs. "I'm a little skinny for the Weres. I still don't eat as much as I should, which makes me a little thinner than normal, but I'm all muscle." I dropped my shirt. "I wasn't always like this. I used to have curves. Come to find out, Weres have a super high metabolism."

"So when you go to McDonald's you get what? Three meals?"

"Five."

"*Madre santa.* That's crazy. Okay. I have no idea how much to get for you and I'm not sure that Luciana is going to let you leave so soon after you got here."

This wasn't something that could be ignored. There was no way the coven was going to let another Were onto the compound, but I had someone who could help.

I pulled my cell out of my back pocket, but as promised, I had zero bars. "Do you have a landline?"

"Sure, but I have to get Luciana to turn it on." Claudia pointed to the antique mounted to the wall next to the back door.

That seemed like the craziest thing. "She has a switch for the phones?"

Claudia nodded. "In her living room. Keeps it all locked up."

"Doesn't that seem a little overboard?"

"Yes. One of the many reasons why we need some change." She paused. "I hate to ask, but I'm going to have to tell Luciana—who are you going to call?"

I thought about it for a second. I wanted to call Dastien, but no way would Luciana go for that. "My mom. She'll make a grocery run for me."

"Okay. Just give me a second. I'll explain it to her." Claudia headed for the door. "Be back in a sec."

I paced around the room, getting more annoyed by the second. What if there was an emergency? A fire or someone hurt or something? The compound was way too cut off from civilization. That didn't seem safe.

Claudia gave me a thumbs-up when she came back. "We've got five minutes."

Luciana was unbelievably stingy. I ground my teeth, trying to stay calm. "Great." I quickly dialed Mom's cell and tapped my fingers along the wall as it rang. "Hey, Mom," I said when she finally answered.

"What's going on? Where are you calling from? Are you okay?"

I sighed. She said the same thing every time she answered the phone these days. I wished for once I were calling just to chat. "I'm on the coven land and—"

"Why are you there? I thought I told you—"

"It's dangerous. I know, but the Tribunal didn't exactly go my way. I have to stay here until the next full moon."

Mom gasped. "No. *Mija*. That's not okay. I'm on my way. I'll talk to Luciana. She can't—"

"Mom. Calm down. It's fine." I paused. That was total bullshit. "It's not fine. It sucks, but I've agreed to

137

put up with it. The bigger problem is that I can't leave and there's not enough food here. I'll eat everything in a day, and I…I need it. Dastien's not here and my wolf is on edge and…"

"I'll go to the store," she said, understanding what I was asking without having to ask it. "I'll bring enough to stock the fridge and will keep coming as often as you need."

I closed my eyes and leaned against the counter. "Thanks, Mom."

"Don't worry about a thing. Mama's here. I'll take care of it."

The tears from earlier threatened to come back, but I blinked them away. "Thanks." It seemed no matter how old I got, I still needed my mother sometimes. I was lucky to have her so close by. "I really appreciate it."

"*Te quiero mucho.* See you soon."

"Are you okay?" Claudia said when I put the phone back.

I raised an eyebrow at her. "Seriously? You're asking me this question?"

"Right." She looked at the ground. "I understand you're mad. I'm sorry."

"You forced my hand when you could've asked nicely. I understand that you're not in a good place, but I liked you. I would've done everything I could to help you. Now, I want to get this done and go back to my life."

She nodded, still staring at the ground.

Being a bitch to her felt like kicking a puppy, but I couldn't help it. I was pissed. It didn't have to be this way. "Let's talk about what we're going to do next."

"What do you mean?"

"Well, you need a new leader. Let's start there. Who do you think is a good candidate?"

She shrugged. "I'm not sure. That's the problem. No one is even close to Luciana's strength in magic."

"And that's one of the requirements?"

"No. Not exactly."

"How about you tell me exactly while I make myself a snack?" I opened the fridge and pulled out cheese, ham, and an avocado for a grilled sammy. I made myself at home as I started cooking. Once I had everything in a pan, I looked over my shoulder at Claudia.

She hopped onto the counter. "Right. Rules. There's always a leader and a successor, so the current leader picks someone to be third in line. Grams picked you and once Luciana stepped down, she was supposed to name your successor, but that's all changed now. And Grams is—"

"Unreachable." Maybe it was snippy, but I was a little tired of being manipulated. I needed real solutions. "So what happens in this kind of scenario?"

"Luciana should pick someone, but we don't want that to happen. That's why there's always a break in succession. No one person's will or agenda gets pushed on two generations. And since we're extremely divided about some of the things Luciana's been doing...we're in a bit of a bind. You're strong enough that you could pick your replacement, and I think if we position it correctly, then we could get the support of the whole coven."

"Sounds reasonable. So I know you have to have some sort of sight like my visions in order to rule."

"Exactly. And Luciana's visions used to be kind of weak, but she's been getting stronger lately. Which is weird."

"Wait. Why is her getting stronger weird?"

"Because once you reach a certain age, your affinity or abilities start to settle or even lessen. But with Luciana, it's the opposite. That's another reason we're divided. The few in our faction suspect she's using dark magic to boost her power and most in the coven want no part in that."

I checked my sammy. Perfectly golden. I tossed some more butter in the pan as I flipped it.

"Wow. That looks really amazing."

"Want me to make you one?"

She shook her head. "No. I eat something like that and I have to eat nothing but lettuce and work out for days to burn it off."

"Right. Well, I have the opposite problem. It gets old, this whole eating all the time thing. I kept almost losing control of my wolf before. But now, as long as I eat I'm pretty okay. Me and the wolf have an understanding."

Claudia pressed her lips together for a second, as if carefully considering what I'd said. "It's weird hearing you talk about the wolf that way."

I shrugged. "It's weird to me, too, but that's the only way I know how to describe it." I checked the sammy. Not quite toasty. "So, who here has abilities that could be considered leadership material?"

"No one. That's the problem. I've even asked friends in nearby covens, but they won't respond. They're too afraid of Luciana."

I snorted. "She's such a bitch." I thought for a

140

second. "What about you?"

Her mouth dropped open. "Me?" She pointed to herself like there was anyone else in the room I could've been talking about.

"Yeah. When we first met, you helped me find Dastien. That could be a good start."

She shook her head. "That's nothing. I helped amplify your own powers."

"What about Raphael?"

"He's good at spells. Other than that…"

"Poor guy." I winked at her.

Claudia laughed.

My sammy was done. I put it on the plate and cut it in half. The bread gave a lovely crunch as the knife sliced through it. "Do you have any chips?"

"Yeah." She hopped off the counter and opened a cabinet. "Snacks are all in here." She pulled a bag of tortilla chips and a bag of Cheetos. "I also have Limón potato chips, and pretzels."

"I'll take the Cheetos." I grabbed a root beer from the fridge and sat down.

Cooking for myself was going to be a pain in the ass. How was I going to get anything done? I suddenly yearned for the cafeteria and stocked common room fridge.

I could do this. I had to. Losing control here would cost too much. "So, you don't have any leads, no covens will help us, and we can't talk to Grams."

Claudia tilted her head. "That's not entirely accurate."

I set the sandwich down. "What part?"

She looked off to the side, slowly nodding as she thought about it. "We could talk to Grams."

"What, like have a séance? Use a Ouija board? What are we talking about here? And isn't that really scary? I mean, I don't know about you, but the kinds of scary movies that give me nightmares start out with something like that. I don't want to spend the rest of my life being chased by demons."

She slashed her hand through the air. "It's a little dangerous, but manageable. With the right spell."

I couldn't believe I was actually considering this. "Any chance we can do it during daylight hours?" I shuddered.

"No. We'll get Raphael and a few of the others to help, too. If we can make sure to get just Grams, then we should be fine. And we'll ward the house to keep out evil entities."

Evil entities? "This sounds like a terrible idea."

"What sounds like a terrible idea?" Raphael said as he came through the kitchen door.

"Your sister wants to have a séance to find out if Grams has any ideas on a replacement for me."

"No." He didn't even think about it. There was no hesitation in his voice whatsoever. "That's way too dangerous."

Claudia hunched her shoulders. "Even if—"

"No."

The twins stared each other down for a minute before Claudia conceded. "Fine. But I still say it's an option."

I finished my sandwich and wiped off my fingers. "What do you think Luciana's really up to? If she's threatening war with the pack and gaining power in a bad way, then she has to have a plan."

"We don't know," Raphael said. "There's been

some major discontent brewing in the coven for years, but now…it's reached a fever pitch. It's crazy. And it's not just Luciana. It's people I thought were normal, chill, before. Now, they're all crazed." He shook his head. "It's not right. And it's not right that we cornered you into this, but we need whatever help we can get."

He was right. It was messed up, but we had to get past that. There had to be a solution, but I didn't know enough to figure it out yet.

I got up and busied myself cleaning up my dishes. When I was done, I turned back to the twins who were quietly whispering about what to do or not do with me next.

Sometimes having Were hearing was a little awkward. Or completely awkward.

I cleared my throat. "I'm just going to go upstairs and get settled. We can figure out the next step once I get unpacked and my mom brings more food."

"Okay," they said in unison.

The good thing about packing light meant I could pack up quickly if I got the okay to leave early. The bad thing about packing light was that I was unpacked pretty quickly. I opened my laptop and tried to connect to the Wi-Fi in the house, but all I got was an endlessly spinning 'looking for networks' notification.

This was going to be a long three weeks. I already felt like I was crawling out of my skin. Being without my connection to Dastien was like missing a limb I hadn't realized was attached before. The absent bond was a constant pull and distraction. A scab I couldn't stop picking at.

It was gross and awful. But I had to get a grip.

I started doing some vinyasas—practicing the yoga that Meredith said would keep me centered, trying to gain the upper hand back from the wolf that wanted to break free. The floorboards creaked as I moved through my sun salutations. I focused on my breath moving evenly and the sound of the wood moaning as I flowed from position to position.

Midway through my fourth downward dog, I laughed. Weres were so weird. The past few months felt so surreal. I still couldn't believe that I'd actually nearly killed Imogene. When the wolf was fully in control of my human body, I wasn't myself, and that was dan-ger-ous. I was starting to get used to the occasional fight. The alphas were pretty good about keeping everyone under control, but the freshman— the newbies—had to be watched a lot.

For what felt like the millionth time that day, I wondered what I'd gotten myself into. I'd been drawn into this weird world that I was expected to know how to navigate, and I simply didn't. I hadn't the foggiest.

The pressure to figure it all out was a heavy weight on my chest. The stakes were too high and I'd sacrificed too much for me to fuck this up. And of course, the probability of fucking up was unusually high.

I sighed. If I made it off coven land without killing anyone or getting killed, I'd call it a win.

Chapter Eleven

When I'd finally worked up a sweat and my arms felt like two cooked spaghetti noodles, I popped down on the ground for savasana. The small area rug did little to stop the loose floorboards from poking me in the back. After a second, my breath was back to normal. I rolled off the rug and lay down on bed.

Relaxing must've made me lower my guard. I wasn't even aware that I'd opened myself up to a vision until a figure walked into the room.

The woman's hair was heavily grayed at her temples, but the rest was dark as pitch. She had it bound in a tight bun at the nape of her neck. Her loose dress was vibrant pink. Brightly colored flowers were embroidered on the edges. A traditional Mexican dress. She looked straight at me and winked.

What? Could she see me? "Hello?" I sat up, but the *figure didn't respond.*

Of course she couldn't see me. This was a vision of something that happened a long time ago.

The woman knelt on the floor, setting down a brown leather book as she threw the carpet to the side. A teal-colored circular pattern was inked on the book cover.

I studied her face, trying to place her. The woman's features were familiar, but not. She had to be family if she had free reign of the house...

It couldn't be Grams, could it?

She slammed her hand on one end of a floorboard, and the other side popped up. Then she placed the little book into the hiding spot.

Finally, she looked up at me and winked.

I hopped off the bed. I waved a hand through her, and I knew it was a vision, but she'd looked straight at me. "Grams?"

She shook her head and pointed down at the floorboard.

Just as quickly as it started, the vision was gone. I was left standing in the guest room, alone.

I didn't hesitate. I dropped to the ground, threw the rug to the side and popped up the floorboard.

Nothing. I couldn't see anything except spiderwebs. Yuck. I really didn't want to put my hand in there. Not even a little bit. But curiosity got the better of me. I squeezed my eyes shut, and reached inside.

Still nothing.

I grabbed my cellphone from my bag and turned on the flashlight function. It was empty. There wasn't a book in there anymore.

Why would I see that book if I wasn't meant to find it? Or maybe it was a useless vision. Lord knew I had enough of those in my life.

But she'd looked straight at me. As if telling me to find that journal. No one had ever noticed me in a vision before. If someone had asked me if it were possible five minutes ago, I would've said no way.

Now, I wasn't so sure.

"Tessa!" Claudia shouted from downstairs.

"Yeah?"

"Someone's here to see you."

For a second I got my hopes up that it was Dastien or Meredith, but I knew better. I'd have to look into finding the journal later. I straightened the rug back in place and headed downstairs.

"Daniel," I said when I spotted the visitor. "What do you need?"

"I'm here to start your training." He was wearing a pair of jeans and a pressed button-down. His hair was still wet from a shower, but I smelled a faint hint of cloves under his soap.

"Training?" I asked.

"Yup. Mom wants me to make sure you're well versed in our ways. You're not here for too long, so I figured it was better to get started on it sooner rather than later."

Daniel was the guy that the coven—or maybe just Luciana—had wanted me to end up with. And apparently they still did. The *brujos* didn't have mates like the pack did, but I'd bet my life that if Luciana could arrange my marriage to her son, she would. All the better to bind me to the coven.

I hoped Luciana wasn't trying to manipulate some sort of relationship between us by sending him here. Because that so wasn't going to happen.

This was perfect. Dastien wasn't going to like this at all. "All right. Where do you want to work?"

"They have a room here for working craft. We'll head that way."

I nodded. "Okay." He led me to a room down the

hall behind the living room. When he opened the door, the first thing that hit me was the smell. So many different dried and burnt things. The room was dark. Only a small window opposite the door let in a little bit of light. The walls were painted black. Black counters topped the waist high cabinets that surrounded the room, and black-painted shelves took up every inch of wall space starting a foot on top of the counters. I wasn't counting, but I guessed they held hundreds, if not thousands of glass bottles.

It was like the Metaphysics supply room on steroids. The bottles were older. Some of the glass bottles had that old-timey warped look to them. The handwritten labels had yellowed with age and were marked with beautiful, scrawling scripts. A beaten wooden worktable took up the center of the room, and stacks of books were piled underneath—I made a mental note to keep an eye out for any brown books with a teal pattern. A small iron cauldron, some measuring stuff, and a few other odds and ends cluttered the working surface.

Now this was what came to mind when I thought of witches. "What's all this stuff?"

"For spells. Each family has a fully stocked room. We try and make sure that we have anything we might need in case of emergencies."

"Do you have a lot of emergencies?"

He laughed. "No. But you never know. That's why they're called emergencies."

I grinned. Maybe Daniel wasn't so bad after all. Not everyone could be judged by their parents. "Right."

"So, I figured there were plenty of things we could

start out with—lighting a fire, levitating an object, becoming invisible—"

The proverbial light bulb went off. "That's how Luciana snuck into the full moon ceremony."

"Exactly. But I thought it'd be more useful to you to learn a basic protection spell."

I did my best to not look disappointed. "Okay."

"You're in a place where you don't trust anyone. I thought it'd be better in light of that, but hey, if you want to start with lighting candles, we can do that, too."

I waved a hand through the air. "No. You're right. I'm being dumb. Protection will be much more useful. It'd be good to not get spelled again—like what your mom did—"

Daniel winced. "Sorry about that."

"Did you do the spelling?"

"No."

"Then why are you apologizing?"

"Because she's my mother. Look, I know that maybe things would've worked out differently between us had you not gotten bitten, and I was a little—okay, probably a lot—disappointed about it, but fate is what it is. It wouldn't have happened if it wasn't meant to be."

Daniel was shorter than Dastien by inches, but still taller than me. He was fit, but not like the werewolves. Not ugly by any means, but I felt zero attraction to him. Not that attraction hinged entirely on looks, but the chemistry was missing. That zing. With Dastien, it was so strong that I sometimes couldn't feel anything else when we were together.

Whatever Luciana had planned, marriage to her

son was never going to be in the cards.

"So, the good thing about protection spells is that they have more to do with the motion and will than with saying the right thing—which can get tricky for spells in Latin."

I shrugged. "Makes sense."

He dug around in one of the cabinets. "Claudia?" He called.

She appeared at the door with a box of glasses. The generic kind that came in sets from Target—eight tall and eight short. "Sorry. Forgot you wanted these." She set them on the worktable. "Want me to stick around?" she asked me.

"Nah. We've got it covered," Daniel answered.

Claudia kept her eyes on me. I shook my head. "Thanks." I'd be fine. If I couldn't handle this guy, how was I going to be able to handle his mother?

"We're going to make them shatterproof," he said as Claudia left. "Once you get that down, then you can extend it to any object or person. You can even cast spells so that anyone who wishes you harm can't enter your room or house."

"Like a supernatural security system?"

"Exactly!" He grinned.

That would totally come in handy. "Cool."

He dug around under the stack of books until he found what he was looking for. He opened to a page, and it looked like a book of Celtic knots. The pages were worn and a little wrinkled, but the colored knots still stood out brightly on the faded paper.

He flipped a few pages. "The spell knots are color coded. Some knots—" he flipped to the back of the book—"require using two kinds of intent. So, if a knot is drawn in more than one color, you know when to switch intent." He went back to the beginning of the book. "But that's getting ahead of ourselves. This is a basic knot that can make an object or material stronger. If we perform the spell correctly, it'll make the glass unbreakable for as long as a week, depending how successful we are."

"Nice." I was a total klutz, so this could actually come in handy. I might never crack another iPhone screen again.

"The key is starting and ending the knot in the same place. That's what holds the spell together," Daniel said.

"Wait. Do we literally draw the spell? Like with a pencil or something?"

"Nope. It's mostly mental. You trace a knot with your fingertip wherever you want to spell applied."

Okay. This was getting ten times harder. "If you're not using a pencil, how do you know where the knot starts and ends?"

"That takes practice. It's best to envision a point and start there. Then you just have to remember to go back to that point when you end. Don't worry. We have plenty of glasses to work with, so we can do some trial and error. By the time you've gone through the box, you should have that knot down."

"Got it."

He started me off by tracing the paper with a finger over and over. It seemed like a waste of his time to stand there watching me, but every time I messed up, he corrected me. It was harder to stay on the lines than I expected.

Once I made a successful knot twenty times in a

row, Daniel said we could move on to the first glass. "Remember to make sure you're incorporating your will into the knot. You have to believe—you have to *know*—that the glass isn't going to break."

That seemed a little counterintuitive. How was I supposed to know it was going to work if I'd never done it before?

"Here goes nothing," I muttered to myself as I picked up the first glass. It was a tall one with a slightly squared shape.

Don't break. Don't break. Don't break. I thought to myself as I traced the knot onto the glass with my fingertip. When I was done I placed the glass on the table.

"What now?"

He reached into a cabinet and dug out a large plastic bucket, a hammer, and two pairs of goggles. "Now, we try to break it." He handed me a pair of goggles, and I popped them on.

I placed the glass in the bucket and lightly tapped it with the hammer.

The glass didn't just shatter—it turned to dust. It completely disintegrated as soon as the hammer touched it.

"Whoa!" Daniel said. "You barely tapped it. I've never seen a knot backfire like that."

I tried to keep my cheeks from heating. That was a total disaster.

"Let's try again. This time really focus on thinking about protecting the glass."

"Right." Because I'd totally done the opposite before.

I did the same thing. I put all my will into

believing the glass wouldn't break. I chanted it in my head as I drew the knot.

Once again, I put the glass in the bucket.

Instant dust.

Okay. Something wasn't right. "Are you sure this is the right knot?"

"Pretty sure. That's why it says 'Unbreakable' at the top of the page." He grabbed a glass from the box and started tracing a knot on it. When he was done, he threw the glass on the floor. It bounced. Literally bounced. Like a ball.

"Clearly, I'm not very good at this."

Daniel scratched his head. "I don't know. It's so odd. I've seen knots not work before, but I've never seen a glass turn to powder." He grabbed a short glass this time. "Again."

By the time the doorbell rang a few hours later, I'd nearly gone through the whole box and there was a thick layer of glass dust on the bottom of the bucket. My stomach growled and I knew it was past time to eat. This whole thing was testing my frustration, and on an empty stomach, that wasn't wise.

"I need a break."

"Yeah." Daniel sifted through the glass powder with a long-handled spoon, still partly in shock at my total spell ineptitude.

A knock sounded on the door.

I opened it and saw Mom. She pulled me in for a hug. "How are you doing?"

"Okay. Frustrated. My first lesson isn't going so hot."

"Then I'd say you need a break. Help me with the groceries. I want you to see what I got."

I stepped into the living room to see two worker men hauling in another fridge. "What's that?"

"I didn't want you to worry about the food so much, so I brought another fridge. Call me when you start hitting the secondary fridge. That way you'll always have enough."

That was an incredibly good idea. I couldn't believe I hadn't thought of it. "Thanks, Mom. This is above and beyond. I really appreciate it."

"It was Dastien's idea."

"You talked to Dastien?" I was suddenly jealous of my own mother.

She nodded. "I wanted to make sure I was getting enough."

Wait. I was missing something. "You have his number?"

"He's your mate. Of course I have his number."

That was news to me. "Do you guys talk? Often?"

She shrugged. "Sometimes. We traded numbers when he came to pick up your stuff for St. Ailbe's. I knew then what was going on. Your father was a bit slower to accept things, but it's important to me to support my children, no matter what life brings their way."

I had no clue she'd done that. I knew she supported me. That was clear in everything that she did, but this was something else.

I followed the workers into the kitchen. Claudia was trying to move the table over to make room in the corner for the second fridge. Now this, I could help with.

I didn't want to show off too much for the workers, but I went to the table and lifted it just enough before taking a few steps back.

Claudia shot me a look of awe, and then started scurrying around and scooting chairs out of the way. After the workers left, we went out to Mom's car. She'd folded the seats down, and every bit of space was filled with food.

"You bought the whole damned grocery store."

"What do you think took me so long?" She bumped her shoulder against mine. "Now, let's get this stuff put away."

"First things first." I smelled a delicious mix of bread, cheese, and tomato sauce and found the source in her front seat. I snagged a slice of my favorite pepperoni and jalapeño pizza and inhaled it. "Okay, let's go," I said as I wiped my hands on my jeans. I grabbed as much as I could carry and still see over, and made my way back inside.

It took us an hour to get everything organized in such a way that the fridges could close. The last thing mom brought in was the stack of four extra-large pizzas. "Lunch. Three for you. One for your cousins. You can heat them back up in the oven."

"Thanks. That's awesome."

Mom sighed. "I wish I could stay." She hugged me. "Be careful. If you need anything, just call. Remember, I grew up here. I know these people and what it can be like."

"I know. I appreciate it. I'm going to be okay. Thanks for the food."

"Of course, *mija*. Anything for my girl."

"If you talk to Dastien again, tell him I'm okay."

"I will," she said as she stepped out the door.

I popped the pizzas in the oven and wondered

what Dastien was doing. Being apart was a constant aggravation. I'd been doing my best to focus on the lesson with Daniel, but it seemed like every time I slowed down or stopped moving, I felt this yearning—this longing that I couldn't ignore. And we'd only been apart for hours. This was going to be a whole bunch of no fun.

Maybe if I climbed on the roof, my cell could pick up a signal, but that would mean breaking the rules...

As the smell of pepperoni and cheese filled the kitchen, I pulled out plates.

"What's going on?" Daniel said as he walked into the kitchen.

I guessed he'd been busy trying to figure out what I'd been doing wrong. "My mom brought food. You hungry?"

"Sure." He sat at the table and my cousins joined him. The way they talked with each other reminded me of my friends. Suddenly, it wasn't just Dastien I was missing, it was everyone.

Adrian might be able to get on coven ground, but that would probably only fly once. If I were lucky, maybe twice, and Luciana would definitely try to get her hooks into him. So, I had to save that for when I had really good reason to contact him.

As I tucked into the second pizza, Dastien occupied my thoughts. He was probably fine. Maybe chatting with our friends.

The image of Imogene kissing him flashed into my mind.

What was wrong with me? I really wished I could un-see things. But once I had a vision, it was never gone. When I was in Imogene's room a few months ago, I'd touched her necklace and glimpsed an intimate moment between the two of them.

I guessed that was why she got to me. She'd known Dastien much longer than I had. He said he hadn't meant to lead her on, but she'd been led nonetheless. Her ulterior motives for speaking against me weren't all that secret.

She wanted Dastien back. I knew it. Hell, everyone knew it. But I had to trust Dastien. I had to focus on why I was here, and know that my bond with him would always exist, even if I couldn't feel it. Still strong. Just hidden.

But it was hard to remember when I felt so cut off from him.

The pizza settled like a ton of bricks in my stomach. I put the last one in the fridge and went back to my room. A shower and a nap would do wonders for my attitude. Or at least I hoped they would.

Chapter Twelve

Three days into being at the compound I'd proven to Daniel, Claudia, and Raphael that I was a walking disaster when it came to magic. Every spell I tried backfired. I attempted to light a candle, but it exploded, splattering me with melted wax. Thank God for my Were healing abilities. That wax was freaking hot.

I tried to levitate an object and it flew through the roof, making a nice hole in the ceiling. That had stopped practice for a while. But at least now I could say I knew some serious home repair skills.

When Daniel suggested we try an invisibility spell, I'd succeeded in turning my clothes invisible. That had been mortifying. And if Dastien knew what'd happened, and that Daniel actually got an eyeful, he'd flip. The guy would be blind or dead. As it was, I suddenly felt really exposed around Daniel. No one had gotten such an intimate look at me in…ever.

I felt like a complete moron. It wasn't like I was failing on purpose. I was following the spells to the letter, but nothing worked for me. It seemed the harder I tried, the worse the damage got. I was seriously starting to wonder if I belonged with the coven at all.

I'd met a couple other people around the compound, but for the most part, I was a bit of a pariah. How I was supposed to befriend all these people, let alone figure out which one was supposed to be the next leader, was beyond me.

To add insult to injury, I was a hot mess when it came to missing Dastien. I hated the needy feeling that was eating me up inside. It was like I was drowning and anxious all the time. And it was all because I was missing my mate. My other half.

Pathetic.

I'd been fine being alone before I met him. Why did I suddenly feel like half a person?

During the mornings, the other coven members had meetings and classes. Any group lessons were held at the little schoolhouse down the road a ways. Daniel told me that the older brujos helped the younger ones with their studies there. Most of them did homeschooling lessons during the afternoon, but Daniel had finished his work for the semester way early, so he usually spent afternoons attempting to teach me.

While he was busy in the morning, I took to exercising. The need to change grew stronger everyday, but I'd agreed to live as a bruja, which meant no shifting. A deal was a deal. I'd stick to it even if it killed me.

As I made my fifteenth lap around the compound that morning, a car pulled through the gate. The driver was someone I recognized. I grinned, and jogged over.

"Tia Rosa."

"Hola, mijita. Como estas?"

Completely shitty was the truth, but she didn't need to hear that I was going slowly going mad from being cut off from my mate. "I'm getting by."

She grumbled. "That's what I thought." She put on the little glasses that hung around her neck and gripped my face with her hands. As she stared into me, she tugged on the skin under my eyes.

I blinked and jerked away. What was that about?

"Hmmm. Interesting." She pulled the glasses off.

"What?" Had someone spelled me again? Because if so, that totally meant I could leave. Didn't it?

"Let's talk inside."

"Okay." I followed her back to my cousins' house. "Would you like something to drink?" I asked as she settled down on their floral couch.

"No, *mijita*. Sit next to me." She patted the cushion.

We sat on the couch together in sudden silence. I didn't know who was supposed to talk first, but she already knew what I wanted to hear, so I waited.

"The things that they have you doing, those are distractions."

Not what I was expecting. How did she know what I was doing here? "What do you mean?"

"Spells and incantations and parlor tricks are not worth your time. You need to be working on growing your visions. Becoming more aware of the lines in the future."

Was it just me, or was she being incredibly...crazy? It was like I was missing half the conversation. "Lines?"

"Up until this point, you've seen past and present.

You've gotten feelings and premonitions of the future, no?"

"Yes."

She wheezed a little as she talked. It made my lungs ache in sympathy. "You need to have more than premonitions."

I shook my head. That was impossible. It wasn't how my visions worked. "How?"

"By finding that place within that's the source of your power. Then, you will be able to lead this coven."

I couldn't contain the shocked gasp. "No. I can't. That's not what I'm here for. I need to find the next leader."

"Your Grams—my sister—found the next leader."

"She found me, but I'm in the pack. I'm an alpha. I don't know where I really stand yet, but I'm stronger than most. I can't be in two places at once."

"No, *mijita*. You are of two places and you will always be in two places. You think your Grams didn't know what would happen? You think she made a mistake?"

Honestly? Yes. I kind of did think she made a mistake.

"She knew what would happen to you. She knew that your path would be hard, and she prayed over it, but you cannot change what is meant to be."

"Rosa," I said to her, pleading for her to understand. "It's not just me who doesn't want to be here. The coven doesn't want me either." Luciana didn't want to give me to the wolves, but she hadn't paid a visit since my first day here.

"Now that is a useful way to spend your time. You need to be going around and making friends here, getting to know what these *brujos* really think."

She'd lost her mind. It didn't matter if I had friends. This wasn't my job. "I don't even want to run the pack." I wasn't sure if that was the road I was heading down, but I was a strong alpha and it could happen—it almost certainly would happen to Dastien—so at the very least, I was bound to end up the Were version of a first lady. But Tia Rosa was talking about a whole other level of leadership. "Why would I want to run the coven on top of that?"

She grasped one of my hands. Her skin was so soft and papery thin; I had to be careful with her. She was human, both old and fragile.

"As you grow, you learn that life is rarely about doing what you want. We all do what we must, and that is even more true for the powerful ones like you. My sister saw the times changing. To stop war, you must be the link that unifies the pack and coven…and eventually, all supernaturals. When the time comes for the world to know the truth, the people will need someone to look to. A trustworthy leader who knows what it's like to be human."

I couldn't breath. There wasn't enough air.

No longer able to sit still, I pulled away from Rosa to pace the small room. "I can't be that person. I'm just me. I'm a normal girl."

"You're not normal, and it's past time for you to let go of that delusion." Rosa stood and walked to the door. "When you're ready, if you want my help, you know where to find me."

"I'm not sure I'm allowed off the compound."

"Not allowed off the compound to visit *la Aquelarre's* wise woman? I think I'd have something to say about that. You send Luciana my way if it's not allowed."

I cracked a grin. Rosa might be old, but she still had her wits and sass. "I'll think about it."

I opened the door for her, and she patted my cheek. "I'll be seeing you soon."

I was still sitting on the couch, trying to absorb Rosa's words when Daniel stepped into the house. His morning lessons must've been done. I glanced at my watch. How long had I been staring into space?

He started chatting about the spells he wanted to try today, but I held a hand up.

"Dude. Four days of trying something and getting the same results...don't you think we've had enough? I mean, a hole in the roof? Really?"

He crossed his arms. "You're giving up?"

I shrugged.

"Didn't you break the curse on Meredith?"

"Yeah. But I majorly fucked up when I tried to use magic to do it. She almost died. I used my normal powers plus some Were stuff to actually break it." I rubbed my eyes, trying to make sense of everything. "Maybe I'm messing everything up so badly because I didn't grow up around spells and magic, but some of this stuff...it's just not working for me."

"Well you have to learn it."

"Says who?"

He looked away from me with a sigh. "Says my mother."

I snorted. "Yeah, okay." I hoped the sarcasm was thick enough for him to pick up on. "You've been really nice to me and I've had fun, but I'm not sure that we're getting anywhere with these lessons. I keep getting it wrong. I follow the all the steps, and I get the complete inverse reaction. Do you think it's because of the Were in me?"

He uncrossed his arms as he thought. "You might be on to something."

"I thought so. The thing is, I got more control over my natural abilities when I became a Were. That could've come with a cost."

"That's a really smart theory. How did you come up with it?"

"The definition of insanity is doing the same thing over and over again and expecting a different result. As much as people've called me crazy, I don't think I actually am." I smiled. "If something's not working, it's time to try something else. Plus, Tia Rosa came by earlier. She said I needed to work on strengthening my natural abilities." I started walking to the spell room. "Any chance there's a book on that in here?"

"Claudia?" Daniel yelled through the house.

"Yeah," she answered as she came down the stairs. "What's up?"

"Do you have anything on sight here? I think I have a few books at my house, but my mom'll be pissed if she sees that we're working on something that's not on the prescribed list." His cheeks got a little pink.

"Prescribed list?"

He got redder. "She's a little controlling."

I gave him a bland stare. "I've noticed."

We followed Claudia into the craft room. "Should have something here," she said as she got down on her hands and knees and started searching through the piles of books under the worktable.

I shook my head. This was no way to store books. Someone needed to do some reorganization. I knelt down on the floor beside her and started digging through the piles.

After what felt like forever searching and coming up with nothing, Claudia dusted off her hands. "There's another place I can check. Hang on."

I stood up from where I was digging through the books, and Claudia came back with a box.

"Maybe in here?"

Daniel and her started inspecting the books, but something else caught my eye. I hadn't noticed before that there was a hidden door built into one of the walls.

"What's back there?" I asked.

"Back where?" Claudia said without looking up.

"Behind this," I said as I walked to the wall.

"Nothing. What you see is what you get."

"No. There's something here." I ran my fingers along the crease, looking for some sort of a latch. A small, thin piece of metal stuck up about two-thirds of the way up the door from the ground. I pushed on it and the door swung open.

"Way to hold back, Claudia," Daniel said.

Claudia stared open mouthed at the closet. "I wasn't holding back. I had no idea."

The three of us crowded around to look inside.

"Wow. Look at this." Daniel held up a little jar of something that looked like nail clippings.

"Oh my God," Claudia said. "Those are so hard to find."

Okay. They had my attention. "What is it?"

Claudia winced. "It's gross. Trust me. You don't

want to know."

Her saying that made me really want to know. I leaned forward, and knocked a book down. "I'm such a klutz." I bent down to pick it up and paused.

It was brown with a teal colored seal—the one that I remembered my vision. I'd searched my whole bedroom to no avail and then forgotten about it. Then just like that, the book was here.

It was almost too perfect. Like I was meant to find it after I talked to Rosa.

But that couldn't be right. Could it?

"What'd you find?" Claudia said.

"I'm not sure."

I ran my hand over the book and hesitated for a second before grabbing it. Its cover was made of soft, flexible leather. I opened it, and the first page was signed with Grams' name.

For Teresa. Don't forget to use what you have to find the answers.

I shut the book and held it against my chest.

Holy shit. That was my *abuela* in the vision. I'd never even seen a photo of her that young, but now I knew why she'd seemed so familiar. Sometimes I was a little too dense for my own good.

Grams had been a really strong precog. She could see what was going to come, which was why she'd made a good coven leader. Luciana had some precognition, but all she could see were really vague things that might come to pass.

Rosa was right. Grams must've known what was going to happen to me. So, why would she ever name me as the leader? She had to have a back-up plan. I leaned against the countertop with the book. This was too good of a find.

I turned the page delicately. *I know you're in a tough place now, but there isn't anything to lessen the burden you must bear. I followed the roads of time and saw that if I told you what to do or gave you any hints in your life, it wouldn't end well. You needed to be raised away from the coven. It's why I had your mother keep you in California.*

I paused. Whatever she'd seen, my life would've been a lot easier if Grams could've at least taught me about the coven. I wanted to shake her.

I wish I could tell you what's going to pass, but if I do, everything will be destroyed. So, I'll tell you that even at your darkest hour, when you're stripped bare, I will be with you. Don't ever lose faith.

The thing that will set you free is just above your head. Don't be afraid to break through.

When the time comes, and you'll know when it's here, listen to your mate, trust in the one you doubt, and push the one who denies it.

I wish I could say more, but I can't. My hands are tied. What I'm placing on you is a tremendous burden, and it breaks my heart to know that I can do nothing to stop what will soon happen.

Do your best to learn the coven's ways and accept the ability you've always feared. Follow your gut. It won't lie to you.

Know that there are hard times ahead, but stay strong. The worst days only make the best ones that much sweeter. This too shall pass. And happy days will be ahead.

I flipped the pages but the rest of it was blank. That was it. Something horrible was going to happen to me and all I got to help were a few extremely vague words of wisdom? Was that it?

How was this supposed to help me?

"What does it say?" Claudia said.

I shook my head. "It's from Grams. She left me a note."

"Can I read it?"

I chewed my lip for a second. "If I say no, will you be upset?"

"A little."

I could handle a little. "No. It's really personal."

She nodded. "Okay." She turned around and started looking in the closet again.

Maybe I should've just shown her, but I really didn't want to. It felt really private, and I hoarded my privacy as much as possible these days.

Daniel cleared his throat. "So, what now?"

The only thing from Grams' message I could really do was work on learning the coven's ways. "So what do normal people start learning first when they join the coven?"

"Depends on their abilities. We start from there and then grow out," Claudia said.

"So why haven't we been working with my visions?"

"Because that's not what my mother wanted," Daniel said.

"So basically we should've been working on my sight the whole time, but your mother doesn't want me doing that." Luciana never failed to piss me off. I hadn't even seen her and I wanted to rip her throat out.

He nodded once.

"Good to know."

"It's not that I—"

"I get it. Your mom's the one in charge. No worries." But it was good to know that he had a particular agenda. Or, more accurately, his mother did, and he was working for her.

We shared an awkward moment where we just stared at each other.

He cleared his throat. "The thing is," he said slowly, "only someone with sight can teach you about it."

"Then why isn't your mother teaching me?"

"I don't know."

That meant that she really didn't want me to rule the coven. I was here for some other reason. But what was she up to?

"All I can do is tell you what I know and hope it makes sense to you," Daniel said.

"Right. Well, good thing I'm a really fast learner."

"I'm not seeing anything," Claudia popped out from the closet. "I'm sorry."

"That's okay. It would've been too easy to find a book to explain everything to me. I'll just wing it like always."

She smiled, and I hoped maybe she was over me not showing her what Grams had written. Claudia started to leave, but stopped. "I forgot to tell you that I have a couple of people coming over for dinner tonight. I thought it might be fun for you to get to know some more of us. I hope that's all right."

"Sure." I wasn't feeling like meeting a bunch of people, but Tia Rosa had said I needed to, so I'd do my best.

Plus, I was still holding out hope for someone to show up and be the answer to my prayers—a leader for the coven.

"So, what now?" I asked Daniel.

He held up the book of knots. "I brought another box of glasses."

I laughed as I shook my head. "You're a glutton for punishment." I rubbed my hands together. "One box of glass powder, coming right up!"

As Daniel set everything out, I wondered how I was going to figure out expanding my visions. If Rosa was right and she could help me, then maybe it was worth facing Luciana to get permission to leave the compound.

I thought about it for a second, and I imagined how many ways that confrontation could go wrong.

I'd wait until I really, really needed to go see Tia Rosa before approaching Luciana.

Until then, I'd just go with my gut. That was what Grams had said to do, anyway. *And when has that ever gone wrong for me...*

Maybe this wasn't such a good plan after all.

Chapter Thirteen

After turning the entire box of glasses into dust, I hid in my room to read for a little while. I was a total failure, but we'd had a good laugh about it.

The doorbell had sounded twice and voices echoed from downstairs. It was time for me to go meet people, but all I wanted to do was stay in my room.

I reminded myself that I had to branch out, and if I stayed inside my cousins' place for the rest of my time here, I probably would go insane. Even if I tended to be a homebody, I still got out, took walks, went to the bookstore…went to school.

Nothing could ever be as bad as school in Los Angeles.

I pulled on my big girl panties and went downstairs.

Three people had joined Raphael, Claudia, and Daniel. I was nearly shocked to see Raphael. He was almost never at home. He worked long hours with a friend from school. They had a web design company, which seemed odd. Spells and witchy stuff felt like the antithesis of technology, but apparently that was a stereotype that had been proven wrong.

"Teresa, this is Cosette. She's been visiting from the Colorado coven for the past few months." Cosette's curly, dark-blonde hair ran down her back in soft ringlets. Her eyes were dark brown, and a little large for her face, but the rest of her features were small.

"Oh. Hi." I never shook hands, so introductions could be a little awkward, but Cosette didn't offer.

Instead, she gave a regal nod. "I've been begging Claudia to introduce us."

I focused on not making a face. Why did she want to meet me? "Oh."

"I hear that you and I have a few similarities." Cosette twirled a curl around her finger, and I couldn't imagine anything we possibly shared. "We both have some form of second sight and are torn in two directions."

Torn in two directions? "You're a Were?" She didn't look like any born Were I'd ever met, and I knew I was the only one who'd been bitten in ages.

She grinned, and I would've sworn she glowed a little. "No! Fey."

I must've heard her wrong. "I'm sorry. Did you say fey?"

"Yeah. Only we're not anything like Tinkerbell."

"Right. Of course." I thought my eyes might pop out of my head. I knew there were other supernatural beings out there. I'd found that out on my first day at St. Ailbe's, but I hadn't actually run into anything other than vampires. I'd put it out of my head a little.

"I wanted to say hello. There aren't many of us who understand what it's like balancing two supernatural worlds."

"True." And I really didn't know what else to say to her about it.

Someone tapped my shoulder and I turned. "I'm Shane. Live two doors down."

Shane had his dark hair buzzed short, and a big colorful tattoo ran up his arm. I wanted to stare at it, but didn't want to be rude. He was also tall and ripped to the point that he would've fit in perfectly at St. Ailbe's. Boy must work out hard for that body.

I realized I was staring after all, and awkwardly shoved my hands in my pockets. *Way to check out the neighbor. Real slick.* "Cool," I said, trying to go for nonchalance but once again, failing.

"And this is Elsa." Claudia motioned to the girl curled up on the couch. She looked like a child with a pair of large, green glasses. "She doesn't talk much."

Raphael walked to the front door and muttered something so softly, that I wondered if he was merely mouthing the words rather than saying them. Then he ran a finger along the painted wood, and I knew exactly what he was doing.

When the ends of the knot met, the pressure in the house suddenly increased, making my ears pop.

"What spell was that?"

"No one can listen in now," Raphael said. "Most of *la Aquelarre* is meeting in the schoolhouse today, so we should be fine either way, but always better safe than sorry."

Maybe I should've been annoyed that I wasn't told about the meeting, but I couldn't bring myself to care. "Why aren't any of you there?"

"Because we know talking to you is more important that hearing whatever Luciana has to say,"

Shane said.

Oh, no. This couldn't be what I thought it was. "I thought you said that the coven was split?"

"It is," Raphael said.

"This isn't in half. There are like forty—"

"Sixty-two," Shane said. "We don't all live here on the compound, but if everyone is called in…"

Shit. There were more members than I'd thought. "Fine, sixty-two, and what, five others plus another half-witch visitor? That's not split. That's not enough."

"It'll have to be enough," Claudia said. "We need to make this work. If we don't, the coven is going to go fully dark and a lot of lives could be lost."

I sat down in one of the wingback chairs and closed my eyes. My pulse was pounding in my ears, and the wolf was rising. Something brushed against my hand, and I opened my eyes.

"Eat it," Raphael said.

I glanced down to see the PowerBar. My cousins were starting to get used to my eating habits. I gnawed my way through the tough, tasteless bar as I thought. With every new thing I learned here, defeating Luciana seemed more and more helpless. The deck was stacked and I didn't—couldn't—see a way around it. It would've been better for these people if they left the coven and joined the pack. They could defect and stay on St. Ailbe's land.

Were there consequences to leaving? The only way to find out would be to ask. "Can you leave the coven? You could stay at St. Ailbe's. There's enough room. And you'd be safe until we figured out what to do next."

"No. That's impossible," Claudia said.

"Why?"

"We all take a blood oath to formally join the coven." Shane crossed his arms, staring down at me while I gnawed on my snack. "Once you're in, it's hard to leave. Especially for people like us whose families have been members for generations. The blood oath grows exponentially in strength with each generation."

"And you all took this oath?" I waved the bar around the room at them. "Even though you disagreed with Luciana?"

Claudia nodded. "With the exception of Cosette. Where else were we supposed to go?"

"I don't know, anywhere. The world is a big place." Was it better to live here than to venture out into the unknown? I didn't think so, but then I couldn't make their choices for them.

Although, I did have to figure out a way to save them. The urge to beat my head against the wall was strong, but I could only do this one step at a time.

With introductions finished, we sat down to dinner. Claudia had cooked two pans of lasagna—one for me, and one for everyone else to share. I shoveled salad and garlic bread onto my plate and let the conversation flow around me as I ate.

"Other supernaturals won't stand for Luciana's behavior. The witches might have numbers, but if all of us in opposition join with the pack, it'll be an even match," Cosette said.

"And just which side would you be on?" Shane asked.

"I'm on the side that isn't dealing in dark magic.

This might not be my coven, but there's a reason I'm in Texas instead of Colorado."

Elsa cleared her throat and everyone looked to her—I had yet to hear her say a word. "The fight is coming, no matter what we do. I think trying to break up *la Aquelarre* is also a waste of time. We should break our covenant, as it's already cracking. Then, when the rest stand up, we'll be on the side of the victors."

"That's assuming that we'll be the victors," I said.

"If we're not, then a dark time is ahead for the world."

Right. Like I needed one more person to tell me this was all *really fucking serious*. I got it.

"So, why isn't anyone listening in on the meeting?"

"Sam is. But the talk will be more of the same. Witches are the most powerful blah-blah-blah. Wolves are evil monsters, blah-blah-blah. Let's takeover the humans and rule the world." Cosette shrugged. "It's Luciana's usual Pinky and the Brain routine."

I chewed through a last hunk of garlic bread and set down my fork. The bread and PowerBar would have to do for now. "Save the rest for me?"

"Where are you going?" Claudia said.

"It might be rote of all of you, but I've never heard Luciana's rant. It's as good of a place to start as any."

Raphael stood up. "I'll go with you."

"You don't have to." If I got caught, I didn't want him to get in any trouble. I said as much and he shook his head at me.

"Trust me. It'll be better for you if I'm with you. I

know how to handle Luciana."

Somehow I doubted that, but we headed out to the main road—the only road in the compound—together.

Houses and other buildings butted up against the dirt road, but there definitely wasn't enough space for more than sixty people. I wondered who decided who lived on the compound and who didn't. Was it based on some sort of hierarchy?

The night was quiet, and if I closed my eyes, I could almost pretend I was back at St. Ailbe's. The scents were nearly the same, but notes of oil from the nearby cars, and dinners being cooked intruded on my illusion.

The little steeple of the schoolhouse cut into the sky up ahead. It wasn't that tall, but the white paint stood out against the setting sun. "So do you go to school there?"

"I used to." Raphael paused. "When we get there, try to be as quiet as possible. Luciana didn't invite you for a reason."

"What do you mean?"

"Luciana wants something from you, and she's letting you get comfortable. Lazy. You going in there will show her that you're not comfortable. In my experience, it's much better to have your enemy underestimate you." He paused to pick up a rock from the ground. He tossed from hand to hand before dropping it. "I know you're having trouble with spells, but if you could maybe learn some defensive stuff, that'd be good."

I shook my head. "I don't know. Nothing I'm doing works."

"Well, then maybe we can make something up for you. A charm to keep bad energies away could help. I'll talk to Claudia about it."

I nodded.

The schoolhouse was still a little ways away, but Raphael started walking between the houses. "You've got really good hearing, right?"

"Yup."

"Good. There aren't any windows in the back. Not any at our height, at least. Less chance of being noticed. You can press your ear to the wall."

I probably didn't even need to get that close. My hearing was damned good. "Yeah. That'll do." As we neared the schoolhouse, I realized I definitely wouldn't need to do that. The walls of the old building were thin, and the people inside were yelling. I grasped Raphael's arm to stop him, and suddenly I felt different. Like I was outside my own body.

I shook my head, trying to break free of the feeling, but I couldn't.

"Are you okay?" Raphael asked.

"Fine. Just got dizzy for a second."

Raphael faced me. "I thought Weres didn't get dizzy."

"Well, this one did. Let's go. And be quiet."

We stepped close to the back wall of the schoolhouse, and Raphael pressed his ear against the wood. I stayed back a little ways. Hearing the voices wasn't a problem. It wasn't like they were talking quietly. At all.

"The pack doesn't understand and they never will," Luciana said. "The humans are weak. The wolves don't think we're as strong as they are and they hardly see us as supernatural. They think us a subset of humans. We're not human."

That was what she thought? That the Weres saw them as humans? It was entirely inaccurate. From everything that I'd seen and heard, the Weres really respected, and sometimes even feared the witches.

"The pack here will never accept witches as equals," said a man.

That voice. It seemed familiar. I couldn't quite place it, but something about the sound made me irrationally angry.

"The only way to make sure we're positioned as leaders when supernaturals are revealed is to eliminate the pack structure. We need to show the pack that our coven is strong. We need to fight for our voice. We've hidden here too long—"

Shouts of agreement filled the night.

I stepped closer to the wall as I tried to distinguish the voices, and stepped on a twig. I winced, and hoped that no one inside had heard.

But I wasn't that lucky.

"Someone's listening." I heard the whisper under all the yelling. I wasn't sure how I heard it with all the commotion, but my wolf must've sensed the danger.

I grabbed Raphael's arm and that dizzy feeling came back. He yanked free. "What?" he whispered.

"They know we're here," I mouthed.

He gave me funny look. "Impossible," he mouthed.

I started to walk away, but suddenly the schoolhouse was quiet. The side door slammed against the wall as it opened and I froze in place.

"See. This is what I'm talking about. She's

supposed to be one of us, but she's spying, and turning our own against us," Luciana said, and the gathered group voiced their agreement.

I turned to look at her, and was surprised to see a familiar face standing beside her. It'd been a while since I last saw him, but I'd never forget him and his chin-length blond hair streaked with gray. Especially since he was wearing another slick three-piece suit.

Rupert Hoel.

Everyone else in his family had shown up, so it wasn't all that surprising that he had, too. But what was shocking was that he was here, with the coven. I'd been too busy chasing my tail to realize who was behind this whole clusterfuck.

This time when I yanked Raphael's arm, he didn't pull free. The dizzy feeling was back. Stronger.

I closed my eyes.

"Are you okay?" Raphael said.

I opened my eyes. We stood behind the last house before the schoolhouse.

What just happened?

I turned in a circle. *How did I get back here?*

As I realized the only possibility, cold sweat broke out on my forehead.

I'd just had a vision of the future.

Oh no. Oh hell no. This was so not happening.

Chapter Fourteen

I spun, stomping back toward my cousins' house, but Raphael stopped me.

"Are you okay?" He asked as he gripped my arm.

"No." I snapped, jerking away from him.

That was rude. I needed to calm down, but this whole seeing the future thing had totally thrown me for a loop.

I took a breath and tried to calm down. "I'm sorry, but I'm so beyond not okay. We need to go back to your house."

He looked from the lit up windows, then back to me.

"I swear. We need to go back. I just…" I started walking again.

"Okay. Okay. We'll go."

I was already walking. Nothing could drag me back there.

In my normal visions, I was always removed— distant from what was happening. This was like living the same moment twice. Or almost the same thing. Like déjà vu on crack.

But what was even more disturbing was seeing the ass-Hoel with Luciana. Was he the reason she wanted me here so bad? Was it revenge for ruining his attempt at a coup? Or was he really teaming up with Luciana?

If someone had asked me a few hours ago if that was even possible, I would've said the idea was nuts. Luciana hated the Weres. But if I trusted the vision—and I did—Mr. Hoel was standing in the schoolhouse right now. With her. At a coven meeting.

If Mr. Hoel was plotting with Luciana, I had to tread carefully. He'd almost gotten four of the top alphas killed. He'd sold our location to the vampires. His endgame had always been about power, and I'd bet my life that his plan was still the same. Everything I'd overheard during my vision backed this up. He was making another play to get more power, take down the Seven, and out supernaturals to the rest of the world.

Only this time, he was using Luciana to divide the pack. Same story, different day. So, how did I beat him this time? The stakes were higher. Fighting the witches would only result in lots of people dying on both sides.

That wasn't the way to come out to the humans. Showing them our violent side would make them afraid. It'd be witch hunts all over again.

So many scenarios ran through my head that I hadn't even noticed Raphael had stopped walking until he spoke. "What the hell happened back there? Why did you chicken out?"

I wasn't ready to talk about it, but I guessed it was unavoidable. "No. I just...no." I didn't know how to put what happened into words. "I had the worst déjà vu. It was like the Matrix had a huge fucking glitch."

"A glitch in the Matrix?"

This was going to sound totally insane. Hearing what future visions were like was totally different from experiencing one.

I needed more visions like I needed a hole in the head.

I waited until we were down the road a little more. I didn't want to be overheard. "I guess I had a vision. We went to the schoolhouse, but as soon as you put your ear to the wall, they knew we were there. Anyhow, it was turning into a bad scene—Luciana and the others were pissed. Then I jolted back to where we were right before you asked me if I was okay for the second time. In the exact same spot."

A slow grin spread across his face. "See. You can do it. See the future. We should start testing it out. We should—"

I tuned him out as I stared up at the stars. It was a clear night, and now that we were far away from the meeting—a quiet one, too. If I closed my eyes, I'd bet I could forget the last fifteen minutes had happened.

For about the millionth time, I wished Dastien were here.

Oh no. I had to get word to him. He had to know that the pack was in danger.

"You wouldn't happen to have a cell that works?" I asked. Even if I couldn't really talk to him, he needed to know that Mr. Hoel was here and working with Luciana.

"No service out here. And Luciana is the only one who knows how to turn our phone on. But..."

I knew it. He'd been holding out on me. "Please. Just this once. I need to talk to Dastien. He has to know what I just saw."

"The only landline that's always turned on is in Luciana's house. She's busy at the meeting and Daniel's at our house—"

"You mean Daniel has a working phone?" And he hadn't told me? He was so going to hear about this.

"And Internet. All of us have to ask permission before we make a call and she goes over the log on every phone bill."

What was this? A fascist regime? No wonder they hadn't told me about the phone. The more I learned about Luciana, the more I confirmed that she was a complete psychopath.

"I'll be gone before she gets the next phone bill. You can put all the blame on me."

He thought for a second, and I crossed my fingers. Short of leaving this compound, I wasn't sure what to do. But getting word to Dastien was imperative.

"This way," he said finally, and I let out a sigh of relief.

He paused in front of a white house four houses down and across the street from his own house. "I'm going to get you the portable from inside. Probably better if we stay out here in case she comes back."

"Sure." Even given the circumstances, I was nearly giddy with the thought of hearing Dastien's voice.

Raphael reappeared a second later with the phone in his hand. "Be fast. I don't know how much time we have before the meeting ends."

I nodded. "I appreciate it." I quickly dialed Dastien's cell.

Meredith answered. "Dastien's phone."

Why did she have his phone? "Hey, it's me."

"Tessa?"

"Yeah."

"Oh my God. Hang on. I'll get him. Just give me one second." I heard doors slam as she moved through the building.

"What's going on? How is he? Why do you have his phone?"

I heard her and Chris arguing but it was muffled, so I couldn't hear what they were saying. A second later, Chris' voice came on the phone. "Hey. So Dastien's been a mess. He's locked in the feral cages. We're heading to them now. I'll put you on speaker and hopefully he'll change forms."

My heart dropped. "What do you mean he's in the cages?"

"The lack of the bond has been really hard on him. Just hang on a sec. Let me get him for you."

The sound of doors clanging closed echoed through the phone.

"All right," Chris said. "I'm putting you on speaker."

"Dastien?" I said.

"Oh thank God," Meredith murmured, her voice sounded tinny.

"*Cherie.*"

I gasped at the gravelly tone in his voice. "What's going on? Why are you in the cages?"

He muttered something in French.

I really was going to have to learn his language. "English," I said as I rubbed my forehead. There were too many things going wrong tonight.

He paused his ramblings and switched to something I could actually understand. "It's hard for me, this distance thing," Dastien said. "I was okay at first, but I just... I was going to break the deal—go get you—so Dr. Gonzales drugged me. I woke up here. It's easier as the wolf...if I order something as a human, it's hard for everyone. They have to obey... How are you?"

I winced. I was better than him, that was for sure. "I'm okay. Worried about you now."

"How are they treating you? Are you eating enough?"

"I'm fine. I'm having some weird vision stuff though. I just wanted to talk to you. I don't have long. The coven's having a meeting and I'm using Luciana's phone—the only one on the compound."

"Merde. That doesn't sound like a good idea."

"I'm glad I took the risk. You need to not be in the cages." I closed my eyes and pictured him. I wished I could actually see him. I'd been able to reach him over distances a few times before, if I concentrated, but with the bond silent...

"Don't worry about me. I'll be okay as soon as we're back together." He was lying. I didn't need our bond to know that. If he'd been knocked out and locked up, he was so far beyond fine it wasn't even funny. "What's wrong with your visions?" He asked.

Explaining that would take way too much time. "It doesn't matter. The important thing is that Mr. Hoel is here, spouting his usual bull and plotting with the coven. This is bigger than we thought."

Dastien let out a string of curses.

"And if you're in that cage, then you're not keeping an eye on the pack."

Raphael tapped his wrist. I turned my back on

him.

"I've used up all my time. You've got to figure out what's going on in the pack. If Mr. Hoel is back, then that means there could be another revolt on the way."

"*Merde*. You're right. I'm going to do better. It's hard, but… I have a few ideas about what he might be planning, but joining forces with the coven? There's a piece that we're missing, and you can't come home until you figure it out. I think—"

"You need to get off the phone. You're pushing it," Raphael said.

I shot him a look. "I know," I said to Raphael. "I've got to go, Dastien. It's not safe for me to be on the phone."

"Go. Be careful. I love you."

"I love you, too."

"Bye, *cherie*."

"Bye." I hung up and gave Raphael the phone and he disappeared back inside Luciana's house.

Raphael came back outside from Luciana's house and started speed-walking back to his place. "The farther away we get from here the better."

I tended to agree with him. I had to jog to keep up, but I didn't mind the exercise.

Tonight had been a real awakening, and not just because of the visions. I'd been hanging around my cousins' house, content to learn witchy things with Daniel, but there were bigger things going on. Before I thought that might be the case, but now I knew and my priorities were changing.

First on my list was figuring out what Luciana and Mr. Hoel were up to. I also needed to make more friends around here. I needed to see if I could figure out a way to get some of the coven members out from under Luciana's thumb.

I wasn't sure if I'd find a new leader. Rosa and Grams had both said I wouldn't, but I wasn't giving that up entirely. Even if I had to be some kind of touchstone, I couldn't be in two places at once. And I really would rather be with the pack.

By the time I got back to the house, I was emotionally exhausted. How could so much be going wrong? I certainly hadn't caused all the issues within the pack, but man, my timing sucked.

I blew out a breath and went into the dining room. The table was cleared of dishes, but everyone had returned to their seats.

"She did it," Raphael said.

"Did what?" Daniel asked.

"She saw the future."

I rolled my eyes. The earnest tone was grating. "I didn't exactly see the future. I lived a few minutes of it, and then I was suddenly back in time."

"You think time travel is more plausible?" Shane asked with a smirk.

I opened my mouth and shut it. "No," I said with a laugh. I guessed that's what I'd made it sound like, but the idea was funny. "Sorry. It was definitely a vision, but it was really jarring. I'm still trying to wrap my mind around what happened."

"How did you know it was a vision?"

I went to the spare fridge, pulled out the tray of lasagna, and cut off a big piece. As it was nuking, I got myself a soda. "I didn't. Not until it was over. But I guess I was dizzy when the vision started."

"Dizzy?" Cosette asked.

"Yeah. It was the only indication. I touched Raphael's arm and this dizziness came over me—like the ground became a tilt-a-whirl. When the vision ended, that feeling came back, only stronger. I swear it was like the earth moved. And then I was back to the first time I grabbed Raphael's arm." I shook my head as I bit into a piece of garlic bread.

Daniel leaned across the table toward me. "That's a hell of a lot better than my mother's visions of the future."

"How so?"

"She only gets vague images. Sometimes just an impression of one object. It can be a little useless and most of the time, we can't figure out the meaning until whatever the event was has passed. But from what you're saying, you actually live through it. So you actually know what's going to happen if you go down that future path." He leaned back in his chair. "Think about how that could benefit the coven. We'd know exactly how to deal with every bump in the road."

"It might not be that easy." The microwave beeped and I grabbed my food. It had dried out a little, but still smelled good. "The thing is, I don't know how to control it. I don't know if it was actually tied to Raphael or if it was just something that happened. Before, I could touch an object and see what it had been through. Or for people, sometimes I'd see what they were thinking or feeling. Now if I just get visions willy-nilly with no warning…how am I supposed to control that? How can I make myself have one or not?" I took big fork full of pasta and meat sauce, but no one said anything. They just stared at me. I waved the fork around. "That wasn't a rhetorical question. I actually want someone to answer."

Cosette shrugged. "I have no idea. I assume it's possible, but I don't have visions, nor am I close to anyone who does. We're going to have to do some trial and error."

"Since your lessons weren't going well anyway," Daniel said, and Claudia started cracking up, "we'll put a stop to those and start doing vision stuff."

"Okay." I shoved another bite in my mouth. This was going to be a nightmare. "What about Tia Rosa?"

"Our crazy aunt who left the compound?" Raphael said. "What about her?"

"She removed the spell that Luciana put on me last time. That puts her pretty high in my book, and I think she might know more than she's letting on. She came by and said she'd be able to help."

"She doesn't have visions," Daniel said. "We would know if she did."

"But she has some sort of ability. And her sister did." Rosa was Grams' sister, so technically she was my great aunt. "She said she'd help me, but that I needed to go see her."

"Yeah," Claudia drew out the word. "She and Luciana don't really get along."

That made me trust her even more. "Again, I'm not seeing this as something wrong with her. I definitely don't get along with Luciana, and if we'd stayed out there tonight, we would've had a massive confrontation."

"Thank God you had the vision then," Raphael said. "None of us can afford to get on Luciana's bad side."

"We are on her bad side," Claudia said.

Raphael rolled his eyes. "Fine. I don't want to be *even more* on her bad side."

I nearly laughed at the exchange.

"So, what's the plan? Do I start touching things?"

"I don't think that'll work," Elsa said. She didn't speak up often, but I liked her style—only talking when she had something of real value to add to the conversation. "You have to start doing things. Making choices. When you take the wrong path, fate will put you back where you belong."

"Fate? That seems risky."

"Fate got you your mate," Elsa said.

Girl had a point, but that didn't make it any easier to swallow. There had to be a way. The others chatted a bit while I sat and ate. One by one, they left as the night wore on, until it was just me and my cousins.

Even if I hadn't learned more spells, I was learning more about magic and life at the compound. The magic part seemed like a total crapshoot. Not anything that we could rely on, but maybe Rosa had some tips.

"Fine. Then tomorrow I'm going to go ask Luciana for permission to visit Rosa."

"Am I the only one who thinks this is a terrible idea?" Raphael said.

"It is a terrible idea," Claudia said.

"Thank you—"

"That's why it's so brilliant." Claudia cut him off before he could finish. "Let's take some risks. It just might work out for us."

"This is more like it. A little adventure never hurt

anyone." Or it could go horribly wrong. But if making decisions was what would set off visions of the future, then I needed to take control. None of this waiting around business.

Dastien was suffering and I wasn't having a good time either. It was time for me to kick a little Luciana ass.

The first real step started tomorrow. I just hoped I was making the right choice.

Chapter Fifteen

Since Luciana always dressed conservative in her long skirts, it made me want to wear my funkiest outfit. Instead, I decided to pretend to be the good little *bruja*. I wanted off coven land more than I wanted to antagonize her.

Claudia lent me a floral dress that tied at the waist. It brushed the tops of my knees, so it wasn't long, but it wasn't short either. I even braided my hair into two pigtails. I slipped on some flip-flops and checked myself out in the mirror. The outfit gave me a girly, innocent vibe.

I met Claudia, Raphael, and Daniel in the kitchen. "Ready?" I said to them.

"Sure. But if things start to go south, let me handle my mom."

I narrowed my gaze. "It's not going to go wrong. This plan is genius." Okay. So maybe I sounded a little more sure of myself than I actually was, but confidence was more than half the game. At least, that was going to be my assumption. Hopefully that was partially correct.

We walked to Luciana and Daniel's house and knocked.

"Yes." Luciana opened the door. "Is there something you need?"

I wanted to grind my teeth, but instead, forced myself to relax and give her a sweet smile. Or what I hoped was a sweet smile. "Tia Rosa came to visit yesterday and invited me over to her house. Lessons with Daniel haven't been going that well—I seem to not be getting a handle on things—and she offered to help. But I'd have to go to her house."

"Rosa hasn't stepped foot on the compound in over twenty years. You want me to believe that she was here? Yesterday?"

I tried not to show my shock. She hadn't been here since before my *abuela* died? "I don't know why she's stayed away, but she came to talk to me. You said I was to come here to learn the ways of the coven, but I seem to be having a bit of a disconnect." She started to speak up, but I talked over her. "It's not Daniel's fault. He's been really patient with me, but it's not working. I think Rosa can help. May I go?"

Her eyes narrowed and I swore I could feel my cousins tensing on the steps behind me. "I'm going to need to call her. Wait here."

Claudia started whispering. "Shhh," I said. I wanted to listen in on the conversation.

I closed my eyes and focused on the sounds in the house. Luciana's steps as she walked along the old hardwood floors. The push tones rang out as she dialed Rosa's number.

"*Hola,*" Rosa said as she answered.

"Rosa." The venom was thick in Luciana's voice.

If I didn't already trust Rosa, I would then. However Rosa had gotten away, I wanted that for the rest of the coven.

"Ah. Luciana. I'm surprised it took you so long to call."

Take that, Luciana.

"You were here?" There was a touch of shock. She thought I'd been lying. I guessed that made sense. If I were less than honorable, I would've tried to break away from the coven ground on day one, but a deal was a deal. No matter how hard it was to keep.

But I guessed that just made me stubborn. Or stupid.

"Of course. You have my great niece. Holding her hostage. Such poor form, even for you."

"You know you're not supposed to come here."

Oooh. There was dirt there. I couldn't wait to find out why Rosa was supposed to stay out of the compound.

"And yet, I did. How did you find out I was there?"

"That's beside the point."

Ha! Rosa for the win.

"Teresa asked you for permission to come see me." Rosa paused, and when Luciana didn't say anything, she continued. "I suggest you grant her request. Unless you want me to come back—"

"No. I'll grant her request." A beep sounded.

She'd hung up on Rosa.

Holy shit. How had she gotten Luciana to bend so quickly? There was definitely a story I needed to hear.

The front door swung open before I could think much about it.

"You're allowed to go to Rosa's and back. Nowhere else. You're allowed no phone calls. And you're absolutely not to go anywhere near any of the dogs. You're here to give the coven a chance and if you fail to honor our deal, there will be consequences. If you're not back on our land before sunset I'll consider you in breach, and the coven will be forced to take measures."

I nodded. "Understood." Too bad she didn't know that as soon as I was off the coven's ground, I didn't need to call Dastien to talk him. The idea that my bond would be back in a few minutes had me giddy. I could barely keep myself from doing my own version of the happy dance.

I forced myself to walk, not run, to my car. Luciana's gaze was practically boring a hole in my back.

"She's not casting anything, right?" I said under my breath to Claudia.
She glanced back quickly. "No. But she looks mad as hell."

I couldn't afford to glance back. As soon as I was in the car, I let out a sigh of relief. Claudia got into the passenger seat, and Daniel and Raphael got into the back.

I started the car and slowly drove through the gates. The bond snapped back with such a force, my vision went black for a second. I couldn't see. I slowed the car, and then I heard Dastien yelling in my mind.

What's going on? Where are you going? Are you okay? Damn it! Answer me! Dastien said in a rush, not letting me get a word in.
Calm down. I'm fine. I'm going to Rosa's.
I'm on my way.
You can't. We're not supposed to have any contact.

I'm here for a reason and I don't want to fuck it up.

He was quiet for a long time, but I could feel him there with me. His longing and pain. He was sad. Depressed. It made me rethink this whole staying apart. I was here for a reason, but was it really worth the cost?

Dastien wasn't in the cage anymore, but I barely had to touch the bond to sense he wasn't doing well. His hunger gnawed at me.

Are you eating? It was my turn to ask the question.

I miss you.

I guessed that was answer enough. *Me too.*

I took a turn a little too fast, and everyone in the car reached for the oh-shit bar.

Careful, cherie.

I got it. I got it. I just couldn't help it if I was more than a little anxious to get to Rosa's. I wanted answers, fast. It was one thing to know that Dastien wasn't doing well. It was another to feel it. I had to wrap this up before my mate lost it.

Hey. Why don't you go see what's in the cafeteria? I'm sure there's something really good.

I know what you're doing. I'm okay. I'm heading that way. I just didn't eat enough while I was in the cages.

But you're doing okay now?

I'm doing better. I'll be fine. Just get what you need done, and come back to me.

Okay.

I wanted to be there for him, but I couldn't be. Instead of turning straight toward St. Ailbe's like I wanted, I started down the road toward Austin. The car was a little too quiet, so I turned on the music.

"What's this? Above and Beyond?" Daniel said from the back seat.

I looked in the review mirror. He was smiling, and seemed to actually be enjoying it. "Yeah. How'd you know?"

"I download their podcast every week. Makes for a good Friday, you know?"

"Yeah." I glanced back at him again before focusing back on the road. "I know exactly what you mean." I just didn't expect him to feel the same way I did.

It made me wonder, if things had been different and Dastien didn't exist, would I have given him a shot? He wasn't a bad guy. He'd been really nice when explaining all of the magic stuff, and as much as I wanted to hate him, I didn't. I'd actually had fun with him.

Tessa. Dastien's warning growl came through the bond.

I couldn't help but laugh. *I was just wondering. But that didn't happen—you exist. So it's a moot point. Don't get upset.*

Don't make me come over there.

Don't threaten me with a good time.

He laughed and it made me smile. For a second, I felt okay. I could get this all figured out.

I turned up the music and pressed on the accelerator, passing a few cars in the process.

As soon as I got to Rosa's, I'd have some answers.

This might all work out.

***

I hopped down from the car in front of Rosa's house. Her flowers were still bright and blooming. Her happy plants made me wish I knew how to garden. Mom had given me an orchid once and I'd killed it dead in days. Needless to say, me and plants were not a good combo.

The door swung open before I reached the porch.

"I didn't think I'd see you quite so soon, but welcome, *mijita*. And I see you've brought some others."

"Yes. I hope that's all right."

"Of course. Come in. Come in." She stepped away from the door, motioning us in. "Claudia. It's been too long." She embraced her, muttering endearments in Spanish. She did the same with Raphael.

When she turned to Daniel, she paused, grabbing his hands. "I'm glad your mother hasn't influenced you."

Daniel sighed. "She is who she is."

"Yes. And you're not responsible for that. She's been going down this road since long before you were born. Don't take it on yourself."

Daniel blinked a few times, and nodded.

I turned away, wanting to give him privacy as Rosa pulled him into an embrace.

"Can I get anyone something to drink? Eat?" Rosa said as she closed the door behind us.

The most delicious scent hit me as I walked inside. My stomach growled. Even with all the extra food Mom had brought, I wasn't eating enough. It was so much easier to eat more when it was just sitting there for me. "Whatever you're making, I'll take it."

"You caught me at a good time. I just finished a

batch of tamales."

Oh my God. Mom never made Grams' tamales. She said they took too long, but they were my favorite. No one made them like her. Chances were good that Rosa used the same recipe.

I walked into the kitchen. There were three plates filled with the corn-husk-wrapped goodness. I piled a clean plate high and started digging in. As I bit into the second one, I felt a little funny. I looked up from the plate to see everyone chatting in the living room, but it was like I wasn't there anymore. The only one who saw me was Rosa.

Suddenly the afternoon was flying by. It was like everyone was moving really fast, and I was slow. Barely moving. Like watching a movie on fast-forward. I felt like I was totally out of my own body. I took a step and the world tilted.

I was going to be sick.

I stumbled my way to the bathroom, barely making it in time before I started booting. My sides ached. Cold sweat ran down my skin.

Christ. I thought Weres didn't get sick. What was wrong with me? Something wasn't right.

I lifted my head from the toilet and I was suddenly back in the kitchen.

I'd had a vision. Of the future.

I dropped the fork and stepped back from the plate on the counter. "What the hell is in these tamales, Rosa?"

Rosa had that same observant look. "I may have put a little poison in them. Bad stuff. Enough to incapacitate a Were."

"What! Why would you do that and then offer

them to me?" Had she lost her mind?

"Really, *tia*. What if one of us ate one?" Claudia said.

"If you had asked for one, I would've given you one that wouldn't make you sick." She gave a raspy laugh. "I wouldn't go to all that trouble only to throw them all away. Tamales are hard to make. But I had to show Teresa how her gift worked."

She could've done that without making me live through the experience of puking up tamales. And I didn't see how making me sick would spark a vision. "I didn't *do* anything but try to eat a tamale. Isn't there some way that I can trigger visions when I actually want them? I need to figure out what Luciana is planning and why Rupert Hoel is hanging around."

"There's no controlling what you have. You have to trust that it's there to guide you when you need it."

I'd never considered myself an atheist. Mom had dragged me to church often enough that I believed in God. But in that moment, when I had to really trust that some higher power would give me a vision when I needed it, I wasn't sure I had enough faith. "So, I really can't do anything to spur them on?"

"No. I wish I could help you, but they come when they come." She shrugged, and put on the glasses that hung around her neck. "As for the tamales, *estos son muy bueno*." She grabbed the smaller plate. "*Pero estos...no*." She upended the pile into the trash.

"Man, what a waste," Raphael said.

"I proved my point. It wasn't a waste." She walked into the living room and I followed her. "The visions will never be what you want—completely controllable—but we can get to a place where you sense a vision coming on. That hint of a premonition can tell you if you're making a wrong choice."

"You mean I need to trust my gut." That's what Grams had said in her note. I'd been hoping for more, but maybe that was as good as it got.

"Yeah," Daniel said as he stepped into the living room. "That's not what I was taught at all. Mom's always said they were controllable."

"And you think your mother would really tell you the truth?"

Daniel looked at the ground and I felt sad for him. He hadn't chosen to be born to her. It must be awful.

"I wanted you to come here so that you'd know that the magic you're trying to do is inside you," Rosa said to me. "You don't need all the trappings. Especially now that you're wolf as well as witch." She looked at the other three *brujas*. "For that matter, none of you need all the trappings, but that's something that Luciana and I always disagreed on. It's one of the many reasons why I left."

Raphael leaned against the wall. "I thought you left because you lost your powers."

Rosa murmured a quick prayer in Spanish. "No. That's not true. Luciana tried to take my abilities. That's when my sister, your *abuela*, left to go stay with Tessa's mother." She wheezed a breath that was so shaky it made my lungs ache in sympathy, and turned to me. "When you were born, Tessa, my sister named you heir, and then kept you safe. Apart. You had to be strong before you came back or Luciana would try the same with you."

I knew most of that, except for the whole magic-stealing part. That sounded really bad. I didn't even know it was possible. "How can she take power from someone else?"

"Not easily, *mijita*. Not very easily." Rosa patted the cushion next to her, and I sat. "Now I have a question for you."

It seemed only fair. "Sure."

"What did you think when you saw Dastien for the first time?"

"Mine." The word was out of my mouth before I could think about it too much. Sure, that was what I thought now, but was it really what I'd thought when I first saw him?

That day, I'd definitely had the feeling that my life was about to change. When I saw him, it wasn't like he was a stranger. It was like I already knew him. And I didn't want to be apart from him. I wanted him to be mine.

"You really thought that when you saw him?" Daniel asked.

I shrugged. "Yeah. I guess I did."

"Wow," Claudia said. "The coven always sets up matches seen in future visions. You were supposed to be with Daniel. That's why we were so surprised when you were bitten. Why so many are eager to follow Luciana in the fight to get you back. We all thought that you'd gone off the intended path." She sat in the blue velvet chair across the room from Daniel. "This gives me so much hope. Maybe I don't have to be with…"

I wanted to ask Claudia who she was supposed to be with and why she didn't want that, but Rosa grasped my hand as she lowered her glasses. "Just like you knew with Dastien. Like you knew with the tamales. The visions will come when they will. They'll show you what you need when you're off the path, but by the time you see them, it might be too late to change the outcome." She relaxed back against the couch. "As the pack and the coven fight and the humans become aware of us all—you will have to play a careful balancing act. You are unique in that you're not just human or Were or *bruja*, but all three. You will be the touchstone for many."

I squeezed my eyes shut. "I don't want that much power."

"Fighting your destiny will only cause discord for everyone." She cupped my cheek and I met her gaze. "*Mijita*. This is in your hands. You can choose to remain stubborn and resist or surrender to your gifts and move forward. You decide."

"I'm not even a very good witch. I can't do the most basic things. Are you sure I'm the one?"

"I'm very sure. So was your Grams." Rosa turned to Daniel. "What were you teaching her?"

"We started with knots and a basic protection spell. Every glass that she tried it on turned to dust. Not just broken or shattered, but a fine powder."

"And what were you thinking as you were doing this?"

I shrugged. "Don't break."

"Aye. See. There is your mistake. You think 'don't break,' and your mind focused on the breaking part. Try again, only this time, believe that the glass will be *muy duro. Uno momento.*" Rosa got up and went to the kitchen. A few minutes later she came back carrying a crystal goblet. "This belonged to my *abuela*. It's one of the only things I have of hers. You

206

will make it strong. And then you will see."

I leaned away as she tried to hand it to me. "No. No way. I destroyed a whole box of glasses. No way am trying it with something so valuable to you."

"If there is no risk involved, you won't try your best. I won't hate you if you break it, but I will be sad." She held the glass out to me. "You will do this thing. You will believe in yourself. And I will be proven right." She poked a finger at her heart. "I know it here. I feel that it's true. So much so that there can be nothing else that happens."

This all sounded nuts. That said, she'd been right about how to break the curse on Meredith. It'd taken me a bit to understand what Rosa meant for me to do. I hadn't quite gotten it at first, but I figured it out eventually. I had to believe that this time would be the same.

I took the goblet. Intricate etchings ran along the outside of the cup and the stem was delicate and diamond shaped. I was afraid I was going to break it just from holding it too hard. I ran my finger along the top of the glass and it rang. I couldn't resist it, so I gave it a gentle flick.

A beautiful ring sounded. "This is real crystal."

"Yes. It's old and lovely. Make it strong."

I gingerly placed it on the table and wiped my hands on my jeans. "All right. Here goes nothing." I reached closer and began tracing the knot.

"Stop."

I looked up at her. "Did I do something wrong?"

"That—" Rosa motioned a finger in a knot-like way. "Is just the trappings of the coven. It can mean something if you need help, but the magic comes from what's inside. You do what you need to do to make it feel real. It could be a knot. It could be words that rhyme. The most powerful *brujas* I ever met didn't need anything at all."

Right. Because that wasn't intimidating at all. "Okay." I stared down at the fragile goblet. I closed my eyes, and instead of picturing crystal, I pictured steel. It was hard. Unbreakable.

Strong. Strong like steel. Strong like diamonds. I listed everything hard I could think of as I pictured the goblet in my mind. I willed it to be unbreakable with everything I had.

"Okay," I said. "I tried my best."

"Do. Or do not. There is no try." Daniel laughed at his own joke.

"Shut up," Claudia said.

"Oh, man. This could go south so fast," Raphael said. He'd finally left his post by the door, and came closer to see what would happen.

"Be quiet. She did fine. I know she did it," Claudia said as she stepped beside her brother.

I swallowed. That was a whole lot of pressure for one old lady to put on me. My hand shook as I handed Rosa the glass.

She moved to slam it against the coffee table, and I grabbed her arm. "Wait. Just wait. What if it breaks? I really did try, but I've fucked this up a lot and this seems to be a big deal to you and I'd really hate to—"

Rosa yanked away and slammed the goblet against the wood without breaking eye contact with me. Instead of a crash, the lovely ring of crystal sounded.

"Holy shit." It felt like it took my heart a second for it to start beating again. "I totally thought it was going to break."

"You need to have more faith in yourself. Even with everything you've accomplished in so little time, you doubt yourself. It will be your undoing. Try to manage that."

I nodded more absently than out of agreement. "I'll see what I can do."

You okay? Dastien said through the bond.

Yeah. Some days things happen that are so weird, you know? And all you can think is, did that really just happen? Fuck. My heart was still beating like crazy. It would've really sucked if I'd broken my great-great-grandmother's glass. Whenever I feel like I have a handle on something, it goes sideways and I lose my grip. How do you get used to it?

You're asking the guy who just spent the week in the feral cages because he couldn't keep it together?

I laughed, not caring if everyone in the room thought I was crazy. *We're the picture of the most put together couple ever.*

Cherie. There was a little bit of pleading in his tone.

I sighed. *I just wish I knew what I was supposed to do. Everything's a mess. I'm not where I want to be— even physically.*

You'll be okay. And if you aren't, I'll be right there with you. We're a team, remember? For good and bad.

I blinked my eyes, trying to keep any tears away.

If I was supposed to be the touchstone for everyone else, then Dastien was for sure my touchstone. And now… "Okay. So, I trust my gut. That's about all I can do."

"Exactly."

"Right." That was so not reassuring. It was just a catchphrase people used when they had nothing useful or constructive to say. Except that Rosa was trying to be useful.

But it couldn't be that easy. Life didn't always work out as planned. No matter how badly I wanted it.

Chapter Sixteen

I spent the rest of the afternoon at Rosa's as she tried to hammer in the lesson she wanted me to learn. We all ate tamales, and no one got sick, so that was worth it, but it'd be a while before I trusted her cooking again. The lady was a little nuts.

Then sun was just about to set we got back to the compound.

Driving through the gates. I warned Dastien.

Okay. Be safe.

I will. No more hiding as a wolf in the cages. And find out what the Hoels are up to. There's too much bad shit going on around them.

I'm already on it.

Good. I love you.

Je t'aime, cherie.

With the clunk of the tires over the cattle guard, the bond shut down. It took my breath away, and I ached to turn the car around. I found a spot to park in front of the house, and noticed a figure sitting on the top step.

Luciana.

I didn't have the desire to talk to her, not even a little bit. Especially when I was still smarting from the absence of the mate bond. But I couldn't ignore her.

"How was Rosa?" She said the name with more than a little venom as I got out of the car.

"Enlightening as always." I shut car door with a slam. The guys and Claudia got out and came to stand beside me. Luciana looked from her son to me and back again. I wasn't sure what was going through her mind, but I didn't want to know.

"I'm sure it was." Luciana paused long enough that it became a little awkward, but I couldn't look away from her gaze before she broke away. The werewolf in me wouldn't allow it.

It took longer than I would've thought before her focus shifted to Daniel. I didn't look at him, but I could almost feel him stiffen beside me.

Whenever I left here, I made a promise to myself to take Daniel with me. He might be her son, but he wasn't anything like her. I didn't know what went on at home, but whatever it was, I didn't think it was good.

"Is there something you wanted, Luciana?" Claudia asked.

She grinned then. "I searched your room, Teresa. I'm sure the mongrel in you will know as soon as you enter, so I thought I'd give you a little warning."

I clenched my hands, trying to maintain control. The idea of her pawing through my things was more invasive than I could stand. "What gives you the right to go through my things?"

"I'm the leader here. I'm the one in charge. As long as you're on my grounds, I'm allowed to make sure you don't have anything here that I need to confiscate."

I laughed. This whole conversation was absurd. What was this? A summer camp? Did I need to hide my candy bars under my mattress? "And what items would be forbidden?"

"That's for me to know."

Right. "You just wanted to go through my things, didn't you? Try to force a vision. I get it. I've been there before." I might have to tolerate her while I was here, but once I was gone, I was going to make sure this bitch went down. All I wanted to do now was go to my room and make sure she hadn't taken anything…or left anything behind. "If you're so worried about me and what I might be doing, why don't you come ask me?"

"I don't worry about you. I'm merely protecting my own. You might be the next leader, but I'm the leader until I die."

"Are you sure about that?"

"Absolutely."

"Then why am I here?"

"Simple. As long as you're here, the pack is weaker."

"I can leave any second."

"Then leave. Give me the excuse." Luciana smiled. She knew she had me, and the second I stepped foot off the compound without her permission, she'd be skipping off to war.

The woman was infuriating. I'd thought I was the center of her plot, but now that I knew what Dastien was going through, the truth was clear. Screwing with him disturbed the whole pack, and he was such a powerful alpha that his unease would be rippling through the pack bonds. The Weres were tied so closely together that everyone would be hurting.

The entire pack structure was weakened.

I was exactly where Luciana wanted me to be. I couldn't go back to the pack—at least not yet—without starting a major shitstorm. But every moment I stayed here made my pack more vulnerable.

This conversation was over. I pushed past her, not caring that I almost knocked her over. I opened the door and stormed inside the house, taking the stairs two at a time up to my room.

It reeked like Luciana—cloves and something sour. I opened the windows, AC be damned. I needed the scent of her out of my room or I'd never get to sleep.

I threw my keys on the nightstand and started systematically going over the room. I opened myself up to visions, but besides things with various visitors, Mom, my cousins, and Grams, I didn't get anything good. Nothing that even hinted at Luciana.

If her visions were like mine, then she needed to touch things to see anything. So how had she managed not to seep anything of herself into the room?

She must've worn gloves. But how was she planning to get a vision wearing gloves? It didn't add up... Unless she really was just searching my room?

Once I was convinced everything I'd brought with me was right where I'd left it, I sat down on the bed. What was I supposed to do now? Luciana had made a move, and now I needed to make one back. I had to gain control of the situation. I was stuck in reaction mode. Ever since she'd showed up at the Full Moon Ceremony, I'd been on defense. It was time for a little offense.

It took a lot to get me angry, and the last person who'd gotten me this mad had almost had her throat ripped out.

I was way more fucking pissed at Luciana. She wasn't just screwing with me. She was messing with the whole pack. And Rupert Hoel was helping her.

Tomorrow I was done playing nice. It was time for some action.

The witch was going down.

***

I'd had some rocking nightmares in my life, but as I laid in my bed, trapped in my dreams, a tiny part of me knew this was the worst one ever.

I was on campus, standing in the courtyard. The damp grass cool on my bare feet. I wore a pair of black cargo pants. A backpack weighed heavily on my shoulders. Glass jingled as I took a step. I reached into the pockets and pulled out a vial.

The same potion that made vampires explode.

The scent of the forest was suddenly dampened by the noxious fumes of rotting meat. Vampires swarmed the campus and the alarms sounded.

Wolves fled from the dorms and surrounding buildings.

A vampire approached me, and I threw the vial, saying the words to ignite it.

Another group rushed onto campus. Fire surrounded their hands.

The *brujos* were out in force. Spells flew through the air in little vials causing explosions that lit the

215

night.

I reached out to Dastien, but his presence was gone. I couldn't reach him. Something was wrong.

And then I didn't have time to take in what was happening. The fight crescendoed and it took everything I had not to die.

I dodged a vampire while throwing spells as fast as I could.

A wolf took a running leap at me, and I dropped to the ground, letting it soar overhead.

I could barely stay ahead of what was going on. It was war. It was bloody. I was covered head to toe in black vampire goo.

A half-decayed heart still beat in my hand. I threw it on the ground and tossed a spell at it, turning it to ash.

My hands were half human and half wolf claws. I didn't want to turn to fight like the rest of the Weres. I needed both abilities if we were going to survive.

As the vampires and witches advanced, wolves spilled around them, fighting as their allies.

Something slammed into my side and took my breath. A heavy, furred body landed on me. My hands caught around its neck as it lunged to bite my throat open.

From far away, Dastien's howl rent the night. Finally. I could feel his howl echo through the bond as I tried to get the mass of fur and claws off me.

One of the traitorous Weres.

He started to shift, just enough so he could talk to me as his claws sunk into my neck. "You're dead, mutt," Mr. Hoel said.

I choked as hot blood spilled from my body.

***

I shot up from bed covered in sweat. My hands went to my throat, as I gasped for breath.

"Holy shit." That had felt so real. My muscles actually ached from the fight. I went to the bathroom and splashed water on my face. When I looked in the mirror, I stumbled back a few steps.

Four red slashes lined my throat.

That wasn't just a dream. That was something else. A vision of the future?

How could things get so bad that something like that could happen?

I didn't want that future, but how did I stop it? I sat down on the edge of the tub, putting my head between my knees.

What was I supposed to do now? Confront Luciana or not?

My skin was itching. My wolf wanted to be free. Ached for it. She'd been pretty silent since I got here, but this was too much.

I went downstairs in the dark to hit the second fridge. The food was nearly all gone. I'd have to call Mom in the morning. I grabbed some ham, cheese, mustard, mayo, and bread. A few sandwiches later the wolf was okay. At least for now. I wasn't sure how much longer I could eat her into submission.

My T-shirt was damp, sticking to my skin. I wished I could take a shower, but I didn't want to wake Claudia and Raphael.

I wanted to call Dastien so badly. I ached to hear his voice. For him to tell me that it was nothing more than a really fucking bad nightmare. That we wouldn't let this happen. It wasn't our future.

The panic started back up, and I stood to pace the small kitchen. Five steps across, five steps back.

It was three in the morning and I was going out of my skin.

I flipped on the light on the stove's hood the next time I passed by it. I didn't need any light to see by. The moon gave me enough, and my vision was good at night, but the dark house left me feeling uneasy. Or maybe I was just uneasy.

Footsteps sounded upstairs. So much for not waking anyone up.

A minute later, Claudia walked into the room. "You okay?"

"Nightmare."

"No fun."

"No." I stopped my pacing and leaned against to counter to watch her.

Claudia got a glass of milk, and sat at the table. She took a long drink of milk before she spoke. "I think we could've been good friends, you know. If we'd gotten the chance."

"Yeah?" That was surprising. I didn't think I knew her well enough to know that.

"Yeah. I mean, our moms are pretty similar."

This was something I wanted to hear more about. I knew pretty much nothing about my mom's sister. They didn't really talk. "Where is your mom?" I asked as I sat down at the table.

Claudia shrugged. "My mom and Luciana didn't get along. There was a lot of tension there, and Mom...well, she's a little more hippie than anything else. About three years ago, she said she'd had enough. She and my dad were leaving the compound for good. My dad couldn't really stick around if she was leaving, even if he wanted to. He wasn't part of the coven. They asked us to go with them. But I was seventeen. I wanted to stay. I felt like I *needed* to stay. So I did. Raphael wanted to go, but he wouldn't leave me here…so here I am, wondering if I made the wrong decision. Sometimes I want to call her to come back and get me, but I feel like that would be giving up. I set out to fix things here, and I'm not leaving until I do."

She sounded like me. Stubborn to the end. "And the guy? You're supposed to be marrying someone?" She'd mentioned it at Rosa's house, but only enough to spark my curiosity.

She groaned. "He's a classic douchebag."

I snort-laughed.

"What?" She asked.

"You just always sound so proper."

She giggled. "Yeah. I guess. But that's the best way to describe him." She leaned toward me. "He spends hours in front of the mirror. *Hours.* To make sure that his hair is spiking just the right way. He orders his mother around. 'Get me a glass of water.' 'I'm hungry. Make me a sandwich.'" She scoffed in disgust. "And that's what I'd have to deal with for the rest of my life?" She leaned back in the chair. "No, thank you."

I laughed. "You know, I think you're right. We would've really liked each other. I hope we still can be friends. Helps that we're family, too."

She grinned. "You know, I was thinking that it's a good thing you found Dastien. I hear that Daniel kisses like a lizard."

I shuddered. "Gross. Yeah, Meredith may have mentioned something about that."

Her smile faded. "I'm glad you were able to break that spell. How did you do it?"

"I'm still not sure." I thought for a second. "It was pure desperation and a bunch of willpower. I just had to break the curse or else my friend would've died."

I started fixing another sandwich. "I wish I had more answers. I'm just going to hope that everything works out okay." I set down my knife. "So, I think tomorrow I'm going to ask some tough questions. I want to get to know some more of the coven members. Do you think you could take me around?"

"Of course."

"Luciana's in with a really bad Were, and it spells big time trouble. This nightmare...I don't know if it was all this talk with Rosa or the confrontation with Luciana or if it was some kind of premonition, but if I mess this up, things will get ugly. I need your help."

"Anything you need. I was the one who forced you to come here. I knew things were going down and I didn't know what else to do."

I shook my head. "As much as I hate being away from Dastien, I think I was meant to be here."

She was quiet for a second. "May I ask you a question?"

"Sure."

"How did you know Dastien was the one for you?"

Not exactly the question I'd expected. "I just knew. We had a rough patch right after I changed. We kind of danced around the idea of each other.

Well, I was dancing around the idea of him, and he was avoiding me because I was adjusting to being a Were. To be fair, I was annoyed at him for biting me. And there was drama with his ex, but it ended up that none of that mattered. When it's right, it's right." I paused. Something told me that she wasn't just asking me to dig. There was something in her tone that made me wonder if there was a guy she wanted to be matched with. "Who is he?"

She looked away. "There's no one. I just want there to be. Someone who's just for me. I want what you and Dastien have, but I haven't found that yet. Even if Luciana is pressuring me, I'm not giving in."

"You're really cut off from the outside world here. You might need to leave to find the one."

She sighed. "Maybe. But I can't leave. Not yet."

"We'll fix the coven so you can. I won't let Luciana's mess hold you back."

She blinked a few times. It must be hard living here. Feeling stuck.

We were actually a lot alike. Both stuck here. Both wanting something else. I could understand that. Somehow, I'd make sure she got out, but we had a lot to accomplish and the clock was ticking.

I put away the sandwich stuff and started up the stairs with Claudia.

"Night, *prima*."

"Night."

The second time I got in bed that night, I felt more confident about my path. I wasn't alone here. I had family. Friends. I could do this. I just had to believe in myself.

God. I hoped I believed in myself enough to fix

this mess.

Chapter Seventeen

I had nightmares all night long. They plagued me.

Images of death. Destruction. My friends suffering.

But that wasn't the worst of it. Not by far. The worst were the images of Dastien cheating on me with Imogene.

Those had me waking up crying. Even when I was awake, knowing it was a dream, my heart still felt broken. The hurt lingered. I couldn't shake it.

After that, I gave up on sleeping around five in the morning, and spent the rest of the time thinking about what I was going to do.

I had a plan in place and breakfast cooked by the time Claudia came down. I just had to convince her to go along with it.

As soon as Claudia was on her second cup of coffee, I decided it was time. "I want to go to the schoolhouse today. It's the best place to meet people."

Claudia set her mug down. "Luciana said you weren't allowed."

I gave her a stare that said I-really-don't-give-a-fuck.

"She's not going to like it, and more importantly, I

don't think anyone's going to be friendly. Not in that setting."

"I have to try. Otherwise, I say screw the whole coven, let's grab who we can and run."

She looked at the ceiling for a second, and I imagined her praying for patience. "There's a lesson in an hour. I guess we could say that you need to learn whatever it is that they're teaching. I'll leave it up to you to figure out the rest." Claudia took a dainty bite of egg.

I gulped down half a glass of orange juice as I tried to come up with how to ask my next question, but I didn't see any easy way around it. "If this goes bad, then would you fight against me or for me?"

She set her fork down. "What do you mean?"

"I mean, say Luciana wants to fight regardless of anything we do. Whose side are you on? Can you fight against your own coven?"

She blew out a big breath. "In some ways being part of the coven is easier than having your pack bond and in other ways it's harder."

That gave me nothing. "How so?"

"Well, from what I hear, your pack bonds can be a bit on the invasive side. You can borrow power from each other, but you can also see too much of each other."

Pretty spot on for someone who wasn't in the pack. I'd used the pack's power to help break Meredith's spell, and I got a headful of Dastien's emotions on a daily basis. "Yeah. So, the harder?"

She pushed her plate away. "I don't have to obey an alpha like you do, but there are consequences for going against the coven. For trying to break away."

"What kind of consequences?"

"I could lose myself. My soul. It could kill me."

This was way more complicated than I'd thought. "Right. So, extreme measures have to be taken." That made me wonder... "How did your mom get away?"

Claudia fidgeted a little.

It was probably rude for me to ask, but I had to. If my aunt could leave, then so could Claudia.

"I promised to stay and help Luciana if she'd let my mother go."

"And your mom let you do that?"

"She didn't know. I can enhance people's abilities and Luciana would never say no to more power. I told her I'd stay, take the vow, and help her if my mom was allowed to leave." I started to speak but she cut me off. "It was dumb, but my mom needed to go. If she didn't, it was going to be bad. She and Luciana were fighting everyday and Luciana's patience had run out. I was scared for her. So, I did it. And Raphael stayed to help me. He's the only one that knows."

That was a huge sacrifice she'd made for her mother. "So, what were you going to do? You can't want to stay here."

"And be her pawn? No. I don't want to be here. I don't know who I am or what I want, but it's not this." She met my gaze. "My plan was to find you. You were our only hope. If you can't fix this, we're all lost. And to some of the people in the coven—" she shrugged—"maybe that's okay. They're fine with what they're doing. They think they're right and that witches are better than both wolves and humans. Plus we have so much more reason to want revenge. The wolves were never persecuted like we were. We burned, and for some hiding here, it still chafes."

"So what happens if you were to come with me? Stay with the pack?"

"I don't think anything. At least not while you were alive. Luciana wouldn't dare. And I'm pretty sure with your abilities, we could find a way to break the curse without the unfortunate side effects."

Yeah. I didn't want to try that unless it was really necessary. Those side effects were pretty extreme.

I stood to put my dishes in the sink and dropped it on the ground. I winced as it rattled, but didn't break.

"That unbreakable spell is really handy," Claudia said.

"No kidding." I picked up the plate. "Let's find out who's chafing. It can't be just a handful of you. There's got to be more. I'll offer my protection. I'll fight for you. But you have to take the first step."

She nodded. "That's all we can ask for." She glanced at the clock. "Class starts in an hour."

Enough time for me to clean this up and figure out a plan. "Good. I'll be ready."

She got up and went upstairs.

I was almost done with the dishes when Raphael came down. "You coming to the schoolhouse with us?"

He nodded. "Someone's got to look out for you two."

I wiped off my hands and hung the dishtowel over the edge of the sink. "Tell me this—waste of time or no?"

"Eh, we'll see."

"What's your story? You have powers? A

226

specialty?"

"I'm good at defensive stuff. Claudia enhances others' abilities."

"And Daniel?"

He shoved his hands in his shorts' pockets. "Much to his mother's disappointment, he's got a little of everything, and not much of anything."

Poor Daniel. Every time I learned something new about him, I felt worse. "Right. I bet that frustrates her."

"Yup. That's why she was so ready for you to marry him. Gain some power that way."

"Yeah, I'm not sure it works that way. Moot point anyhow."

Claudia came downstairs. She was dressed in her usual peasant shirt and cut off skirt. Both the twins always wore a pair of worn-in brown leather flip-flops. Claudia's thick, nearly black hair was separated into two braids. "Let's do this."

I stumbled as I walked, but Raphael caught me.

"You okay?"

"Yeah. Sorry. I don't know what happened. Apparently, I'm dropping things and tripping over my own feet today."

"Give yourself a break," Claudia said. "You didn't get much sleep."

I was tired, but it wasn't that. Or it wasn't *just* that. My limbs felt like lead. They were heavy. Like I was moving through sludge. But I wasn't dizzy.

Claudia was right. It was exhaustion. I'd been through a major emotional upheaval the past couple of weeks and it wasn't going to get any better any time soon. It was weighing on me. That was all.

The schoolhouse looked prettier during the day. It had a large porch on the front and the wood was painted a bright white that gleamed in the sun. Large windows let a ton of light into the main room, which was filled with tables. Kids worked in groups of threes. A few older ladies walked around, pointing and making comments.

"Follow me," Claudia said.

I did, and Raphael took up the rear.

Claudia didn't knock. She just walked in. Everyone stopped.

One of the women rushed to the front. She was wearing a pair of wide-leg jeans and a flowing top with a paisley print. Her hair was fully gray, but it hung long and wavy down her back. "Claudia. Raphael. You know that Luciana doesn't want her here with the other students." The woman moved toward us with her hands out, as if to say we shouldn't go any farther.

"I understand that, but Daniel has been having trouble teaching her a few things, and we thought it'd be best to bring her here. She needs to learn, and what better way than how I did?" Claudia gave her a brilliant grin.

Whoa. Way to throw the guy under the bus, Claudia. But it was working. The lady had stopped trying to herd us back toward the door.

The lady rubbed her hands along the front of her jeans. "Yes, well…"

"Look, I don't want to put anyone out, but I've been kind of hiding in their house, and I'm going a little crazy. The learning isn't going well, and I just want to meet some more people. If this is my coven, then shouldn't that be normal?"

"Yes, but you're not...I mean...it's just that Luciana—"

"Why don't we just let her try a little bit?" Claudia asked in a voice that was so sweet it was almost sickening. "If she wasn't meant to be here—if it wasn't good for our coven—wouldn't Luciana be here already?"

That stopped her. "I...Yes, of course. That's very wise of you, Claudia."

Way to go, Claudia. I spotted Cosette and Elsa at a table in the back of the room. Daniel and Shane were in the back, too. I wondered if Daniel would be pissed at Claudia, but he gave her a thumbs-up.

"I'm sorry for being less than welcoming," the older woman said. "I'm Mary. If you find a spot, maybe with..." She looked around the room. "With Cosette and Elsa. Then we can continue on our lesson. We're working on a spell for spiritual healing."

Spiritual healing? Trying not to roll my eyes took way more effort than it should've. I walked around the room and took a spot.

If I made it through this class without being completely condescending, it'd be a miracle.

Spiritual healing? Were they serious? No wonder Luciana had them all under her thumb. They didn't know how to do anything. At least Daniel had gone straight to protection spells to keep anyone from messing with me or my things.

This was going to be a long day. I hoped it was worth it.

***

To put it nicely, I wasn't going to be healing anyone anytime soon. Thank God that wasn't why people were coming to me for help. Nope. I was just supposed to fix the whole coven.

I cleaned up the ingredients we'd used in the potion—placing the unused stuff into their labeled jars and burning all the odd leftover bits in one giant cauldron that had been 'tainted' by the day's work. As I stepped away from the table to leave, a girl got in my face.

"You're not welcome here. Don't come back to the schoolhouse." Her black hair was pin-straight. It fell in a sheet down her back. Her eyes were a little too far apart and her nose a little too hawked to ever allow her to be called pretty.

"I'm supposedly part of this coven. I'm here to help," I said.

"We don't need your help. You're wasting your time."

"Then why did Luciana drag me here? I'm happy to go home."

As soon as she grinned, I knew she knew something about it. "Don't worry about that. After the month is done, we don't ever want to see you again."

The rest of the class had gathered around her. Besides the people I knew, only the one old lady and two others stood off to the side, looking awkward. The rest looked as angry and put out as this girl did.

"Right. So I do my time, and then I go home."

"If you're still around by then…"

Still around? "That sounds a lot like a threat. Are

you insinuating that my safety is in danger while I'm here?"

"You're the precog. Shouldn't you be able to answer that?" A few people laughed.

It was surreal. I'd been made fun of a lot in my life. This scene wasn't anything new to me. In fact, it was almost tame. I'd been slammed into lockers. Beaten. Accosted. Had a few unwelcome guys try to grab me. Kiss me. Worse. But this?

It was safe to say that I'd never been bullied or made fun of because I couldn't see enough. From experience, I knew that the best reaction was to not react. So I forced myself to keep breathing.

"I've seen enough. I know what's to come, and I'm not the one who should be worried right now." I moved toward her. "Excuse me," I said keeping firm eye contact. "I'm leaving now."

She looked away and stepped back. "Bitch," she muttered as I walked past.

"Don't worry. I've been called much more creative things." I could hear footsteps behind me, and took a deep breath in. From the scent, my cousins, Cosette, and Elsa were following me. I wasn't sure what Shane and Daniel were up to, but I wasn't turning around to find out.

"Well, that went just about as well as could be expected," Claudia said, breaking the silence when we were halfway to her house.

"It wasn't so bad," I said.

"What do you mean?" Cosette said.

"Yeah, those people sucked, but did you notice the ones along the sidelines?"

"Beth, Tiffany, and Yvonne. Yes. I noticed,"

Raphael said.

"They'll be in with us. So, that's more than I had this morning. The rest seem like a total lost cause. I'm assuming most of the adults who disagreed with Luciana found a way to leave—like your parents, Mom, and Tia Rosa—and the rest here are complacent."

"Yes," Claudia said.

I blew out a breath. Well, it wasn't a total waste. We'd learned some good stuff. Maybe not all of it was actually *good* good, but knowing was half the battle.

I texted Mom about getting more food and she promised to come by tomorrow with a truckload.

Until then, I needed to get a game plan. Those dreams were still haunting me. I needed to find out how to make sure none of my nightmares come to pass.

Chapter Eighteen

I'd thought the dreams couldn't get worse. But they did.

I was drowning in the images. I couldn't breathe and my heart was breaking.

Dastien was with Imogene.

Her gaze met mine as I saw them across campus. He was kissing her. His back was to me.

It was worse than a punch to the gut. There was no more air in my lungs. It burned and I couldn't get a breath in.

This was why people cut themselves off from love. This was it. I knew it. It was worse than anything I'd ever felt and I wasn't sure I'd survive.

Just when I thought I couldn't take anymore, the images changed.

I blinked and we were back in Imogene's room. It was a sty, as always. Clothes piled everywhere. Clean mixed with dirty.

She was putting on her gold necklace; Dastien had given it to her and it had triggered a vision for me once. Now I wanted to rip it from her throat.

I moved toward her, lunging for the gold chain, but the image shifted again, and suddenly she wasn't there.

A moan had me turning around.

They were in her bed. They were…they were…they were…

***

"Wake up!" Claudia said.

I blinked. I was sobbing so hard I couldn't catch a breath. The pain—the heartbreak—was still there. Lingering. I couldn't shake it free.

"You have to calm down or you're going to make yourself si—"

She didn't have to finish that sentence. I ran to the toilet just in time to throw up.

When I stopped, I washed my face. I looked at my reflection. My skin was usually pale, but now it looked ghostly.

"Are you okay?"

"I don't know," I said honestly. I didn't know what was going on, but I didn't like it. "I've never had such vivid dreams before. I could smell her perfume. I could smell her…as he kissed her. I can't…" I took a breath. "God. I thought since I was a Were, I wouldn't get sick anymore, but I think I might throw up again."

Claudia reached out to me. "Let's get you back in bed."

I shook my head. The thought of going back to that room made me even more queasy. "No. I can't go back in there. I don't trust my dreams. I can't take it."

"Fine. Then come to my bed."

Seriously? I wasn't so sure that was a good idea. What if I got visions in her bed? I was already a

234

mess… "I've never slept in a bed with anyone other than Dastien." It sounded lame, but it was the best excuse that I could come up with.

"Don't worry. I have a queen-sized bed, and I'm not going to try and steal your virtue." She winked. "Come on." She pulled me toward her room, and I let her.

It was a nice room. A large bookcase took up one wall. I looked through it and saw mostly classics. All of them were vintage. The smell of vanilla wafted from the pages and they made me wish I could really enjoy an old book instead of buying new all the time.

"Pretty good stuff you've got here."

She hmmed. "I don't know about you, but I'm going to bed." She climbed into her big, four-poster bed. It had way too many pillows. So many that when I got in, my feet nearly fell off the end. Quite an accomplishment for someone as short as me.

"One thing." She leaned over me. Her lips were moving, but no sound was coming out. She traced a knot over my forehead with her pointer finger. "There. You'll sleep well now."

"You think?"

She nodded. "It's a protection spell. It's something my mom used to do to me when I was having a hard time sleeping."

"Did you have nightmares as a kid?"

"A lot. But not so much anymore. And I never had one so bad that it made me throw up."

"Yeah. I've never felt anything like that before." I didn't know what else to say. It was already a little embarrassing that she'd seen me in such a state. But she was family. Even if I felt like I was only just starting to get to know her.

I rolled over and tried to think happy thoughts.

I didn't know if I could take another dream like the last one. My heart couldn't handle the stress. It was too hard.

I said a little prayer as sleep overtook me. *God. Send me good dreams.*

***

I woke up to the sound of a car honking. I sat up, going from sound asleep to totally awake in an instant. Claudia's side of the bed was cold, and from the light streaming in the window, it was way past morning.

Two days of total horrible sleep must've really done a number on me. A clock ticked on Claudia's bedside table and I tilted it toward me. Two forty-five. In the afternoon.

I'd really slept. Claudia's spell thingy must've been the real deal.

I got up and went into the hallway. There was someone downstairs.

"—brought the food and—"

I knew that voice. "Dad!" Raphael looked a little startled as I flew down the stairs and jumped into Dad's arms, knocking Dad back a few steps. It was overkill, but the nightmares and everything had left me feeling a little off center. I missed him. I missed home. I missed a lot of things.

"Hey there, baby." He ran his hand down my back. "How're you doing?"

I pulled away, even though I didn't really want to.

"I'm okay."

"Well your mother bought the entire grocery store."

I stepped out onto the porch to see her pulling things from the trunk. "Mom."

"*Reina de mi vida.* How are you doing?" She put down everything she was holding and pulled me close to her.

"Better now."

"Good. *Te queiro mucho.*"

"Love you, too." I grabbed the stuff she'd set down. "Thanks for this."

"Of course, anything for my baby."

We set to the task of putting everything away. Claudia and Raphael made themselves scarce and honestly, it was really nice of them. Not necessary, but appreciated.

After we had it all unloaded and put away, Mom pulled out a dining chair and sat.

"Now tell your mother what has you upset."

I looked between my parents but they were both giving me that look. The one that said I'd better tell them or else. Sure, I was old enough to blow that off, but I didn't want to. I sat in the chair at the end of the table. "I've been having nightmares the past two nights and they're sticking with me."

"You've had nightmares before."

"Not like this."

Dad sat down in between Mom and me. "You know, dreams are usually driven by our fears and—"

"Unless they're visions of the future."

"And do you think that's what it is?" Mom leaned into Dad as she talked. They were always doing that.

Supporting each other. I guessed that was why I felt okay jumping in with Dastien. I was lucky to have a good model of a healthy relationship.

"No. I don't think so. They're nightmares. At least some of them are. Others...I don't know. They might be visions." I thought about the battle on the St. Ailbe's quad. Even if I didn't want those to be visions, I thought they might be. "But there are ones with Dastien and it's not good."

Dad laughed.

That wasn't the reaction that I was looking for. "Glad my nightmares amuse you."

"I'm sorry." He sobered a little but the smile was still there. "There was a little while when your mom and I were long distance, and she used to have the worst dreams. She'd call me ranting in Spanish. It was completely nuts."

Mom slapped his shoulder. "It wasn't nuts. They were nightmares and they *felt* real." She shook her head. "But your dad is right. My fears were consuming me, and my biggest one was that something would happen to take your father away from me. From cheating to death. I dreamed it all."

Dastien cheating would definitely be a relationship killer. "That's exactly it." God. It felt so good to be normal.

"Don't worry. Dastien is committed to you. It's just because you're apart and you're an emotional person. Don't give it a second thought."

For the first time since I woke up, I finally felt better. This was totally fine. My fears were taking me for a ride at night, but I just had to tell them to shut the hell up, and all would be good.

My parents got up, and I stood.

The floor came up to meet me. Or more accurately, I met it.

"Whoa." Dad crouched beside me. "Are you okay?"

I sat up and shook my head. "God. What is wrong with me? That's the second time I've tripped. And I threw up last night and dropped a plate. What is up with me?"

"You didn't trip. You fainted," Dad said.

"Is it your wolf?" Mom asked. "Do you need to shift?"

"No. I should be okay. It takes weeks for that to happen." I paused to think.

Something changed two days ago. I'd been feeling weak ever since. What had changed?

I'd gone to Rosa's. Learned some things.

And Luciana had been in my room.

There were times that coincidences were simply that. But for me lately, nothing was a coincidence.

Luciana had spelled me. Or cursed me. Or had done something else invasive and unforgivable.

I had to fix this. Now. It was time I dug around in her place.

"Mom. Dad. Thanks so much for coming," I said as I stood again and managed to stay on my feet. "But I think it's best if you go now." The both started protesting as I hustled them out the door. "I'm serious. Things are about to get ugly here, and I think you should go. It's safest."

"But what about you?"

"Don't worry about me. It seems like someone around here has forgotten that I'm an alpha. I'm a *bruja.* And I've been bullied too much in my life to take it anymore."

"Luciana cursed you. They're not just dreams," Mom said. She was a smart lady. I hoped that when I grew up, I was half as good as she was.

"Don't. Just go. I'll be okay." I wasn't so sure about that. Luciana had spelled me twice. This time she was completely out of line. She'd broken her side of the bargain, and now I could break mine.

Chapter Nineteen

As soon as my parents were gone, I went to my room. I'd known as soon as I fainted that something was wrong. That was what happened to Meredith when she'd been cursed. It wasn't the same, but it didn't matter. I hadn't gotten a vision from anything that was in my room.

When I was searching my room, I'd been looking for something missing. But what if she'd planted something?

I started digging around. I tore apart the room inch by inch. I emptied the closet, knocking on the walls and floorboards, looking for some place she could stash something.

It wasn't until I moved the mattress that I found it. She'd cut a hole in the box spring so that it wouldn't make a lump. I pulled apart the torn material and reached between the springs. My finger brushed against something and a dirty, oily feeling came over me.

I jerked my hand back, cradling it against my chest. I knew exactly what it was.

No. She couldn't have. No one would mess with magic that dark.

A gris-gris.

A few months ago I hadn't even known what a gris-gris was, but after Imogene accused me of cursing Dastien and using one, I'd done some research. It was a little pouch that carried a curse and was usually inscribed on the outside. Sure, they could be used for good, but I'd bet everything I had that this one was evil.

I didn't want to touch the thing again. I grabbed a discarded sock from the floor and stuck my hand in it. I picked up the little pouch between two fingers. Whatever was inside jangled as I moved, but I didn't want to open it. Messing with one of these was dangerous, and letting anything out of it could release a whole world of hurt.

I placed it on the bedside table and stepped back.

As shocked as I was to see it, it didn't entirely surprise me that Luciana had sunk to this level. What surprised me was that I hadn't noticed it sooner. Only now did I smell the rotten stench of whatever nasty ingredients were inside; Luciana must've warded the pouch against my Were senses.

No wonder I'd slept so well in Claudia's room. She didn't have a curse under her mattress.

The front door slammed shut. Raphael and Claudia's voices were muffled by the distance. Daniel said something, too.

I thought about telling them about the gris-gris, but my gut was telling me that I needed to deal with this alone. If Rosa was right, I needed to start listening to my instincts.

I quickly straightened my room, and put the gris-gris in the drawer of my bedside table. I'd deal with it later. Maybe it was dumb, but I needed to investigate Luciana at least a little before I left. I had to see if this was the kind of thing she was into. I needed into her craft room.

I put on my running gear and laced up my shoes.

I waited until I heard my cousins and Daniel in the kitchen, and then went quickly downstairs.

"Going for a run. See you guys in a bit," I said.

"Have fun," Claudia yelled as I left.

I took off down the front stoop and made a few laps behind the houses. That way, if anyone saw me, they'd think I was just exercising.

It might've been better to wait until night, but some things needed to be handled on the spot. This was one of them. I'd had enough waiting.

If I left now with the gris-gris, maybe I could even prove that Luciana had broken our deal, but I didn't want to hide behind the Seven. I wanted to take her down myself. I needed more information. The more I had, the better my argument would be. I needed it to be airtight. I hadn't been joking about burning the compound to the ground if I were double-crossed.

Luciana had taken me from my mate. She'd cursed me. Twice. I was done.

It was unfair to damn the whole coven because of one person, but in this case, Luciana had already corrupted almost everyone.

As I circled the compound, I used my Were hearing to listen to the conversations inside the houses.

I nearly slowed when I heard her voice in the schoolhouse.

"To prepare the spell, we'll need the following

ingredients—"

That was all I needed. She was teaching, which meant she'd be occupied for a while. Daniel was in my house, and even if he went home, I didn't think he'd tell his mother on me.

I dashed toward Luciana's house. The quicker I went, the less chance I'd have of someone seeing me. Or at least that's what I figured. I'd never been a very sneaky person and my few escape attempts from St. Ailbe's had only proven that.

I carefully went through the backdoor and closed it softly behind me.

The house smelled overwhelmingly of cloves. Sage burned somewhere too, but it wasn't enough to combat the cloves. Piles of garbage took up a lot of the room. Stacks of newspaper and flyers. Trash from take-out. Things in shopping bags that had never been used.

Luciana was a hoarder. My nose crinkled. It wasn't dirty per se, but it was dusty. There was no way someone could really clean with this much junk everywhere.

I watched my steps as I moved deeper into the house, not wanting to disturb anything. The layout was pretty similar to the one in my cousins' house. From what I could tell, most of the houses at the compound looked the same. It made sense if the same contractor had built all of them.

I wandered toward where I thought her craft room might be. If there were something I could use against her, it'd be in there. I let my feet carry me along until I found myself staring at a navy blue door. Fingerprints smudged the black lacquered doorknob.

My gut said that I wouldn't like whatever was beyond that door.

My palms were sweating as I reached for the knob and hesitated, not quite touching it.

All the hair on the back of my neck stood on end. This wasn't a place I wanted to be, but I needed to go in there.

In and out, I told myself. I'd be fast. And then I was leaving the compound. Going home to St. Ailbe's. Home to Dastien.

"Fuck it," I said to myself, and gripped the knob, twisting until it opened.

I immediately put my hand over my nose and mouth, to stop myself from gagging. How had my Were senses not smelled it sooner?

The floor was shiny black and almost entirely covered with a pentagram. Candles burned at the five corners of the star, and from the orientation in the room, it looked like the star was pointed downward.

Seeing what was on the altar at the center of the pentagram made my hands shake.

A dead black-feathered chicken lay across it next to a bowl. Inside the bowl was a picture of Dastien and me. We were on campus, sitting in the quad. There was a notebook in my lap, but I was laughing at Dastien. The picture was wrapped with some kind of fine, dark brown string. The color of my hair.

I wanted to grab it, but the tips of my toes were at the edge of the circle surrounding the pentagram. I'd watched enough movies and read enough books to know that crossing that circle could be bad news. I'd either alert her I was here or unleash something ugly. Either way, I wanted no part in that.

A brown matte substance was sprinkled all around the floor. I squatted down to get a better look, but I didn't want to touch it. I gave it a sniff and it smelled of iron. I hoped it was blood from the chicken, but it could've been from anything.

I stood and took in the rest of the room. A closet in the corner of the room was half opened. A few black robes hung inside, but the door wasn't open enough for me to see anything else.

The walls were stuffed with books. Lots and lots of books. I watched where I placed my feet as I went around the circle. As I stepped on a half-rotten floorboard, a loud creak sounded.

I paused, waiting to see if I could hear anything, but the house was still silent.

I wiped my palms along my jeans and stepped closer to the bookshelves along the back wall. Some of the books looked like the ones at my cousins'. Others were in a language I'd never seen before. I'd been careful not to touch anything so far. I'd been even more careful not to have a vision here. From the state of things, I had a feeling this room held more than I ever wanted to see. But holding back was a chickenshit move, especially when I'd come here to gather proof.

What should I touch?

I glanced back at the altar. The dead chicken's head lolled, revealing the deep slit along its throat. With the picture next to it…I couldn't think of many things more horrible.

I swallowed and turned back to the walls. I closed my eyes, held out my hand, and let my gut instincts take charge. Blindly, I reached for whatever I could.

Flashes of dark and light. Smells of death. Decay. Burning things. Rotting.

It was too dark to see anything. Too quiet.

And then there was a voice. It sang and my heart sped.

I didn't have to know Latin to know this was bad. The tune, the cadence, told me everything I needed to know. I made out the word 'Satani' and chills ran along my skin.

The scent of sulfur filled my senses. It was suddenly hot. Scorching. It felt like I was baking alive. Burning.

I screamed and threw what I was holding.

A knife. It spun into the closet as I ran for the door.

I wasn't thinking as I fled the house, leaving the door to Luciana's craft room wide open. I didn't care about getting caught anymore. I just needed to be gone.

The feeling that I would never be clean after touching that knife filled me.

That smell. Sulfur. The scent of hell.

Were demons real? Could Luciana call one to her? Even if she could, why would she?

I was halfway to my cousins' house before I slowed down. I hadn't noticed if anyone had seen me leaving or was following behind.

As I hit the front stoop of their house, a realization hit me and even in the Texas heat, I was cold.

Daniel had to know his mom was doing black magic.

He seemed to be on our side, but why wasn't he doing more to stop her? He hadn't told us about it. Or at least he hadn't told me about it, but there was no way he could be oblivious of that kind of evil in his own home.

Was he fooling us all? Was he really siding with Luciana?

I crashed down on the couch in the living room. The floral print that I'd found hideous before now seemed positively charming. I'd take anything over a black lacquered floor.

"Who's here?" Claudia said as she walked down the stairs. "Oh. Are you okay?"

I grunted, not lifting my head from the couch. "Not really." My voice was muffled from the cushions.

"What's wrong? What happened?"

I shook my head. "I think I saw a little sliver of Hell just now."

She sat on the chair next to me. "What do you mean?"

I didn't look at Claudia. "I decided to sneak into Luciana's house."

"You did what?" She yelled.

"I went into her craft room." I finally met Claudia's wide-eyed gaze. "Did you know she was practicing dark magic?"

She opened and closed her mouth a few times before speaking. "I had my suspicions. Her aura is really dark. Black as pitch. But I didn't want to really believe."

"You don't have to believe. You don't need to take it on faith. I found a gris-gris in my box spring. That's what was giving me the nightmares. I'm leaving, but I wanted some more evidence first, so I went there hoping for…" I shuddered. I hadn't even thought to bring anything with me. I'd just run. "There's an upside-down pentagram on her floor and a dead chicken on her altar. Plus a picture of me and Dastien wrapped in what I think might be my own hair. But that's not the worst of it."

"What's the worst?"

"I had a vision while touching some sort of ritual knife—"

"There are a lot of ritual knives. That doesn't mean that this one was bad."

I narrowed my gaze at her. "This one was bad. I touched it, and I was in a dark room. It was scattered, but I felt alone. Terrified. So scared I could barely breathe. The smell of sulfur was so strong. And I felt like I was burning alive. Whatever that knife is—whatever she's done with it—it's evil. It's possible that it wasn't always bad, but it is now."

Claudia blinked a few times before covering her face with her hands. "I didn't know." She pulled her hands down. "I swear. I didn't know."

"I believe you." And I did. I didn't know much about my cousin, but I knew for sure she wasn't evil. "The question is, how much does Daniel know? How much does the rest of the coven?"

She shook her head. "I don't know. I don't think Daniel knows anything. He would've said something. He's not allowed into the craft room at his house. He always uses ours." She rubbed her hands along her temples. "I would've said that we'd never allow that kind of darkness in *la Aquelarre*, but I guess I was wrong." She sighed. "This coven might not be worth saving."

No shit.

After my reception at the schoolhouse and the fact that only a handful of people had even come by to say hello, I'd been thinking more and more that the coven was a lost cause. *La Aquelarre* needed to be dissolved. Disbanded. Whatever it was called, but it needed to go away.

But after what I'd seen in Luciana's house, no fucking way. This place was bad news and just breaking the coven up wasn't going to cut it.

My gut was telling me to run. Now. Fast. Before anything else happened.

I wasn't sure if I'd even closed Luciana's back door. She was going to know I'd been there. And if she was really involved in dark magic, she was going to retaliate. She didn't want me around. She wanted to control me. To manipulate and use me. But I wouldn't allow that.

Dastien had been right. Caving to her had been a bad idea. I should've never come here.

I stood up. "If you come with me—if you and whoever you know, and I mean know, is good—come with me to St. Ailbe's, the pack can protect you. But I'm leaving. If I ever come back here, it won't be on friendly terms."

Claudia blinked as she tried to take in my words. "I…I…I've got to get Raphael. And the others. We need to pack. I can't just go right now. We need time."

The urge to go now was riding me hard. I'd left Luciana's maybe ten minutes ago. I wanted to be gone within the next ten. "How much time do you need?"

"I don't know. A day."

A day was too long. I shook my head. "No. We

need to go now. Like within the next fifteen minutes."

She paced away for a second, wringing her hands, before turning back to me. "Raphael is out by the creek. It'll take me time to go get him. Please wait for me. I'm scared of what Luciana will do if you leave and we're still here. I just…Please. Do this one more thing, and I swear I'll make it up to you. I'll get everyone as fast as I can."

Crap. I didn't want to leave her stranded. If Luciana did come looking for me, Claudia and Raphael would need protection. I couldn't leave them to deal with the backlash of what I'd done.

"I can give you one hour—and I don't even want to do that—and then I'm leaving with or without you. My offer of protection will stay on the table, though. You're welcome with the pack, but I'm not sticking around." I stood up and felt woozy. I slammed my hand down on the table to keep from pitching forward.

Claudia shot over to me, steadying me. "Are you okay?"

"I don't know. I think that gris-gris is still messing with me."

"A gris-gris!" Claudia said with eyes wide.

"Yeah." I was so tired. I hadn't been sleeping, and I probably wasn't eating enough. And I hadn't shifted. It was all weakening me. My body needed to run free, but I'd been following the rules.

"Okay. I'm going to know about that, but just give me a little time to go get the guys. We can be good to go in an hour. I'll make it work. And then we can figure out what to do about the gris-gris and everything else once we're off the compound."

I took a breath to calm my nerves. I still wanted to leave right this minute, but I didn't want to screw Claudia over. She was going to be leaving everything she knew. Of all people, I knew what that was like. "Okay. Okay. But be fast."

She rushed off out the door, and I hurried up to my room. I packed up everything. I didn't want to leave even the littlest bit here. When it was all done, I opened up the bedside drawer.

The gris-gris was still there. I dug through my bag and grabbed out a sock. I picked it up with the sock, and then folded it inside the cotton. I placed it carefully in my messenger bag.

I glanced at the little clock on the bedside table. Claudia had been gone for thirty minutes. I hauled everything downstairs, and piled it by the door.

What now?

I thought about leaving anyway, but another wave of dizziness almost made me topple to the floor. I sat on the couch to wait, taking a few calming breaths.

Soon I'd be gone. Far away from here. The next time I saw Luciana, I'd be taking her down.

Exhaustion started to weigh on me as I waited.

Even as my eyes grew heavy, I could feel the vision coming on. Pressing against my barriers. I couldn't fight it off and I couldn't stop myself from falling asleep.

***

The only reason I knew I was asleep was the slight hazy glow the room had taken on. It was brighter but duller than how it had looked a split second ago. The couch dipped beside me.

My breath caught. "Grams." Her long black hair was streaked with white, and loosely braided. She was wearing a traditional Mexican embroidered dress, and smelled of roses.

"Sí, amor. I sat here a long time ago, in the hopes that I could link with you one day. I'm sorry that I couldn't stop this from happening. I fought it, but every path I uncovered seemed to lead to the same place." She smiled, and I ached to sit up and hold her, but I didn't want to destroy the illusion. "It's time for you to wake up and fight. You know what you want, but you've been catering too much to everyone else. I know why—you didn't understand the way things were. The way it worked. You have to know the rules to know when to break them." She paused. "Break them. Fight. Or lose everything you love."

The image of Dastien cowering in the feral cages, upset and alone, filled my mind. Of his broken spirit. Of him withering.

I'd been wrong. As always. I'd tried to do the right thing, and I'd ended up hurting those around me.

I'd tried to help Meredith and it'd almost killed her.

Now, I'd tried to help the pack, and it was only hurting my mate.

"That's right, amor. Time to wake." She clapped her hands, and I blinked. "Wake! Before you lose it all!"

She clapped her hands again. And I jolted awake.

***

The scent of cloves burned in my nostrils. I tried

to sit up, but couldn't.

My hands were tied. My legs were tied. I was chained to the floor, blindfolded. Gagged.

And then I smelled it. The faint scent of blood. The decay of the chicken.

I was in Luciana's craft room.

I'd woken too late.

Chapter Twenty

The strangest things occurred to me as I lay there against the cool floor. Like the fact that the last time the pack was in danger, it was Dastien and the others who'd been tied up and left to die. But I'd been there to get Dastien. I'd seen him go. I'd seen him be taken. My abilities and determination had saved him and the others.

No one knew I was gone. Dastien wouldn't be coming for me. Neither would Claudia or Raphael. No one in this coven would stand up to Luciana for me.

As I waited for whatever was to come next, I knew that I'd cut myself off from my mate. There was no way to reach him. There was nothing I could do. I was stuck until I figured a way to get myself free.

It was almost funny how bad my luck was. I hadn't gotten a vision telling me that something bad was going to happen, so I'd figured it was okay. Except that I'd ignored the gut feeling telling me to get the hell out of the compound.

This was why I hadn't wanted to trust the visions. I didn't want to depend on seeing something, because right when I needed help the most, they'd failed me. I could only trust what I could hold on to with my hands.

So why had I ever let myself be separated from Dastien? We were a team. Infinitely more powerful together than we were apart.

The floor moaned as someone walked toward me. "She's awake."

Mr. Hoel. If I could say anything, I would've ordered him to let me go. I was more alpha than him. No matter what he tried, I could've overridden it.

Silent spells worked with my witchy stuff, but could I do the same with my alpha powers? I reached for the wolf inside me and pushed my demand toward Mr. Hoel—*Set me free!*

Nothing happened. No one moved. I bit back a wave of despair.

"Did you bind her yet?"

"Yes. Of course," Luciana said. "We'll start now."

Someone struck a match. The faint smell of wood burning filled the room.

I could feel the magic before Luciana said anything. Her spell seeped under my skin and my back bowed in pain, and I screamed through the cotton stuffed in my mouth.

I struggled against the bonds, but whatever they were made of was too strong for a Were—or at least *this* Were—to break.

It was like slime was sliding under my skin. Oily. Dirty.

I screamed again as I struggled. It felt like I was getting bit by a million fire ants all at once.

The chanting started and then it was all I could do to breathe.

I was being sucked dry. All my power was draining away. Separating.

A hand held each of my shoulders. One was bigger, stronger than the other.

I didn't understand the words, but I could feel my power being absorbed by them. My alpha powers were going to Mr. Hoel. My *bruja* to Luciana.

The hands let go of me and I thrashed as much as my bonds would allow. I didn't care as they bit into my skin.

The smell of sulfur choked the room and the chanting got louder.

Tears rolled down my cheeks. Something was burning under my skin. Like I was on fire inside.

I screamed until my voice was hoarse, but it didn't do any good. The sound was muffled against the cloth. Overrun by the chanting. But I couldn't stop. So much pain.

Suddenly the room was quiet except for my screams and breathing.

Hands unchained me from the ground, and I was dragged across the floor. A door shut, and I was sobbing. Unable to stop.

My powers were gone. I could feel them missing. Like they'd chopped off my arm. I felt dead inside. Drained. No more.

They'd taken a piece of my soul.

I thought I'd die there. That I would never get to go home. I'd never see my parents again. Never see my brother.

And Dastien.

There were so many things I wished I could do. That I wished I'd done. And now, here I was. Tied up.

All my powers drained. In the dark.

It was a while before my harsh gasps slowed. Before I could think clearly. It could've been minutes or hours, but when I did, I knew three things.

I was alive.

I had to get out of here.

And I had to stop Mr. Hoel and Luciana. No matter what. Even if I started a war. Even if it outed us all to the humans. Even if it cost me my life and the lives of others.

They were evil.

Somewhere in the dark, I found clarity. Focus.

I remembered Grams' words from the journal.

…you that even at your darkest hour, when you're stripped bare, I will be with you. Don't ever lose faith.

That was how I felt now. Stripped bare. But I didn't have faith. It was gone. I was broken. They'd already taken my powers. They'd ripped something so vital from me it was like my soul was rent in two.

I wiggled around in the space as I sobbed. Something brushed against my face and I jerked, knocking my head against the wall before I realized it was just a robe. One of the robes I'd seen in here earlier.

Something about the feeling of the cloth against my face made me calm down. I was forgetting something.

I shook as I lay there.

I should never have broken into the craft room. And I should've run as soon as I got the vision from that knife—

I sucked in a breath. The knife.

The tiniest spark of hope flared inside me.

It had to be in here. *Please, God. Let it still be in here.*

My hands were tied behind my back, but I could roll a little and feel the walls. I moved around and found a way to sit up. Sort of.

I frantically searched. Praying. Hoping. *Please, let Grams be right.* It was here. I knew it was.

I felt along all the walls and still nothing. Exhausted I relaxed against the floorboards.

Come on, Tessa. Keep looking. It's got to be here.

I needed to sit up more. I wiggled until my back was against the wall, and then rolled until I was sitting. My head clunked into a shelf, and something rattled.

I froze. Was that the knife?

Something else Grams had written came to mind.

The thing that will set you free is just above your head. Don't be afraid to break through.

I hit my head against the shelf harder, and the rattle came again.

I didn't want to hurt myself, but I'd heal. I was still a werewolf, even if Mr. Hoel had a hold on my alpha powers. I wasn't afraid.

I positioned myself just under the shelf, right where I heard the rattle.

One. Two. Three.

I slammed my head into it, and the wood splintered. Pain flared across my forehead and I smelled my own blood, but something cool and metal landed in my lap.

I managed to get an awkward grip and sawed at the bonds at my wrist. As soon as I got the ones off of my arms, I ripped off the mask over my eyes, then the gag.

"Fuck."

After freeing my legs I held my breath and listened.

I wanted to run out of the house, but what if Luciana and Mr. Hoel were still here? What if they were waiting?

I'd been dumb enough. I needed to be smarter now.

I counted to sixty three times, taking care not to rush.

Not a sound in the house.

They were gone. Using my powers in whatever way they wanted. But not for long.

I opened the closet door. I was still in the craft room.

The bowl on the altar was gone. In its place were two mason jars. They glowed with a light so bright, so pure, it dimmed the shadows even in this room of darkness and evil.

I wasn't scared of crossing the circle anymore. I knew what was in those jars, and it belonged to me.

There was a faint smell of sulfur as I crossed the circle. It was hot. At least twenty degrees hotter than the temperature outside the boundary.

I wanted to break the jars right then and there, but Luciana would know I was out and that her plan had failed. I couldn't afford that yet.

I gritted my teeth. I had to deal with the empty feeling for a little bit longer. *Not much longer,* I promised myself. *Just enough time to take these motherfuckers down.*

I grabbed the jars, cradling them to my chest, and

ran as fast as I could to my cousins' house.

***

Claudia flew out from the kitchen as soon as I stepped through her front door. "Where have you been? What's in those jars? Are you bleeding?"

The cut on my head had already healed, but I wiped at it anyway. "I'm not bleeding anymore. My powers are in these." I held up the jars. "Luciana did some spell on me. I need to go. Right now. I'm getting my keys and my things. When I leave, I want nothing here that they can use to spell me again. Not a single piece of hair. Nothing."

"Holy shit," Raphael said from the top of the stairs. "Are you okay?"

"No. I'm not okay." I went to get my things, grabbing out a shirt from my duffle. I wrapped the jars in the T-shirt so they wouldn't break. I tucked them carefully inside my messenger bag before grabbing my keys. Then I scooped up the rest of my stuff and headed for the door. "Anyone who wants to leave can come to the pack. I'm not waiting a second longer." I didn't pause as I strode toward my car. I took the jars out of my bag, set each one in a cup holder, and then threw everything else in the back. I didn't want them out of my sight.

I buckled my seatbelt as I drove over the cattle guards. My bond to Dastien slammed in place, but it was weak. Barely there. I heard him cry out, but couldn't even make out what he was saying, only a vague feeling of fear and anger. I couldn't answer. I didn't have the strength to.

I was in the zone as I drove. Maybe it was shock. Or maybe I was ready to kick some ass. Or maybe I was traumatized. All I could see were the road stripes as I hit the accelerator. I focused on the road. I pushed my car to go as fast as it could. Nothing was getting in my way. I was going home.

Chapter Twenty-One

As I pulled through the gates of St. Ailbe's, I was still numb. My hands shook as I grabbed the two jars from the cup holders, and cradled them to my chest. I left the rest of my stuff in the car. I didn't need it. There were two things that I really needed.

A shower and Dastien.

I bumped the car door with my hip, closing it, and as I turned, my breath caught.

Dastien stood at the edge of the parking lot, waiting for me. Meredith, Donovan, Mr. Dawson, Adrian, Chris, and Dr. Gonzales were there too, but I hardly spared them a glance. Dastien alone filled my vision as he took slow measured steps toward me. He was wearing a pair of sweats and nothing else, which meant he'd shifted too quickly to go home for clothes.

I walked straight to him and no one said anything. His arms wrapped around me, and I buried my nose in his chest.

He muttered things that I couldn't understand, rubbing his hands up and down my spine. "Are you okay?"

"No." I stepped away from him, and started toward the dorm. I didn't pay attention to what anyone was doing. I kept moving. Any questions, any comments fell on deaf ears, as I moved woodenly.

I didn't stop until I got to my bathroom. I closed the door and started the shower. I placed the glowing jars on the counter and stared down at them.

It was like two stars were trapped inside. In the one with my alpha powers, the light flickered and swirled with a glowing red orange center and yellow and white along the edges. The energy in the *bruja* jar shone vibrant blue and green on the outside with a pure, bright white center. It looked like they should be burning, but both glasses were cool to the touch.

I took a quick shower, and when I was done, I felt maybe ten percent better. But I couldn't scrub away that oily feeling. I couldn't shove aside the knowledge that something had been stolen, and even if I could get it back, I might never be the same. I'd never trust in the same way again.

The worst part was, I didn't trust myself anymore.

I felt like everything I'd done since the Tribunal was a mistake. I tried to let go of my anger and frustration, but it wasn't easy. If only I could learn lessons the easy way…

I reached through the shower curtain for a towel, but found it much closer than it was supposed to be. I peeked out to see Dastien leaning against the wall, holding a towel out to me. I hadn't noticed when he'd come in, which said how out of it I was, but I was glad he was there. I wrapped myself in the towel and got out. The first thing I did was grab the jars.

Dastien watched me without a word as I left the bathroom.

Everyone was in my bedroom. Meredith and

Chris stood up from where they were sitting on my bed when I walked in. No one was talking. I was back early, and they knew that I wouldn't be here—not speaking—unless something terrible had happened. They all had to know something was wrong. Majorly wrong.

I didn't have a free hand to make sure the towel was tightly wrapped, but I couldn't bring myself to care.

"What's in the jars?" Donovan said.

A tear slipped free and I shook my head.

"*Cherie.*" Dastien's voice rolled through me. His body heat warmed me as he stepped close, his chest brushing my back and I closed my eyes. "What's in the jars?"

I kept my eyes shut tight as I held up the one in my left hand. I didn't think I could take their sympathy and hold it together. "Alpha." I held up the one in my right. "*Bruja.*"

It was quiet for a second before Donovan spoke. "She's been stripped."

It was chaos after that. Questions. Arguments about whether or not it was possible. About how it could've been done.

I couldn't handle it. Not then. Especially not in a towel.

I turned to Dastien. "Hold them please. Don't break them."

He nodded, and took the jars.

I moved to my closet, and grabbed out some clothes. I'd feel better once I had clothes. Probably.

I quickly dressed in the bathroom. It was only then—as I brushed my hair—that I looked at myself in the mirror. My eyes were a dull brown. My skin looked pale and tinged with green. My cheekbones stuck out, and my eyes were sunken in their sockets.

I looked sick. Half-starved. Weak.

I put my hair in a loose braid and went back into the room.

"—Even if it were possible, it would be black. No one would do that. Not when the cost is so high. It's impossible for—"

"Believe me, the scent of sulfur and the heat and the fire under my skin—when she dies, Luciana will pay a high price for what she's done." My voice sounded flat even to me. "*La Aquelarre* is lost. Rupert Hoel is working with them. He's the one who wanted my alpha power. She wanted my witchy stuff. They absorbed some of it into themselves, and drained the rest into these jars. And now I'm left with nothing. My only hope is that when I open the jars, I'll have everything back. That it won't just escape into the world at large, and I'll get back whatever they're still carrying. But we don't have time to research or do anything about it now. Luciana will attack soon, and we need to be ready."

"Can we stop it?" Meredith said.

"It's coming whether we want it or not. The coven never cared about me." I pointed to the jars. "That's what Luciana wanted, and she got it." I swallowed. "All we can do now is prepare for a fight." I glanced at Dastien. "I'm hungry, I think?"

Dr. Gonzales stepped forward. "You look sick. Can I help?"

I shook my head. I didn't want anything from her bag o' tricks. "I don't think anything's going to fix this except opening those jars, but I need to hold off until tonight. If I open them now, they'll change their plans. We might not be ready for them next time." Meredith moved aside as I went into my closet, digging through to find a backpack. The backpack that Claudia and Raphael had given me. I didn't have any potion vials left, but it still had some other weapons.

I unzipped it, and held it in front of Dastien. He carefully put the jars inside. "Wait. I should wrap them again." I grabbed a couple of T-shirts, making sure that they were properly cushioned, and then zipped the pack.

My dream of the war on the quad was coming. My gut was telling me that particular nightmare was true, and I had to trust it.

"At midnight, the vampires will come. Then, the witches. And then the traitors from our own pack. We need to figure out who's good and who's bad. And we need to get ready. Luciana and Mr. Hoel don't know that I saw what's going to happen." I wasn't sure if Mr. Hoel was going to kill me tonight, but it was a strong possibility. Maybe if we were ready, I could avoid it. Maybe not. "Can we clear the cafeteria? I want to eat and I want to talk to you, but we can't trust anyone. Not anyone outside this room. Not yet."

Donovan nodded. "Don't you worry, lass. We'll keep you safe."

I shrugged the backpack over my shoulders and started for the door. "That's why I came home."

***

267

The cafeteria was pretty much empty, but one growl from Donovan, and the place became completely empty.

"I'll get you some food," Dr. Gonzales said. "You sit."

I nodded and made my way to our normal table. Dastien took the backpack from my shoulders. "I'll take care of the jars," he said as I looked back at him.

"Okay." I trusted him more than I trusted myself at this point.

As I sat down, I sighed. It felt like I was getting a little piece of normal back.

Maybe everything wouldn't be okay today or the next day, but we'd get there.

A tray appeared in front of me, and I stared eating and telling the story. Everyone stayed quiet at the table, except for a few laughs when I told them about my attempted witchery. Even I could admit that blowing a hole in the roof was pretty funny.

"So, that's how I ended up here." I'd gone through three trays of food while I was talking. Mr. Dawson sat straight and started to speak, but I held up a hand. "A few questions for you guys before anyone says or asks me anything."

"Please," Donovan said.

"I'm still feeling drained, even with the food I've eaten. I'm not around the gris-gris, but it's still weakening me. I need that gone before tonight. Any ideas?" If I was going to beat Mr. Hoel, I was going to need all the strength I could get.

"Did you bring it with you?" Donovan asked.

"Yes. It's in my messenger bag in the backseat of my car. Wrapped in a sock."

"We'll burn it. Best way to release whatever's got a hold of you," Donovan said. "As for the jars, I do believe setting the power free will bring it back to you. It takes a lot to pull it from you—as you saw. It's contained for now in the jars, but once we break the seals, the power should be yours again. You'll be right as rain."

I stared at the table and swallowed. Dastien reached for my hand under the table. "I can barely hear Dastien and I can't talk to him in my head anymore."

"It'll all come back. You'll be whole again," Mr. Dawson said.

"Will I?"

"We'll make sure of it."

"As one of the Seven, you need to figure out which wolves we can trust," I said to Donovan.

"Sebastian has been working on it. It seems Rupert has a good number of wolves supporting him. About half."

"That's more than I'd thought," I said. This didn't bode well for tonight.

"I thought we fixed the problem wolves months ago," Mr. Dawson said with a frown. "The ones who acted out with Rupert were punished, but now...it has to go deeper than we thought. Someone more powerful than him..."

"What about the humans?" Chris asked. "If there is a war, we're going to need to alert them."

"I think telling them now is a bad idea," I said. "We're going to have a battle. There are two outcomes, we win or we lose. If we win, then any that get away will lick their wounds before coming back.

Luciana said some covens were with her, but I met a witch from Colorado who said her group was with us. Luciana could be full of it, but there will be some who will back her, even if we defeat her tonight. So, we win tonight. Then, we slowly out ourselves in a good light to the humans and prepare them for the dangers of the supernatural. Then, when the big war comes, we try to handle it as under the radar as possible. If we lose tonight, then it's all moot. We won't be around to worry about anything."

I flashed back to my vision. The sounds of battle surrounded me. I heard Mr. Hoel yelling at me. I could almost taste the iron of my blood filling my mouth.

"Tessa?" Dastien asked.

I blinked. "I'm fine," I said.

"Liar. Tell me what's wrong."

He was right. I wasn't fine, but I couldn't tell him all about my vision. Some things were left better unknown. If he was distracted during the fight, it could cost him his life.

If that nightmare came to pass, then I'd be glad that we hadn't tied ourselves together, and the ceremony was interrupted. Dastien would have to find a way to survive. "I'll be fine." It was a less of a lie. One way or another, I'd figure it out. "So what's next?"

"You need to rest," Dr. Gonzales said. "Let your body heal."

"We'll cook up some potions to fight the vamps and we have a few anti-witchy spells I researched while you were gone. One blinds them for a few minutes, so they can't cast anything at someone.

Another one is a blocking spell. I can mix those up," Adrian said.

"I'll grab your stuff from the car," Chris said. "We'll burn the gris-gris in the lab and get started with Adrian's spells."

I checked the time. It was two in the afternoon. "But class is still going on?"

"I'll kick them out," Adrian said. "Some things are more important than teaching the freshman metaphyiscs."

He had a point. "You'll come to my room?" I asked Dastien, but I was sure of the answer.

"Of course."

"Do you want me to come?" Meredith said.

"No. I'll be okay. But thanks." I just wanted to be alone. Dastien didn't count though. He was a part of me, even if I couldn't really feel the bond right then.

Dastien wore the backpack as we headed back to my room. I wasn't feeling as sickly as I had been before. But that empty feeling haunted me. I couldn't shake it—wouldn't be able to until those jars were a distant memory.

I climbed into bed without taking off any clothes, and Dastien followed, tucking me to his side.

"Sleep." His chest vibrated under my ear.

"I'm scared to fall asleep. The dreams— nightmares—were so bad."

"None of it will ever come to pass. I won't let it."

He might not have a choice.

I breathed in the scent of him. The forest. The earth. The bit that was just him.

"Relax," he said as he untied the band around the bottom of my braid. He ran his fingers through my hair, massaging my scalp lightly. "You're home now. Sleep."

There was a command in his words, and without my abilities I couldn't even pretend to fight it. My eyelids grew heavy and the world faded from view.

Chapter Twenty-Two

I woke with a start. My heart was beating so fast. It thundered in my ears.

A beep sounded, and I rolled over.

"Are you okay?" Dastien said.

I lay back down. "Sure." Only I wasn't so sure. Something was up. I was so revved that even my teeth tingled. "Who texted?"

Dastien checked his phone. "Adrian. They found the gris-gris and burned it." He clicked on my bedside lamp. "How're you feeling now?"

"I don't know," I snapped and instantly felt like a jerk. That question was getting old. "Something woke me up," I said, changing the subject.

"Probably the gris-gris being destroyed." He grabbed my chin, and forced me to meet his gaze. "How're you feeling? Be honest."

I sighed. He was only trying to help, but I didn't have a great answer for him. "I feel weird. Unsettled." I paused. "Should we be doing anything? I feel like we're just lying here and there's so much to be doing. We're wasting time."

"I think you've done enough to help the pack. You've sacrificed. I've sacrificed. They're doing the busy work. The prep. Sometimes it's good to delegate. Trust our friends. They'll get it done." He got up.

"Aren't we delegating?" If so, there was no reason for him to be leaving.

"Yes, but there *is* something that only you and I can do. Come on." He held his hand out to me, and I stared at it for a second. "Trust me."

I met his golden eyes. "I do." I put my hand in his and let him pull me from the comfort of my bed.

He slung the backpack on, and kept his hand firmly in mine as we made our way to the common room. He let go of me then, but only long enough to stuff a bunch of food and drinks in a bag, before he reclaimed it. "This way."

I thought about asking where we were going, but I had a pretty good idea.

We walked across campus to the parking lot, and he opened the front door to his car. "In."

"Are you sure it's okay to leave campus right now? I just got back and…"

"Yes. We need this. It'll be okay."

I raised an eyebrow at him. "If you say so."

"I say so." He threw the bag in the back and got in the seat, handing me the backpack. I couldn't help but peek. I unzipped and looked at the two glowing jars. My energy was still there. I had to keep reminding myself. It hadn't gone anywhere. Not really.

A year ago, if I could've put my visions in a jar and buried them in the backyard, I would've done it. I would've done anything to get rid of them and be normal. Now I wanted them back so bad I itched to snatch the jars and smash them.

"Ready?" Dastien asked.

"Yeah."

As he drove, playing soft piano music that soothed my soul, I stared out the window. "Are you mad?" I asked.

"No. Why?"

"Even though you were in the feral cages? Even though I was wrong, and you were right?"

He sighed. "We were both wrong. I was wrong because it was worth trying. We had to give up a lot, but if the witches had been honorable, it would've been for the greater good. And you were wrong, too."

I bit my trembling lip.

"You're wrong because you're a good person. You saw the evil there, but you wanted to fix it. You wanted to protect the pack. And that's the most honorable kind of wrong you could ever be." He paused. "Wrong is the wrong word."

I laughed but it sounded a bit desperate, even to me. "Wrong, huh?" He'd used the word a million times.

"It is. It's not you. This wasn't your fault. You didn't ask to get stripped. This is Luciana's fault. This is Rupert's fault. All we did was try our best."

"We failed."

"Not yet."

He was right. We still had a chance, but it felt like I'd already failed. I'd gone to the compound and I hadn't accomplished anything.

As we pulled onto the worst road in the history of roads, I gripped Dastien's hand tightly. It was good to feel him, to be with him. He calmed me.

Dastien stopped the car as we reached the clearing, and went into the back of the car—pulling out the bag of food and a blanket. While he was busy, I hopped down out and started walking.

He caught up in a second. "Let's go by the pond."

"Okay," I said.

This was the first time I'd been around him since I accepted that he was my mate—since that first vampire attack—that I couldn't feel what he was feeling. It was both disarming and unsettling. It was like there was a great cavern between us and I couldn't reach across to him.

I'd thought I missed him before, but being next to him, I missed him even more.

He glanced up at me from where he was putting the blanket. His eyes hadn't dulled from glowing yellow. I didn't have to be able to read him to know that this was bothering him, too. He was way more obsessed with our bond than I was.

"Are you okay?" I asked.

"I wish we could break the jars now. I don't like this distance. You're here but you're not, and it's driving me crazy."

I sat down heavily. "Me, too."

He sat next to me and pulled me into his lap, pressing his forehead to mine. "We'll be okay. It'll take more than this to take us down."

"I know."

"You were hurt, and that hurts me, but I'll be here for you. No matter what."

His words made me feel a little better. "Do you think we'll ever get to live here?"

"I know it. I will make it happen no matter what."

He was so determined that I almost believed him. Almost. "Some things won't be in your control."

"I don't care. If that's what you want, I'll make it happen. Trust me. This will be okay. It might be a while, but we'll make it okay."

I nodded and rested my head on his shoulder. "Do you think that our bond will come back?"

"Is that what you're afraid of?"

A part of me was. A lot of our relationship was based on our bond and being mates. If that was suddenly gone, if I never got back to who I was before, would he still be with me? "Yes. If I can't be your mate anymore—"

He shook my shoulders until I looked at him. If I'd thought his eyes were glowing before, I was wrong. "You are mine. There's no backing out of it for any reason. I liked you when you were human. Seeking you out in the bookstore. Following you to that stupid party. I couldn't stay away even then. And you're still a wolf. I can feel her there, under your skin. You're going to be fine and even if you weren't, I'd want you just the way you are." He stared into my eyes and for the first time, I broke away first. "Got it?"

I chewed on the inside of my mouth as I let his words sink in. "Yeah. I got it."

"Good. Now let's have a snack and talk about happy things. Like where we should put the house. How many bedrooms? That seems like a good negotiation. I was thinking seven was a good number."

I shoved him. "Seven? How do you figure that?"

"One for us, two for guests, four for kids. Although, maybe we need ten. Ten would be better, right?"

"Ten? Who the hell is going to be visiting us? How

many guests can we have at one time?"

He grinned and his eyes dimmed. Not all the way back to amber, but closer. "Not for more guests, *cherie.*"

I laughed. "You're out of your mind."

He pressed his lips softly against mine. "Only when it comes to you."

***

When we got back to campus, I was feeling much better. A little R&R with Dastien was exactly what I'd needed. Everything would be better when the jars were history, but at least I was feeling more like myself. More confident.

We parked the car, and hopped down, but I didn't get far before stopping. The rest of the gang stood by the edge of the parking lot. Again. With a few extras.

"Jeez. It's like everyone is watching for when I get back. Why is there always a reception here?"

"There're cameras along the fence. Someone was probably looking out for us, but I think we've got some visitors. Isn't that your cousin?"

I nodded. "I guess I forgot to mention that I told them if they needed a safe place to stay, they could come here. With the coven that bad, they couldn't stay at the compound. Do you think the pack will be pissed?"

He shrugged. "They'll get used to it. Things are changing. Better they get used to it now." He pulled me toward the waiting group. "Come on. They're getting impatient."

"I say they blame you instead of me. You started

the whole change in the pack by biting me."

Dastien tweaked my nose. "Well, maybe you shouldn't have been so irresistible."

"Oh barf," Adrian said. "We can hear you from here. How about getting a move on? Some of the pack are flipping out about this."

Dastien and I picked up our pace.

Claudia, Raphael, Shane, Cosette, and Elsa stood beside my friends. I nodded to them, and then turned to Mr. Dawson. "They'll need a place to stay. In the dorms?"

Mr. Dawson shook his head. "There's room for visitors on the top floor of the admin building. Above the infirmary. The freshman are mostly stable, but I wouldn't want to risk any accidents in the dorms."

Huh. I'd always wondered what was up there, but I'd figured it was offices or something. "Okay. In the meantime, how's the prep work coming?"

"Slowly," Chris said.

"It's getting there." Adrian was being a little defensive.

"No you haven't figured out how to make them—" Chris started, but Meredith cut him off.

"Do you trust them?" Meredith asked.

I glanced at the group from the coven huddled in a circle. They looked both scared and defiant.

Wait. Someone was missing. "Where's Daniel?"

Claudia shrugged. "I couldn't find him. We waited for as long as we dared, but Cosette saw Luciana pull up and we left. I can't stand up to her. Not after the blood oath. And if she's doing evil stuff, I just…I couldn't wait." She blinked rapidly as she pressed her lips firmly together.

"Got it. He's a big boy, and his mother won't hurt him," I said, but I wasn't so sure about that.

"She could hurt him worse than anyone because he's her son," Elsa said.

I blew out a breath and turned to Dastien.

He shook his head. "*Non.* You will not suggest that."

His defiant look made me smile. Despite everything, he knew what I was going to ask before I could ask it. "Fine. But I think leaving him behind is a bad idea. We should go get—"

"No!" Adrian, Chris, and Meredith all said at once.

Meredith pointed a finger at me. "We let you go once, and we took care of your mate while he was half-crazed, but we won't do it again. I'll throw *you* in the cages this time. And believe me, I'm one hundred percent serious." Meredith's eyes hardly glowed before I got rid of the curse, but right then, they were so pale and bright, I took a step back. "You will *not* leave campus again until *I* say it's okay."

The power behind the command took my breath away. She had to have been borrowing some alpha energy from Donovan. He stepped forward, squeezing her shoulder. "I think Tessa understands that we're all against her putting herself at risk again, love." Donovan turned to me. "We'll keep an eye out for this Daniel, but he might not be trustworthy if Luciana is his mother."

"He's trustworthy," Raphael said. "He doesn't like his mother any more than we do."

"Are you sure about that? Could he be lying to you to get in with you?" Donovan asked.

Raphael opened his mouth to say something, but then snapped it shut.

"That's what I'm sayin'. It's mighty convenient that he went missing just as it was time for you to leave."

"He has a point," Cosette said. She tucked a piece of blond hair behind her ear. "The timing was too convenient. We would've arrived right behind you, but we were waiting on him."

"I find it interesting that you're in Texas," Donovan said.

Cosette grinned. "The queen said things were getting interesting down here. I came to assess the situation."

"And what did you find?"

"*La Aquelarre* and its allies are evil. The fey will be backing you," she said.

"I thought you were only part fey," I said.

She shrugged, but didn't look the least bit perturbed. "I've been many things, but at the core, I'm fey."

Was I missing something? "But you said you were a witch."

"I have some witch in me down the line, but that's only a small part. We don't lie, but there are many shades of gray."

Right, but I would've felt more comfortable if she'd just be honest. "Claudia, if you wouldn't mind helping us out with some more of those vials for vampires—"

"Vampires?" Claudia shouted. Then her cheeks reddened. "I thought we were fighting the coven," she continued at a much more normal volume.

"We are. But the vampires will be here first."

The scent of fear hit the air, and I knew she was scared.

"I think we probably have all of the ingredients, but I'm not sure if I'm putting the spells together correctly. Would you mind showing me?" Adrian asked.

"Not at all. Let's all go. I'm happy to share what I know about fighting with potions," Claudia said.

As we headed through the quad to the school building, I knew that this was what I was here for. The supernatural community was fighting, but it was also changing. Witches and wolves working together to fight evil.

We had eight hours to prepare, but when the first vampire stepped on campus, we'd be ready. We could do this. We had to.

Even if I died trying, I'd stop Luciana here tonight.

Chapter Twenty-Three

The sun was setting as we finished filling vials. Donovan had been gone for a while. He was with Sebastian and Muraco, finding a way to single out the bad pack members as soon as they joined the fight.

"These potions should be enough for us *brujos*," Claudia said as she gathered up the little glass vials. "The rest of you will be shifting, right?"

Adrian nodded. "Yes. I think we're all shifting."

I shook my head. "I'm not."

"What? Why?" Meredith said. "You'll be much safer as a wolf. Are you still afraid of changing?"

That wasn't it at all. "No. I just have this feeling that I need to be human. I need to be able to talk to the witches. I need to be able to command the wolves. I can't do that as a wolf."

"But you'll be without your magic and you won't have the protection of teeth and claws that you'd have as a wolf," Chris said. "Not changing is a big mistake."

In my vision, I'd been human. My gut told me that if I shifted, the fight could get even worse than I'd dreamt. I wasn't about to ignore that feeling. "Trust me. I need to be human." I shrugged. "Plus, I'm not even sure if I can shift. With the jar and everything…"

"Just because your alpha powers are in the jar doesn't mean that you can't shift. You're still a Were," Meredith said.

"I don't know. Something's telling me not to try. So I'm sticking to two feet."

Chris held up his hands. "Okay. But for the record, I think it's a bad idea."

"Me, too," Adrian said.

"Me, three," Meredith said.

Dastien was silent as he sat on one of the lab stools. His long legs were stretched in front of him.

I raised an eyebrow, waiting for him to chime in.

"I trust you to know what's best. Doesn't matter what form you're in. You won't leave my sight."

I took him in. His long, lean form. The way his biceps bulged as he crossed his arms. His dark curls that were a little too long. I wanted him. So badly. I wanted a future with him. The thought of not being here—of leaving him no matter the circumstances—was a little too much to bear.

He sat up straighter, and I knew he was feeling something through the weakened bond. He couldn't fully read me, but if I could sense basic emotions from him, he could do the same from me. I had to stop thinking about what might happen. The future could change and I'd do my best to make sure it did.

Donovan and Mr. Dawson strolled into the room. The Weres all sat up straighter, waiting to hear what they might say while the *brujos* just seemed nervous. They looked everywhere but at the two men.

Meredith crossed the room to Donovan, and he grasped her hand, pulling her until she was tucked against his side.

"What's the story?" I said. "Any update on the bad wolves?"

Donovan shook his head. "Too many Weres went home after the Tribunal. I couldn't even get hold of Ferdinand. Thought he was stickin' around, but he must be on a plane back to Europe." He sighed. "It'd be one thing if it were just one or two Weres in question and they were easily accessible. I could call them in. Order them to tell me where their loyalties lie and lock up the bad ones. But I can't get in touch, and even if I could, where am I to put them to keep them out of trouble?"

I guessed that was true, but it didn't make me feel any better about tonight. "We'll just have to deal with them as they come."

"The good news is that we've tracked down some that we believe are on our side and called in some Cazadores who are definitely loyal. That's not nothing," Mr. Dawson said. "They're already in place, patrolling the area. They'll stay hidden until the battle starts. We don't want to give the traitors any idea that we know they're coming. Surprise is our best tactic."

"So who's going to be leading them?" Dastien asked.

"Good question," Donovan said. "I am."

"And what about the witches?" Elsa said. "Not all of them are bad."

"If they choose to step aside, no harm will come to them. But I'm afraid if they fight against us, we'll have to fight back. I'm sorry, lass," Donovan said.

"Maybe I can convince them not to fight," Claudia said. "It's worth a shot."

That didn't seem likely. I wasn't sure anyone from

the coven would listen, especially not in the middle of a battle with Luciana leading the charge. "If you don't want to fight, I think we'd all understand." I couldn't imagine trying to go against people I'd spent my whole life with.

"No," Shane said. "We'll do our part. If they're that far gone, messing around with demonic stuff, then they're not the same coven we grew up with. It's something that we'll just have to deal with."

Raphael nodded. "We should've stepped up sooner, but we didn't. It's our duty to fix this now."

I understood the sentiment, but they weren't responsible for Luciana's actions. "You shouldn't take so much on yourself."

Raphael lifted one eyebrow at me. "You're the one whose powers are in jars. I know you were waiting for me. If you'd left the compound right away, this wouldn't have happened."

I hoped I hadn't made him feel guilty for anything. It wasn't his fault. Not even a little bit. "Raphael," I said his name firmly so that he'd know I was being totally serious. "I don't blame you for what happened." He pressed his lips together in a firm line. I wasn't being nice. I really didn't blame him at all. It hadn't even entered my mind, but from the fierce look on Raphael's face, I knew no amount of reassuring him would change his mind.

Claudia stepped next to her twin, leaning on him a little. "Our coven has gone bad. We know what might happen, and we're going into this fight ready to do what needs to be done."

Donovan grunted. "It'll be harder than you think. You'll be armed with the spells for the vampires.

Focus on those. We'll try and cover the witches as much as possible."

"I think they're aware how hard it will be to fight *la Aquelarre*," Cosette said. "But the answer is the same. They know what they're doing."

"And you've permission to fight as well?" Donovan asked. "I don't want the queen to come calling if you get hurt."

"Yes. You'll be safe. For now at least." Cosette shook her head, sending her blonde curls bouncing with the movement. "The fey aren't always the most reliable, but Luciana's magic is bad business for all of us so they'll support the fight. It's too short notice to get help for tonight, though."

"Of course," Mr. Dawson said. "We just don't want any trouble with your people. We've got enough on our hands already."

"I'll handle that."

This was getting us nowhere, and I had one more question. "What about the rest of the students? Has anyone warned them?"

Mr. Dawson crossed his arms. "I called them into a meeting while you and Dastien snuck away. When the alarm sounds, any seniors who choose to do so will join the fight. I ordered the underclassmen to stay in the dorms no matter what. I don't want the younger pups getting in over their heads."

I didn't make a comment about me being new to the whole Were thing, too. I might have been inexperienced, but I wasn't backing down from this fight.

"So, where are we supposed to be? I assume we're waiting outside to ambush them?" Adrian asked.

"Yes," Mr. Dawson said. "The loyal pack members will be hidden in the forest surrounding campus. They'll try to cut down the number of vampires that make it to the quad. As the fight progresses, they'll either press in or move out to cover our backs as needed."

I nodded. "This sounds like a solid plan." Although only a million or so things could go wrong. "I'll be in the center of the quad. As soon as I see both Luciana and Mr. Hoel, I'll smash the jars. I don't want either of them no-showing because I got my powers back too early. Which means I'll be vulnerable for a time."

"I've got your back. Always," Dastien said, and I knew he was telling the truth.

"Luciana is too strong to fight while she has access to my powers. No one should approach her until the jars are broken."

"What happens if you get caught up? If you can't break the jars?" Meredith asked.

That would be bad fucking news. If I didn't break the jars, they'd be using my powers to fight against us. Not even a little bit acceptable. "I have to break them." I checked the clock. "They'll be here in less than an hour. If we're all set, then I'm going to go change into something with more pockets." Last thing I needed was to run out potions mid-battle.

"I think we've covered everything," Mr. Dawson said. "Everyone okay?"

There were a few yes's and some nods. I took that as a sign that it was okay to go. I slipped the backpack with the jars over my shoulders and headed for the door. "Meet everyone on the quad."

I caught Dastien's gaze as I left and once again I felt sad. So sad. I had to make it through tonight, but if I didn't, I needed to know that he'd be okay. I wasn't so sure that was the case.

Dastien caught up with me in the hallway. "You were scared about something earlier, and just now, you looked at me and you felt sad. What aren't you telling me?"

I kept walking. "I'm scared about fighting. That's all it was and it's totally natural."

"No. That's not what I felt from you a second ago. Fear. And resignation." He grasped my hand, pulling me to a stop. "What do you know that you're not sharing?"

I thought carefully about how to word it—I couldn't give Dastien any information that would put him off his game tonight, and my potential death definitely fell in that category. "Look. I've seen what's going to happen—or what might happen—and it's bad. Really bad. I did my best to avoid all this, and it's still coming anyway. So, yeah, I'm afraid, but resigned to the fact that it's going to happen whether I want it to or not." That was at least part of the truth, and giving him any more details wouldn't help.

He wrapped his arms around me. "It's going to be okay. We're going to get through this."

"And if we don't?" The words slipped out before I could stop them.

He leaned back, muscles tensing. "What are you saying?"

I closed my eyes. I shouldn't have said that. "Nothing."

"You're lying again."

"I'm sorry. I'm just in a mood. Let me go get changed. We don't have much time."

"Okay. But I'm coming with you."

"Please." I wanted to spend as much time with him as possible. If this was it, if Mr. Hoel did manage to kill me, I wanted every second I had left to be spent with Dastien.

Chapter Twenty-Four

The night was quiet as I stood on the quad. No birds chirped. No cicadas sang. Not even a breeze to rustle the grass. My hands shook as I waited for the vampires to show. I took deep breaths, partly to calm myself, but also so I'd know when they were close. I'd smell them before I saw them.

Dastien had convinced me to take off my shoes. Apparently they were a bitch to rip through when shifting fully clothed. He didn't try to make me shift, but he made it clear that I should if I needed to. He was hiding between the buildings. I couldn't see him, but I knew he was there in wolf form watching out for me.

I dug my toes into the cool, damp grass and reached into my pocket to palm one of the vials. I had thirty. *Please let that be enough.*

I sensed motion behind me and spun. The smell hit me. Death and decay. Old blood and rotted meat. I gagged as vampires swarmed the campus.

So much for the Cazadores keeping the flow down.

Wolves jumped from the forest to meet the vampires in a clash of fangs and fur.

The alarm sounded, the soft wail alerting the students we were under attack.

It didn't take long for the seniors to swarm out of the buildings in wolf form. I focused on the figures in black floating toward me. Hair like straw. Faces rotted and disgusting.

The wolves bounded toward the vampires, but I waited where I stood. They'd be here soon.

I knew enough about witchcraft to know that I didn't need to say the words aloud. As the first vampire approached, I threw the vial. *In the name of Jesus Christ, I purify you.*

Nothing happened. I froze. With or without my magic, the words should work. Should I shift?

"In the name of Jesus Christ, I purify you," Claudia's clear voice rang out beside me as she tossed another vial. Night turned to day as the potion exploded and the vampire burned to dust.

Thank God for cousins.

I let out a shaky breath and Claudia stepped in front of me. "Careful, *prima*. Your magic must be sealed."

Magic shouldn't factor into throwing potions, but I didn't have time to figure out the problem.

Three vampires had Dastien pinned down and the wolves were being pushed back as more and more of them flooded the quad. The other *brujos* were throwing vials as fast as they could, but it wasn't going to be enough.

"Cover me while I get the jars out," I said to Claudia.

I slipped off my backpack and grabbed the jars. I'd been hoping I'd be able to fight at least a little, but not so much. I needed these jars gone. Now.

Another vampire flew at us, and Dastien finally burst free—he jumped on its back, snarling.

Where in the hell were Luciana and Mr. Hoel?

A voice cried out. "Kill the wolves!" I didn't need to turn around to know who had arrived.

La Aquelarre.

They wore all white. Luciana was wearing one of her long skirts. Really impractical.

She paused her jog to the quad. Her face turned red as she stared at me.

One down. One to go.

As helpless as I was, I needed to wait a few more seconds. As soon as I spotted Mr. Hoel, I could destroy the jars.

Luciana threw a vial in my direction, but it fell way short of me and shattered against the ground, sending off a puff of fire and smoke.

"You don't want to do this," I shouted. "Turn back now."

She laughed. "You're weak. I have your power."

"Do you?"

She raised her arms, and the scent of sulfur filled the quad. The ground rumbled.

She was calling something from below the earth. My pulse sped. This wasn't what I'd seen in my dream. This was way, way worse. If she managed to summon something from hell…

I'd been to enough church masses to know we were all doomed.

"If you do this, there's no going back. You're damning yourself and every member of *la Aquelarre* along with you."

"Listen to her, Luciana," Claudia said. "Think about what you're doing. This is evil."

Luciana didn't even look at Claudia. She was too far gone. Magic flowed around her, like wind, raising her hair and making her skirts flow around her legs. But that wasn't what had me scared. It was the look in her eyes. And the fact that they'd turned completely black. Not even a hint of white was left in them.

I had to stop her before she finished this spell.

A figure in white dashed toward us. I moved to meet him, but stopped just as he dashed between Luciana and me.

"Mother!" Daniel said as he ran in front of her. "Stop! You can't do this. You'll kill us all." When she didn't respond, he turned to us. "We have to stop her."

When Daniel hadn't shown up at St. Ailbe's, I was worried I was wrong about him. It felt good to be right.

"Let's knock her out," I said. "If she won't stop casting, then we just shut her up."

Luciana's lips moved rapidly as the wind grew around her. She raised her arms to the sky and a red light from the ground rose around her.

Daniel shook his head. "It's too late. The spell she's doing...it's a chain reaction. Once it's started..."

"So what do we do?" I shouted.

Enemy Weres streamed in from the parking lot, led by a certain wolf I remembered from my nightmares.

Now. I needed to smash the jars. They were both here, and if Luciana was using some of my power to call up whatever that was, then I needed to cut her off.

Fast.

A vampire swiped at me, and I dodged out of the way and hit the ground rolling. The vampire lunged again, and I heard Claudia shout the incantation just before the vampire's ashes rained down on me.

Shit. This was getting bad.

Before one more thing could go wrong, I threw the jars as hard as I could on the ground. Both jars bounced and started rolling away from me.

My heart dropped into my stomach. "No. Oh shit."

"What's wrong?" Claudia said.

"The jars." I pointed at them as they rolled deep into the fight.

"Is that what I think that is?" Daniel asked.

"Yes."

"I'll get them," Claudia said.

"No." I grabbed her arm before she could go. "It's too dangerous."

"I'll be okay." She ran after the jars before I could stop her.

I didn't have time to watch her. A mass of black fur headed my way and I took off running. I dodged around a tree, but it was still on me. I could hear it panting. I looked over my shoulder and it was already leaping into the air, teeth bared in a snarl.

I dropped flat on the ground, and the wolf soared overhead.

Before I could get up, a vampire was on me. I didn't have time to think as anger heated my blood. I wasn't going to get bit. Not again.

My hands partially shifted and I punched through its chest, ripping out the heart. It collapsed against me and I gagged from the vile stench. I pushed the body off and climbed to my feet, but I was covered in black vampire goo. The half-decayed heart still throbbed in my hand.

Thank God Meredith had been right. I was still a Were. Just not an alpha one.

I tossed the heart on top of the now-still vampire.

Daniel gagged, quickly covering his mouth with his hand. "That's disgusting."

"Understatement of the year." I wiped the vampire goo on my pants and reached into my pocket with my clean hand, grabbing a vial. "Do you mind?" I asked as I held it out to him.

He took the vial and ignited the vampire. "You got any more?"

They weren't doing me any good, so I unloaded my stash on him. "Be safe."

Bright bursts of magic were flaring all around me as wolves and witches fought. I tried to find Claudia but it was chaos.

Where in the hell were my fucking jars?

I spotted Dastien's gray and white fur. The battle had taken him farther away than I'd thought. If something happened, I wanted to be closer to him. I took a breath and started across the quad.

The earth rumbled again as Luciana's chanting grew louder. I swayed on my feet, trying to stay upright, but something slammed into my side hard enough to break ribs. I hit the ground wheezing.

I couldn't stop. I had to get it off me. I had to get to Luciana before she finished calling up that hellspawn.

Jaws snapped at my neck, but I managed to hold

the mass jet-black fur off of me.

Oh shit. It was Mr. Hoel. It was happening.

I heard Dastien's howl, and knew what was coming next.

I struggled to stop him, kicking at the mass of fur and muscle that pinned me to the ground, but I couldn't move. I couldn't breathe.

Mr. Hoel started to shift. It was disgusting. His face half wolf, half human. Grotesque.

This was why people were afraid of werewolves. Because of monsters like Mr. Hoel.

His claws dug into my neck. "You're dead, mutt."

"No!" Daniel shoved Mr. Hoel with all his weight, pushing the wolf away.

I gasped as the weight lifted.

Mr. Hoel snarled, swinging his claw-like paw. I watched as if in slow motion as Mr. Hoel's razor-sharp nails went through Daniel's neck like butter.

Hot blood rained down on my face.

Oh God. Oh God.

Daniel gave a sickening gurgle as he slowly crumpled.

My heartbeat thundered in my ears. It was all I could hear as Daniel hit the ground.

This wasn't supposed to happen. I was the one who was supposed to die. Not Daniel.

Mr. Hoel, still frozen in his half-shifted state, snarled at me. "You won't fight. That's an order."

For a second I froze. I couldn't move. His alpha powers had worked, and I couldn't disobey. He stared at me, his claws dripping with Daniel's blood.

Then something amazing happened.

My whole body burned. My vision went white,

blinding me, and my back bowed up from the ground like a million needles pricked my skin. But it wasn't a bad thing.

This was good. So very good.

Cherie! Move! Now!

My powers. They were back.

If Claudia was the one who'd just broken the jars, I owed her big time. But I didn't have time for thanks.

Luciana's chanting grew louder and I spun toward her. The light around her was gone. Her back was to me, but I knew from the way her chanting had grown frantic, she was pissed.

And she still hadn't seen Daniel.

Chanting back was the best thing I could think of. *In the name of Jesus Christ, I cast you back to hell.* I had no idea if it'd work, but I kept saying it. Hoping something would change.

The third time I thought the words, the ground stopped rumbling.

Thank God.

I lay there for a second, and then I sat up.

Mr. Hoel was backing away from me. He couldn't get away with what he'd done.

I didn't hesitate. Rage swamped my body and I shifted fully.

"The jars!" Luciana yelled, but it was too late. "Where are you, you little bitch?"

Mr. Hoel spun around, toward Luciana's angry tirade, and I took advantage, leaping at him. He glanced at me at the last second, but it was too late. My teeth sank into his neck.

The taste of copper filled my mouth in a hot wave.

Luciana was running toward us, screaming

something unintelligible. I had seconds before Luciana closed the space. When she did, she'd see Daniel, and I didn't want to know what she'd do for revenge.

I knew the second she'd seen him. She stumbled before changing direction. She'd glared with pure rage, but now her features twisted between rage and sadness. I wasn't sure which was worse.

"No!" Luciana screamed as she knelt beside Daniel. Lightning crashed down around the quad as she sobbed. The ground had stopped rumbling, but the scent of sulfur still hung in the air. She might not be able to use my powers to finish calling up whatever demon she'd been summoning, but as she looked at me, hate filling her eyes, I knew it wasn't over.

"You. This is your fault," she yelled.

Dastien howled as he bounded across the quad. He slid to a stop between Luciana and me. Her hands glowed as she stared me down.

I spared a glance around. Fires burned throughout campus.

The vampires were all burning or already turned to ash. Their stench had begun to clear.

Wolves fought wolves. *Brujos* fought wolves. And the handful of *brujos* on our side fought their own coven.

It was bloody. Howls and screams of pain tore across the night.

"Wolves. Hear me," Donovan's thick Irish accent echoed, cutting through the chaos. "You will stop fighting. Now."

At once, the wolves on both sides of the battle stopped their attacks.

When the Weres froze, the witches stopped in place. They looked to their leader for some direction, but she was still sobbing. Kneeling beside Daniel.

He'd saved my life.

Maybe all of our lives. Nothing but his death would've stopped Luciana.

Why had he done that? What was he thinking? I couldn't breathe. I'd been imagining he was a traitor, but instead Daniel had traded his life for mine.

He was gone. It was my fault.

A *brujo* came to help Luciana stand. She whispered something to him, and the man bent to pick up Daniel's body.

She held her head high as she turned to us. "I will bury my son, but I'll be back. The covens are coming." She pointed a long, bony finger at me. "*You* will pay for this."

Two more coven members immediately flanked her, and the rest fell into place as their group hustled away.

No wolf dared to move as the witches left campus. Not under Donovan's watch.

"You wolves who have fought against us are banished from the packs. Consider yourselves lone wolves who will be hunted and killed if you so much as sniff our lands again. You have thirty seconds to get beyond our boundaries before we start chasing. Run. Now."

More wolves than I would've thought—at least thirty—took off running into the trees.

But one wolf stayed. His white coat was streaked with blood. As he shifted, I recognized his long, blond beard. "The old ways no longer work," Ferdinand said. He was the one who'd pushed for the Tribunal. Who wanted me to go to the coven's compound.

It wasn't just Mr. Hoel who was directing the wolves.

It was Ferdinand. One of the Seven.

"I thought it was you," Sebastian said. "You've grown power hungry over the last century."

"And why shouldn't I be? I'm the oldest of the Seven."

"Not by much. And you're the most full of ego. Pride. Anger. You're not worthy to be a member of the council," Donovan said. "We should've done this long ago."

Donovan and Sebastian joined hands, and murmured something in Latin.

Ferdinand shifted with a snarl, and took off running. Donovan, Sebastian, and Mr. Dawson shifted and bounded after him.

I sat on the ground, still in wolf form. Exhausted. Dastien butted his head against mine with a whimper.

I wanted to check on my cousins and the others, but suddenly I was too exhausted to even move. I needed to change back and take a shower. I needed clothes.

After a quick look around the quad, I found the twins huddled together with the other *brujos*. They were crying, but otherwise unharmed.

Dr. Gonzales moved through the pack, checking on the injured.

Dastien bumped against me again, and then started toward his cabin.

This time I followed.

A little rest and then we'd figure out the next step.

Luciana would be back, and we needed to be ready.

Chapter Twenty-Five

After a shower and some food, I collapsed on Dastien's bed.

A towel was wrapped around his waist, but as water dripped down his abs, I found it hard to concentrate.

"Let me get dressed."

I squeezed my eyes shut. We'd have time for us later. Now was not the moment. He opened and shut some drawers. "Dressed," he said, and I opened my eyes.

You okay? He asked through the bond, and I felt his wave of concern.

The bond is back. I really like being able to do this creepy, silent-talking thing with you.

He leaned down, brushing a kiss against my forehead. "Now, tell me something."

"What?"

"What did you know about the fight before it started? There was something—and now I feel your guilt through the bond. So, spill."

I didn't see what good it would do to spill, but it wasn't like I could keep secrets anymore. "I dreamed that Mr. Hoel was going to kill me."

Dastien jumped up, hovering over me as he shook my shoulders. His eyes flashed bright yellow. "And you still went into the fight? Without telling me? Are you insane? Do you not care about your own life?"

I jerked his leg until he sat back down next to me. "No. I'm not insane. I knew it was going to happen. I was going to do my best to avoid it, but the fight was coming. What was I supposed to do? Hide?"

"Yes. Next time something like that is even a possibility, you damn well better hide!"

"And if the situation had been reversed? Would you let me go off and fight while you hid?"

He growled. "That's not the same thing." His voice was gravelly. The wolf was close to the surface.

"It's exactly the same thing."

He squeezed me so tight I could barely breathe. "You okay?"

"No. I'm not okay." He let up a little. "Are you okay? You're the one who…Mr. Hoel."

"I killed him." I thought about it for a second. "You know, I thought I'd feel worse about it. Maybe I will later, but for now, I'm glad he's dead. He killed Daniel. He tried to kill me. He tried to kill you before…"

Dastien ran his fingers through my hair, and I soaked up his touch for a second.

I could've stayed there forever, but we still had a whole host of problems to deal with. "We have to go check on the others." I chewed on my lip as I thought back to the fight. "Luciana was summoning an actual demon."

"Yes. I think she was."

"How do we fight that?"

His breath was hot on my neck. "I don't know."

That was what I'd thought. I wasn't sure how to kill one either, but I was Christian enough to know it wouldn't be easy.

"Don't worry. We'll find a way," Dastien said.

"Maybe Claudia knows something." From what I knew about Claudia, it seemed like a long shot, but what could be the harm in asking?

"Doubtful. Not everyone knows about that kind of magic. And fighting it...depending on what Luciana was summoning, it could've been really bad."

I squeezed my eyes tight. "We have to stop her."

"Agreed."

It was a good thing some of the coven members were going to be sticking around. A little witchy expertise would go a long way. "We need to go talk to Claudia and whoever else stayed on our side."

I tried to sit up, but Dastien stopped me. He pressed a hard kiss to my lips before pulling back. "Don't you ever put yourself in danger like that again."

I tried to smile at him, but failed. "I wish I could promise that, but I can't." I swallowed. "I'm glad to be alive. Is that bad? Daniel died saving me. I should feel worse. He was a nice guy and I was busy doubting him, even when he'd been nothing but kind and helpful. I should be more upset. I'm just so grateful to be alive that it's overshadowing everything."

Dastien pushed a piece of hair behind my ear. "No. We will honor his sacrifice. We can't bury his body, but we'll have a service for him. I'll always be grateful for what he did."

I squeezed his hand. "Thanks."

"Come on. Let's go get this over with. And then lets come back. I'd like to spend the next day or ten in bed with you."

I blushed.

"Mind out of the gutter. We've got time before the next full moon."

I scoffed. "You're so old fashioned."

He kissed me again, and I lost myself in it. I was fully breathless when he pulled back. "I just want to be respectful. But that doesn't mean I can't hold you."

"Deal."

***

The cafeteria was always the place to meet on campus. Apparently, that hadn't changed in the little bit that I'd been gone. Weres sat around eating, but one table stood out from the rest.

Claudia, Raphael, Shane, Cosette, and Elsa sat together, along with two other girls and one older lady.

Beth, Tiffany, and Yvonne.

There was a ring of empty tables around them, like no one wanted to get too close. I was a little disappointed in my fellow Weres, but it wasn't all that surprising. They'd just been attacked by a bunch of witches.

I spotted Meredith, Donovan, Chris, and Adrian at another table and they waved me over. I held up a finger. "One second," I mouthed as I moved toward the witches.

As I pulled out an empty chair, their hushed conversation stopped. "Hey." Dastien stood behind me, letting me take the lead.

"Hi," Claudia said. Her eyes were swollen and ringed with red.

I stared hard at the linoleum for a second. I wasn't sure what to say. I knew I should say something, but anything I could come up with felt insubstantial. Meaningless. "I'm sorry about Daniel. If I could've...if I—"

Claudia reached out to me. "Don't. He knew what he was doing. He stayed back to get the three of them. They played along with Luciana. But he knew who you were. Who you were meant to be." Her soft, understanding words only made me feel worse.

I wasn't worthy of that. I'd cost Daniel his life.

A tear rolled down my cheek, and I quickly brushed it away. "I didn't ask him to do that. Why would he do that?"

"Because he believed in what we were doing. Because he knew his mother had to be stopped and you were the only one who could do that," Raphael said.

Dastien squeezed my shoulder. *You okay?*

I grabbed his hand. *I will be.* I cleared my throat. "I also wanted to thank you. You opened the jars?"

Claudia gave me a small smile. "Had to be done. Otherwise, the night would've gone very differently."

I snorted. That was an understatement. "Does anyone here have any idea what Luciana was calling up?"

"A high-level demon," the older woman, Yvonne, said. "Luciana went dark some time ago, but I swear, we here had no idea it was this bad. Daniel made his sacrifice just in time. Otherwise, we'd all be dead."

I noticed the tables filling up around us, and fought back a smile. They'd come to like the witches. They just needed some time.

"We couldn't have fought it?" I wanted to be extra clear.

She shook her head. "Not and lived."

"So what do we do?"

"That's what we've been talking about," Cosette said. "The fey have magic, but anything that could counter demons was lost a long time ago."

"We need to find ancient white magic again," Elsa said.

"Where would we even start?" I asked.

"Peru," said a voice behind me. I turned to see Muraco. His wrinkles were a little more defined today. Was it a result of the fight or was he aging that rapidly?

"Peru?" I asked.

"The Incas were supposedly deep into both the dark and the light. Some say their white witches fought the lords of the underworld, but there's no way to know whether that's true," Claudia said.

"It's true," Muraco said. "But finding mages who know the old ways and getting them to show you their magic—that will be no easy task."

I chewed on my lip. Going to South America sounded like a terrible idea. I'd been through an ordeal, and I needed to rest before Luciana came back with reinforcements. I wanted that time with Dastien. And when the full moon came, we needed to be here to finish our bonding ceremony.

Plus, I couldn't leave with Luciana gathering more support. The vampires would be back. And who knew what was going on with the wolves who'd taken off.

There was no way I could go. "I can't. It's impossible—"

"Who says it has to be you?" Muraco pulled out an empty chair. His knees creaked as he settled down.

I opened and closed my mouth a few times. I'd been the one on the spot so many times these past few weeks, I'd just assumed it would be me. Which was totally egotistical. "No one." I tilted my head. "Who then?"

"Claudia De Santos. You were born of magic. I think the mages will like you."

She scooted away from the table, her chair screeching against the floor. "Me? No. I'm nothing special. I help others with their magic. That's what I do. I enhance others."

That was true. Back when I first met her, my bond with Dastien hadn't been that strong. She'd helped me strengthen my own abilities so I could find him when he was in the vampires' den. Plus she'd seriously come through for me with the jars. If I hadn't gotten my powers back when I did, I might not be sitting here.

Yvonne laughed. "And you think that means you don't have power?"

"I...I...yes?" Claudia said. Her face was pale as she looked from Muraco to Yvonne to me and back again. "But saving us is Tessa's path."

"No. Tessa's path is to serve as the leader of all. An ambassador that each community can look to for guidance," Muraco said. "But she can't guide the packs and covens at the same time."

I clapped my hands. "Thank you. Thank you. Finally someone with some sanity."

"That's not getting you out of your position," Muraco said.

I stopped clapping. Now that was a major downer. "Right."

"I will take you back with me to Peru, and then we will go our separate ways. You will find the answers in the mountains."

"I'll go with her," Raphael said.

"The mages in my country appreciate spiritual quests, but those are solitary things," Muraco said. "This is something Claudia must do on her own."

Raphael narrowed his gaze at Muraco, but Claudia placed her hand on his arm, stopping the argument before it started.

"Yes. She's been hiding her light," Yvonne said to Raphael, patting his hand. "It's time for her to find it. And in doing so, she'll find the answers to save us."

Claudia looked at me with wide eyes, slowly shaking her head. "I feel for you," I said. "I really do. But I have to say, I'm glad it's you instead of me this time."

"This is going to be a disaster," Claudia said, rubbing her forehead.

Two arms wrapped around my neck, nearly pulling me out of my chair. "You took too long," Meredith said.

I laughed, and slapped at her arms. "You're choking me."

"Serves you right. Ignoring me."

The rest of the gang pulled chairs up to the table as I made introductions. Dastien disappeared for a second, but came back with a plate of food.

"I've been watching how much the Weres are

eating," Claudia said. "You really weren't getting enough food."

"Tessa," Dastien growled.

"Tattletale," I said to Claudia. "I was doing fine."

"Maybe that's why you were feeling so dizzy," Claudia said.

"Maybe. Or it could've been because of the gris-gris Luciana planted in my bed. Or the whole stripping my powers thing. Or the stress. I mean I've been told stress is hell on the body."

Dastien pushed back from the table. "I'm getting you some more food."

I rolled my eyes. "See what you've done. He's going to be a pain in my ass." I leaned back in my chair and watched as the two groups mingled.

They'd fought together, but when I got to the cafeteria, the witches had been sitting isolated. Now, I was back and everyone was hanging out like old friends.

Maybe Muraco was right. Maybe I did have a bigger role to play. Bringing people together didn't sound bad at all.

Dastien came back with two trays. "Eat." He was still growling.

"I'm already full. We ate before we got here aaaaand I already ate another tray full of food."

He stared at me, eyes glowing yellow.

I'm okay. I'm here, and I'm not going anywhere.

He pulled me out of my chair and placed me on his lap. *I don't think you get it. I can't do this without you. I tried, but I was a mess. I don't know when my world started to revolve around you—around us—so much, but it does. And you almost died. So you'll have to excuse me if I try to feed you a little more because I heard that while you were away, you'd been starving yourself.*

That's not true, I said through the bond. *I wasn't starving myself.*

Well, you weren't eating enough.

I sighed. His panic and distress beat against me, and I pressed my forehead to his. *All right. I'll eat.*

He brushed his lips against mine. "Thank you."

I tried to move back into my own chair, but he held me tight. "Okay. Guess I'm eating from here then." I went to grab the fork, but he did it for me, making a huge bite of roast beef and some mashed potatoes. "Okay, mister. This is where I draw the line. You're being ridiculous. Give me the fork."

His chest rumbled with laughter, but he didn't hand it over.

"Seriously. You're not feeding me in front of everyone. It's embarrassing. Give me the fork." I tried to reach for it and he moved his hand.

His chuckled, and I dug my fingers into his sides. "Give me the damned fork." He dropped it as I hit his ticklish spot. His chuckles turned into full-on belly laughs.

I snatched up the fork, and took a bite. Everyone at the table was watching us.

"You've made us a spectacle. I hope you're happy."

He nuzzled my neck. "Very happy."

Claudia quickly looked away, but I caught the hint of sadness in her gaze. I couldn't help remembering her douchebag fiancé. She obviously wanted what I had. Honestly, I wanted everyone to have what I had.

Okay, so maybe not the whole insane, dark witch after me or the vampire attacks or the werewolves on a power trip, but the mate thing…that was the best.

And the friends weren't so bad.

All in all, I was lucky. Lucky to be alive. To have the family and friends that I did.

To have Dastien.

War was coming, and until it was here, I planned to enjoy every minute I had with the people I loved the most.

The Alpha Girls series continues with *Bruja*—the story of Claudia's quest to Peru.
Out May 12, 2015.

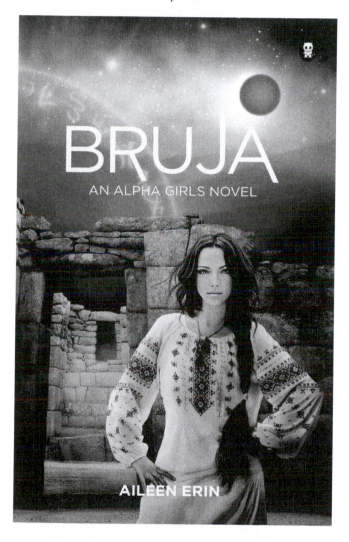

Tessa and Dastien will be back with Alpha Unleashed.
Out October 13, 2015.

For more information on the series, go to:
http://inkmonster.net/books/alpha-girl-series

Acknowledgments

To all my readers, thank you so much! This series has taken off and I owe it all to you! I hope you're happy with this latest installment, and I really hope you like where it's going. I'm excited to dig a little into Claudia's story for next time. She's going to have one wild adventure in Peru, and maybe have a little romance of her own. ;)

Christina: My partner in crime! Another release date done! We're killing it, sistah!

Lola: Thank you so much. This was a tight deadline and I appreciate all of the late night's you've put in for this one. You're the best! You're an editing genius! I've said it before and I'll say it another million times, I can't write anything without your fabulous feedback and comments. Bet you didn't realize when you got me at SHU that you were going to be stuck with me forever.

To all of the lovely ladies at INscribe: Thank you for everything that you do. Working with you is like magic! Christina and I and Ink Monster wouldn't be where we are today without you.

To my Halcyon Bastards: Thanks for helping me maintain my sanity. You're all amazing writers and I'm lucky to call you friends. Counting down till our next chat. Big hugs.

To the lovely Kristi Latcham: Thank you for all of your support and proofing! And being sweet about doing it on an extreeeeeemly tight deadline. Thank you for all of the late nights! You're the best.

To my family and friends: Thank you for all of your support. I know I turn into a bit of a hermit when I'm writing and on a deadline, and more so the past few months! Sorry I checked out, but I'm baaaa-aaaack. I love you all tons!

To everyone at Seton Hill University's Writing Popular Fiction program, big hugs! I'm lucky to be part of such an amazing writing community.

Last, but most importantly, to my husband: Thank you for being so supportive and understanding while I tried to write two books at once. It was an insane task, but you helped me keep my sanity through it. I really can't do it without you! I love you more everyday. You're the one for me. ;)

Aileen Erin is half-Irish, half-Mexican, and 100% nerd—
from Star Wars (prequels don't count) to Star Trek (TNG
FTW), she reads Quenya and some Sindarin, and has a
severe fascination with the supernatural. Aileen has a BS in
Radio-TV-Film from the University of Texas at Austin,
and an MFA in Writing Popular Fiction from Seton Hill
University. She lives with her husband in Los Angeles, and
spends her days doing her favorite things: reading books,
creating worlds, and kicking ass.

CPSIA information can be obtained
at www.ICGtesting.com
Printed in the USA
LVOW04s0258190816
500953LV00030B/395/P